FEB 2 2 2018

SEASON 5.5
FATAL LEGACIES

HAVERHILL
PUBLIC LIBRARY

This item was purchased with
funds from private donors to
maintain the collection of the
Haverhill Public Library.

D0711434

DISCARD

ALSO AVAILABLE FROM
TITAN BOOKS:

ARROW: VENGEANCE
by Oscar Balderrama and Lauren Certo

ARROW: GENERATION OF VIPERS
by Clay and Susan Griffith

FLASH: THE HAUNTING OF BARRY ALLEN
by Clay and Susan Griffith

FLASH: CLIMATE CHANGELING
by Richard Knaak

GOTHAM: DAWN OF DARKNESS
by Jason Starr

ARROW™

FATAL LEGACIES

WRITTEN BY JAMES R. TUCK

Based on a New Original Story
by Marc Guggenheim

Based on the Hit Warner Bros. Series Created by
Greg Berlanti, Marc Guggenheim &
Andrew Kreisberg

TITAN BOOKS

ARROW: FATAL LEGACIES
Print edition ISBN: 9781783295210
E-book edition ISBN: 9781783296774

Published by Titan Books
A division of Titan Publishing Group Ltd
144 Southwark St, London SE1 0UP

First edition: January 2018
10 9 8 7 6 5 4 3 2 1

This is a work of fiction. Names, characters, places, and incidents either are
the product of the author's imagination or are used fictitiously, and any
resemblance to actual persons, living or dead, business establishments,
events, or locales is entirely coincidental. The publisher does not have any
control over and does not assume any responsibility for author or third-party
websites or their content.

Copyright © 2018 DC Comics.
ARROW and all related characters and elements © & ™ DC Comics.
WB SHIELD ™ & © Warner Bros. Entertainment Inc. (s18)

TIBO40535

Visit our website: www.titanbooks.com

No part of this publication may be reproduced, stored in a retrieval system,
or transmitted, in any form or by any means without the prior written
permission of the publisher, nor be otherwise circulated in any form of
binding or cover other than that in which it is published and without a
similar condition being imposed on the subsequent purchaser.

A CIP catalogue record for this title is available from the British Library.

Printed and bound in the United States.

DEDICATION

James Tuck
Dedicated to every fanboy who ever wanted to write
the heroes they love. I am you. Keep moving forward.

Marc Guggenheim
For Lily and Sara

PROLOGUE

MAY 2017
LIAN YU

He leapt, flinging his body off the dock and out into empty space.

He didn't think about missing. Didn't consider that if he did, he would go under the boat, dragged along the bottom of it and chewed to pieces by the propeller that drove it forward at top speed toward the open sea.

His only thought was of his son.

He crashed into the railing, the hard metal ramming into his ribs in a burst of pain he ignored as he hauled himself up onto the top deck. Scrambling over the cabin he jumped down, slamming into Adrian Chase, the man behind the hell his life had been for the last several months. The man who tortured him, who kidnapped the people he loved, who took his son.

Oliver Queen fell on Adrian Chase like the vengeance of God.

The bow in his hands became a club and he

bludgeoned Chase, shoving him toward the back of the speeding boat. Chase stumbled away, unable to fight against the sheer ferocity of Oliver's rage. Oliver pressed him until he was hanging over the rail, pinning him there above the churning propeller.

"Where's William?" Oliver bellowed at him. *"Where's William?"*

Chase smirked through a bloody mouth.

Oliver's fist rose, as far back as he could swing, then crashed into his enemy's face like thunder.

"Where—"

He drove his fist into Chase's sternum.

"Is—"

His fist smashed down again in the same spot. The ribs there buckled.

"William!"

He punched again, his fist a hammer to the same spot now gone soft under his blows.

"You really love that kid, dontcha?" Chase gasped.

A raw animal sound tore out of Oliver as he lifted the bleeding man and flung him away. Chase careened across the deck, crashing into the vessel's control panel. As he slid down he grabbed the throttle, cutting the engine. The boat slowed immediately, causing Oliver to fall back, grabbing the rail for support.

He righted himself and found Chase sprawled on the deck, leaning against the side of the boat underneath the controls, gasping for air. His voice came in fits and starts.

"For an… absentee father, your… devotion is impressive." He gulped for oxygen. "Here you are, worried about your kid… when everyone else you care about is on an island… about to get blown sky-high."

"My friends, and my team, can take care of themselves," Oliver growled. He began to pull an arrow from the quiver on his back. Chase licked his bloody lips and looked up, smiling.

"By using my plane to escape, right?"

"I can't start the engine."

John Diggle let the frustration edge into his voice. The C-130 sat behind him as he and Curtis Holt walked toward Felicity Smoak and Dinah Drake. Samantha Clayton, William's mother, followed close behind them.

"John's right," Curtis said. "There's definitely something wrong with the plane."

"With the plane or with the pilot?" Dinah looked at Diggle. "No offense."

"None taken," he replied. "I'm no ace, but I know how to start a plane. Whatever this was, it's not pilot error."

Nyssa al Ghul and Slade Wilson moved up to join them.

"Either way," Slade said, "we're not going anywhere without Oliver, or his son."

"Actually, we're not going anywhere at all," Nyssa said, holding up a mangled mechanical device. Torn wires hung off it, their frayed ends catching on one another. "I found this ten feet from the wing."

"Please, don't tell me that's what I think it is," Felicity said.

"Depends on if you think it's an on-wing hydraulic system," Curtis replied.

"Can we repair it?" Dinah asked.

"With what tools?" Thea Queen asked as she and Quentin Lance stepped up to join the group.

"So, we're stuck here?" Lance snarled. "Is that what you're saying?"

Diggle rubbed his forehead. "We have to tell Oliver." He gave Felicity a hard look. "Now."

Felicity put a comm in her ear and keyed it up.

"Oliver, do you copy?"

Felicity's voice sounded in his ear. He kept his eyes pinned on Chase, but let go the nock of the arrow and reached to engage his comms.

"I'm here," he answered.

"Chase sabotaged the plane. We can't get off the island."

"There's an A.R.G.U.S. supply ship on the eastern shore—" Oliver turned, looking over at the island where his loved ones were.

"That's on the other side of the island."

"Slade knows where it is. Go. Now."

"They'll never make it in time." Chase's voice made Oliver spin to find him on his feet. The madman turned and opened the door that led into the cabin.

"Besides—" He leaned through the door. "—we're not finished here." He spun, revealing William Clayton trapped in his grip.

Oliver had the arrow out of the quiver and pulled across the bow before he even thought about it. He aimed it at Chase's head, but his eyes were on his son's frightened face.

"Don't do that," Chase said. "Even if you had a shot, you've already told me that you wouldn't kill me." He reached up, tousling William's hair, tugging it hard enough to make him wince in pain. "Or have circumstances finally changed?"

The archer stared at Chase, holding his twelve-year-old son. The man was right. Oliver's mind ran through all the angles, all the openings, all the options, calculating... calculating...

There was a dead man's switch wired into Chase's vital signs, linked to the explosives on the island. Anything short of a clean killing shot would be too tricky. It would run the risk of harming William. He had seen Chase move, fought him before, and he knew that even injured, even at this short distance, the man had the ability to put his son in the path of an arrow.

"If I die—" Chase smirked as the words left him. "—everyone you care about dies. Except your son. What if you don't kill me? I kill him."

"You sonofabitch."

Rage and frustration pounded inside Oliver's head,

while fear for his son and his family pounded in his chest. His voice sounded strangled, even to his own ears.

"William or everyone else. You choose. Right now." Chase rolled his head, looking casual, nonchalant, as he held Oliver's child with an arm around his throat.

Oliver stood, bow drawn, frozen save for the shaking in his limbs.

Chase shrugged. "Either way it proves me right. Either way it's exactly like I told you. Everyone around you, everything you touch, dies."

Oliver's eyes sighted down the still-nocked arrow and pointed at Chase, his mind racing. His son or his team. The innocent life—his own blood, who had done nothing to deserve the terror that rode plain on his face—or the family he had carved from the life he had chosen. Not just his team but his friends, the people he loved.

All the people who were his world.

He slowly lowered the bow.

Chase smiled.

The arrow was inches into his shin before he realized Oliver had fired it. The impact and the explosion of pain pitched Chase forward, tossing William out of his grip. The boy fell over into Oliver's arms as his captor hit the deck, blood pumping out around the shaft.

"Are you okay?" Oliver scooped William up, keeping him from falling. He patted his son, checking him for injury. "Are you alright?" he asked, trying to keep the panicked worry out of his voice, and failing.

"Did he hurt you? Are you alright?" William nodded and Oliver pulled him close, wrapping his arms around him.

He felt so small, frail.

Oliver swore in his heart that he would keep his son safe from that moment on.

"He's gonna be fine." Chase pushed himself up, sliding back to lean on the cabin door as he sat in a puddle of his own vital fluids.

Oliver pointed his finger. "Don't you talk to him. Don't even look at him!"

"You won," Chase said. "Your son has his father back, and he learned *exactly* who his father was, just like you learned who your father was, right here on these very same waters."

"What?" Oliver shook his head.

"William's younger than you were, so he's gonna be fine, y'know? And you have each other."

"What are you saying?"

Chase continued on as if Oliver hadn't spoken.

"Which is good." He nodded emphatically. "Oliver, that's good, because it's gonna be lonely." Chase reached around, his hand going to the small of his back. "Without Mom, and Felicity."

The hand came out from behind his back.

Holding a large-caliber revolver.

He lifted it to his temple.

"No, *Adrian!*"

The gun kicked out of Chase's hand as the bullet

entered his skull. Oliver watched it happen, unable to move, holding William tightly against his chest, shielding him from the suicide.

The first explosion made him turn away from Chase's slumped corpse, to look out over the island of Lian Yu. That explosion rose above the tree line like a rapidly blooming orange flower. More followed, creating a garden of destruction that raced from one end of the island to the other. He stared in horror.

William pulled back from the man he had been told was his father, watching the fires rage across the island.

The boat drifted on the water.

JUNE 2017

1

He drove his knee into the man's back, pushing him to the ground. Even though the man wore a Kevlar vest, he felt the floating ribs fold in under the blow.

His mind flashed back, dragging his memory to the last time he'd experienced cracked ribs. Sharp pain, like an ice pick shoved up into his lungs from underneath, diaphragm spasming but not drawing air.

Unable to breathe.

Unable to stand.

Unable to fight.

He spun on his heel, dismissing the downed man as no longer a threat. Unlike the second man who now stood in front of him.

Same dark uniform as the downed man—military-style fatigues and Kevlar, bristling with weaponry. Same skull mask covering his entire face.

An AR-15 semiautomatic rifle in the Skull's hand.

Pointed at him.

"Back off, man!" the Skull said. The voice through the mask was muffled, hard to make out. His own voice, however, was electronically amplified and distorted for maximum effect.

"Drop the gun and get out of my way."

"I could…"

The shaft had sunk four inches into his opponent's shoulder before he even saw it drawn and fired. The pressure of impact caused four spring-loaded prongs to pop out and sink their barbed points into his skin. A touch of a button on the bow, and the Taser arrow lit the Skull's nervous system with 50,000 volts of electricity.

The Skull fell back, rifle clattering to the asphalt, falling from a useless arm.

Green Arrow stepped over him, moving into the lit, noisy warehouse that was now unguarded in the back.

He settled high in the rafters, looking down on a scene in the large open space. People in matching skull masks moved in a chain, hustling multiple stacks of duffel bags into the trunks and interiors of five cars that formed a line behind an empty car carrier—an eighteen-wheeler that rocked gently to the rumble of its idling engine. The cars were different makes and models and parked close to one another, bumper-to-bumper, scant inches between them. The Skulls moved with efficiency, like a ballet of dark uniforms and bone-colored masks.

"Move faster, but don't get sloppy!" The woman barking orders wore the same uniform as the ones loading the duffels, standing out because her skull mask was electric blue, just a hairsbreadth shy of being neon. The visage on it was stylized to look more menacing than the plain, nearly anatomical, masks worn by her confederates. "I want these cars packed tight. Not one bag left behind."

There were a few others wearing blue skulls, and even a scattering of other colors, all separated from the rank and file. Each held a rifle.

The muscle and the ones in charge.

The last time he'd tangled with skull-masked thugs, they'd been bank robbers and easily dealt with. Felicity had dubbed them the "Spooky Crew."

Felicity…

He pushed the image of her from his mind. He had work to do.

This gang had nothing to do with the Spooky Crew. They were a new thing, grown up like mushrooms after the rain. Heavy with numbers and mostly focusing on the drug trade in Star City. They had moved in during the time he had been occupied with the machinations of Adrian Chase.

Each duffel bag being moved was packed with drugs, all kinds—uppers and downers and all-arounders, heavy on opioids, heavy on junk made in trailers where nobody lived, on the outskirts of the city where the police presence ran thin. Even legitimate prescription drugs used to treat diseases, and steroids for athletes.

These Skulls were covering all the bases.

Moving them in cars loaded on a car carrier was smart. No police officer would look twice, and they'd think very little of it when the truck stopped to drop off a car from its back—a car loaded with drugs, delivered to a community where they would be dispersed to a network of dealers, put on the streets to poison people and destroy their lives.

Not on his watch.

He reached to his ear without thinking, stopping before activating the comm system in his hood.

His hand dropped back down.

Tonight he was working alone, and it was time to get started.

He slid back into the shadows.

The car didn't bounce when the trunk slammed shut, even though the Skull slamming it did so with enthusiasm. It was too full of merchandise, dozens of duffel bags' worth, their weight causing the vehicle to sit low on its shocks.

"Drivers! Load 'em up," the Blue Skull cried out. "Take your time getting them on the back of the truck. I don't want them falling off halfway there." The people with the red skull masks moved to the cars. Before any of them could get into their vehicles, however, the warehouse plunged into inky blackness.

Three red dots streaked through the dark, embers flicked as if from the hand of God. They cut down from above, their swift trajectory ending in three dull ~~metallic~~ *thunks* as the arrows pierced the hoods of three automobiles—the first, middle, and last. The impacts were followed by a trio of low whining sounds that rose quickly in pitch.

At the ten-second mark, they became a shrill scream.

"What's happening?" Blue Skull's voice rose over the din. The words were just out of her mouth when the arrow's screams ended in three simultaneous explosions. Metal sheared from the cars in blasts of noise and light and smoke, flinging a ring of concussive force from each that dropped a dozen skull-masked thugs to the floor.

Men and women, hardened criminals to a one, screamed as if the end of the world had come. Emergency lights came on, and then he was among them.

The hooded man moved with the brutal efficiency of a woodsman, chopping with his aluminum and carbon-fiber bow as if it were an ax, felling Skulls like saplings. A flash of movement caught his eye and he dropped, spinning on his toes and, in one graceful motion, drew, pulled, and fired a green-fletched arrow that sank into a Skull who had recovered enough to raise his gun. It hit with enough force to whirl the man around and sling him to his knees, the gun lost and clattering away into the shadows.

Without pausing he drove himself forward and

swung elbow-to-jaw on one Skull, the blow twisting the mask completely around, blinding the woman who wore it. He let his momentum carry him forward into a flip that snapped his boot into the throat of another, this one with a telescoping baton that fell away from fingertips gone weak and watery.

He kept moving, kept grinding, kept dealing out the punishment for a life of crime. Skull after Skull fell in the dark to his blows, to his rage. He was more than a man in a hood, more than an archer, more than a vigilante.

He was Green Arrow.

Standing over the last Skull he looked around at the fallen criminals. Every one of them had on the bone-colored masks or the red ones.

Where are the Blue Skulls?

The answer came via the sound of the car carrier shifting into gear, and the stitch of automatic gunfire. He dove to the ground as the bullets *pinged* on the scorched and smoldering drug cars. Looking up, he watched as the Blue Skulls rode away, hanging from the back of the empty car carrier.

Pushing off, he climbed to his feet, pulled and fired an arrow. It arced across the warehouse and struck its mark, the rear tire of the car carrier, but the distance was too far, the rubber too thick, and it bounced off, as ineffective as if he had missed completely.

Racing after the departing vehicle, he stopped in the bay door of the warehouse and cursed as the vehicle pulled out of sight. He had the drugs—they weren't hitting the streets—but the thought that the perpetrators had gotten away boiled his blood.

From behind him came the shrill whine of high-performance machinery. It echoed through the warehouse, giving the whine an erratic, almost hollow cadence. Drawing closer.

He pulled another arrow, waiting for what came.

A motorcycle streaked from the night, sliding to a stop beside him. The rider was a woman in dirty white leathers, blond hair tangled from the whipping of the wind. She cracked a reckless smile up at him. Her voice was a smoky growl.

"You want to keep staring," she said, "or do you want to go catch some bad guys?"

Though questions whirled through his mind, he slung his bow on his back without uttering a word, climbed onto the motorcycle, and put his arms around Sara Lance, the White Canary.

The highway glistened, slick from an earlier rain, as it whipped by under them. He leaned with Sara, using his body in tandem to hers as she took the curves at high speed. Soon they were closing fast on the car carrier. Traffic was light with the late hour, and they were heading toward the edge of the city. The handful of Blue Skulls hung onto the metal frame of the speeding eighteen-wheeler.

White Canary leaned back, her voice tearing past his ears with the wind.

"Hold on."

He pressed closer to her back. Bullets tore chunks from the road underneath them, pieces of it peppering their legs. White Canary twisted the throttle hard, making the bike leap forward. She veered left to avoid another spray from the Skulls' firearms as the gap narrowed between them and the truck. The bike screamed up to the rear of the carrier, until it was just inches away.

Canary leaned lower over the handlebars.

She's not—

He didn't finish the thought before she pulled up sharply. The bike lifted, front tire leaving the ground and striking the loading ramp of the car carrier. Sparks showered as metal struck metal with a *clang* and a *bang* and the bike squealed as Sara screamed and forced the thing up and onto the back of the trailer.

The bike slewed sideways and he threw himself off, hands reaching out to grab onto the frame and stop himself from tumbling onto the speeding asphalt below. He latched on and used the momentum to swing up and onto the upper level of the car carrier. The force of the wind stream smashed into him like a bulldozer, almost knocking him back off.

Through the ramps meant to hold the top row of cars he saw that White Canary had also come off the bike, which had tumbled into the space between her and the Skulls. Somehow it hung upside down, engine still chugging. Two of the five Blue Skulls pointed their guns at her. He pulled his bow off his shoulder and had an arrow notched in the blink of an eye.

He was too slow.

Canary did a nimble twist at her hips and her arm extended as a blur. In the dark and at the speed it was done, he didn't see the shuriken she threw until the spinning blades were embedded in the arms of both Blue Skulls. Their guns dropped, bouncing off the metal of the trailer and falling to the street to be swept away as if they'd fallen into a river. From a thigh holster she pulled a pair of nunchaku, the two hardwood handles connected by a length of chain.

"Stop this thing from moving!" she yelled up at him as she began working the weapon, spinning it and whipping it around to build momentum. "I've got these guys."

Part of him wanted to stay and watch her work, but instead he pushed off, leaned into the wind, and began moving toward the cab of the big rig.

She could feel the smile that spread across her face.

Legs braced against the motion of the speeding truck, she worked her weapon, looked at her enemies, and felt that thrill—the joy of oncoming battle—swell inside her chest. This was what she'd been trained for, had been remade for, had been *reborn* for. All the things she had endured on Nanda Parbat, the times and fights since, had brought her to this moment, crafted her to become this thing built for the simplicity of battle. Strength against strength, skill against skill, weapon against weapon.

The nunchaku whistled around her, cutting the air, whipping in a pattern of centrifugal force with her as the anchor point. Her mind expanded, becoming an open field of perception that took in everything—the sway of the vehicle under her feet, the whirl of her weapon, the beat of her heart. The rhythms of her body, her blood in its blind circuit, the very air as it passed her by full of the scent of the night, of the truck on which she rode. Of the city itself.

The copper and latex scent of the criminals that were her prey.

The leader pushed two of the Skulls, pointing them up, yelling for them to climb and intercept the Green Arrow above. They swung their guns to their sides, anchoring the straps, and scrambled to climb up.

She didn't try to stop them. Oliver could take care of himself.

The two she'd stuck with the shuriken began moving toward her. Despite a wave of sooty black smoke from the diesel engine of the truck, she could smell the blood running under their sleeves. She could read the conflict in their body language, as well. She'd hurt them, but in their eyes she was just a small woman and it made them angry.

One pulled a knife from his belt. It was as long as her forearm.

Looks like they want to teach me a lesson.

Her smile widened.

The two came toward her, moving with heavy steps, remaining upright by holding onto the metal beams that comprised the sides. They passed her motorcycle, its engine now silent, its wheels still. When they stepped past it, she moved.

Using the motion of the truck under her, she leapt at the one with the knife, closing the distance as fast as a striking snake. He slashed at her, the blade shining in the low light. She dropped to a crouch, swinging the nunchaku down, the hardwood cracking against his shin, making him shunt forward. Twisting, she moved with the new direction of her weapon, and it struck the Skull's knife-hand. The blade spun in a circle, flying up as its former wielder fell down, crashing into the metal platform of the car carrier.

Time seized up, and White Canary watched the knife spin in the air as if it were in stop motion, everything about it liquid and slow—an eternity between heartbeats, the heightened perception of a warrior's mind. As the knife began to fall, she swung the nunchaku in a backhand, striking the handle. The blade went from a spinning thing into a streak of sharpened steel that had been fired and flew straight and true, embedding itself in the calf of the Skull who once held it. It passed between muscle and bone and wedged into the space between the metal tracks of the trailer, pinning him to the floor.

Sara twisted as the other Skull lunged toward her. He was too close and the nunchaku bounced off his shoulder, not doing any real damage. Hands closed on her jacket, bunching the leather, and he yanked her toward him. This Skull was a bear of a man, long arms thick with muscle, shoulders of rock, and a chest as wide as the grille of a sports car. He lifted her off her feet, swinging her like a toy he intended to smash against the wall.

She could hear his teeth grinding through his mask.

Her left hand clamped on his arm, fingers sliding until they found the soft spot, the place her shuriken had gone in. It had long since fallen away.

Pushing deep into the cut, she dug with her nails, not the least bit squeamish at the feel of his muscle separating. He howled, the sound vibrating the latex mask like a loose drum-skin. Then he jerked, trying to pull his arm away from the blinding pain she was causing him, the motion dropping her back down.

As her feet hit metal she rammed the handle of the nunchaku into his throat, driving with her shoulder and the force of her body weight. Instantly the Skull went limp, his knees banging into the ground before he slewed sideways and crashed, unconscious, on top of his fallen partner.

White Canary stepped over him, looking for the last Skull, the leader of them all, when the air filled with bullets.

2

The two Skulls pulled themselves to the top of the car carrier just as he reached the front half of it. They crouched, swaying with the rhythm of the speeding vehicle, their shirts rippling up their backs as a result of the drag of air rushing past.

The one on the left reached up and jerked the mask off his head, revealing a fighter's face that matched his broad frame. Short-cropped hair, cauliflower ears, nose canted to the side from being broken more than once, and a slick of scar tissue over his left eyebrow likely from leaning into punches instead of ducking away.

The unmasked Skull was steadier on his feet than his partner, who held tightly to the rail beside him, knuckles white. Frozen by his fear, the man didn't move forward.

But he did raise his gun.

Green Arrow drew an arrow from his quiver and fired, aiming at the unsteady Skull's feet. The arrow clanged on the metal platform, spitting sparks and clattering toward his opponent like a skittering animal. The Skull jumped to avoid it. Off balance, he slipped and crashed to the metal platform, the impact shaking the grate. He cried out, finger squeezing the trigger, sending a stream of bullets into the night air.

Green Arrow drew and fired again, this arrow *thunk*ing into the metal grate a foot from the fallen figure. He moved his face slightly into the shadow of his hood as the flash-bang arrow fulfilled its destiny in a blast of sound and light and force. Then he turned back, in time to see the Skull slide away, sent flying by the blast, falling off the edge of the trailer.

The unmasked Skull lunged forward, shooting toward Green Arrow's knees. His arms were outstretched.

He's a grappler.

Green Arrow twisted, pushing off, stepping high to go over the man's back. Something powerful clamped onto his leg and jerked him out of the air, the steel of the car carrier slapping him like a giant's hand, forcing the air from his lungs. The world went staticky for a long moment, all white speckle snow pulsing in a field of matt black, and he fought to keep from falling into it, from being swallowed up.

Pressure on his chest, enough to make the fibrous seams of cartilage creak with sharp pain, cleared his vision. The unmasked Skull lay on top of him, pinning him to the steel grate, massive shoulders driving into Green Arrow's torso as the criminal's fingers dug into the holes of the grate for leverage, adding even more pressure. The archer twisted, bucking to throw the bigger man off him, but the big criminal fought back, driving Green Arrow down again. His face came inches from Green Arrow's, as he bared his teeth like an animal.

A bridge of dark gray metal replaced three missing molars on the left side.

"I will kill you."

His breath was the foul meat smell of a carnivore. Green Arrow didn't answer, saving his own limited breath. His arms were pinned, the quiver on his back driving into him. Options zipped through his mind so fast they weren't even thoughts, but rather instinct. His hands clenched into hard fists, first knuckle extended in a Phoenix Eye. He drove them deep into the unmasked Skull's back, digging hard for the pressure points above the kidneys.

The man on top of him jerked away. The force of him lurching off Green Arrow's chest knocked the Emerald Archer's hand into the metal grate, and torn knuckles sent a burning lash of pain up his arm. His brain shut it away as air rushed into his chest and he rolled on top of the bigger man.

Lunging forward in a mounted position, he tried to drop an elbow strike, but the unmasked Skull was too quick, his meaty hand catching the archer's arm and deflecting it. The Skull didn't try to flip his opponent off him. Instead he drove a hard punch to the vigilante's ribs.

Even through the Kevlar mesh it felt like a hammer.

Green Arrow folded, elbows tight to his side to protect himself, and dove left toward his bow. It lay bouncing on the vibrating grate just a few feet away. His hand closed on it as pain blasted up the back of his leg, the muscles seizing into a clenched knot. Scrambling away he turned to find the unmasked Skull holding a metal tube not much longer than his hand. The end of it crackled and sparked with electricity.

Thanks, Cisco, Green Arrow thought. If he'd been hit with that Taser while wearing his old suit, he'd have been paralyzed, rather than just suffering a cramped muscle.

The unmasked Skull waved the Taser again. "I'm going to shove this down your throat," he growled.

Oliver pulled an arrow from the quiver on his back.

"Shoot me!" the Skull screamed over the wind. "Do it!" A shadow passed across them, cast by a highway overpass.

Green Arrow pulled and fired.

The arrow crossed the space between them like magic...

And sailed right over the criminal's head.

"Ha!" he cried. "You can't even—"

The thin cable attached to the shaft burned across the Skull's bicep as the loop on its end slipped over his arm, sliding all the way to his shoulder. He still looked surprised when the loop cinched closed, and he was pulled off his feet by the grappling hook arrow lodged in the overpass. Green Arrow stepped aside as the big criminal was pulled past him and off the end of the trailer.

He still had a limp as he turned and began moving toward the front of the truck.

The bike still hung upside down, its front tire wedged into one of the support struts for the upper level where Oliver stood. A hail of bullets struck it, and the impacts sang loudly in Sara's ears. White Canary braced against the machine, nunchaku held low by her hip as she waited for a pause in the fusillade.

A few seconds later, the opportunity came.

Over the rumble of the speeding truck and the hollow clang of the bike hitting the side of the car carrier, she heard the distinct dry *clack-clack* of a magazine being changed in an assault gun. Stepping around the hanging motorcycle, she found the Blue Skull raising the carbine in her hands. Whipping the nunchaku up and around she let it fly, spinning like a dervish across the space. The hardwood and metal chain weapon struck the gun, knocking it from the Blue Skull's hands. The rifle swung around her body, still attached to the strap across her torso, causing the masked woman to stumble.

Sara closed the distance between them in three long steps, swinging a knife-hand strike at the Blue Skull's head. Her opponent used her own stumble to duck,

White Canary's palm just skimming the latex of the mask. Closing her fingers, she snatched it off the Blue Skull's head. The woman underneath the mask had a set of wide eyes that might have looked innocent if they weren't pools of molten rage.

Canary planted her feet and spun, bringing her shin up in an arc toward the unmasked criminal's head. The woman raised her arm to block. They connected and blue sparks shot from the blow, the shock causing White Canary to collapse to the metal grate of the carrier's platform. Looking up through a curtain of her hair she found the Blue Skull pulling back the sleeve of her shirt, revealing a gauntlet of metal and wire that wrapped her forearm. She clenched her fist and electricity buzzed around the mechanism.

"You've got a Taser glove?" Sara said. "Not fair."

"And it's going to get a lot worse."

White Canary pulled herself up to stand unsteadily, still holding the mask. The micro muscles of her legs jumped and spasmed. She'd be okay in a few minutes, but until then she wouldn't be able to move—couldn't brace herself, couldn't even kick.

She raised the rubber mask and held it up.

"Got your nose."

"I'm going to watch you scream, then throw you under the wheels of this truck," Blue Skull said, breathing hard, pulling air through her teeth. Sweat from wearing the mask made her skin shine, highlighting cheekbones and brow sharp enough to cut. White Canary read the determination in the criminal's eyes—she had a feral glint deep in them, of someone who would be absolutely ruthless.

Still holding the rubber mask, Sara clenched her fists and dropped into a boxer's stance, regaining more of her footing with each passing second.

"You're gonna have to do better than you have so far, sweetie."

The Blue Skull growled, a low animal sound, and stepped forward, swinging her electrified arm like a club. White Canary ducked back, letting the strike whistle past her face. It came so close that the electricity in the device made her lips tingle. Her own hand shot up, wrapping the rubber mask around the gauntlet, using it as insulation from shock. Tightening her grip, she pushed the gauntlet against the Blue Skull's throat.

A look of surprise appeared on her opponent's face as Sara held it there, watching as the woman convulsed from the shock and her dark eyes rolled up into her head. The acrid smell of melting rubber was stronger even than the diesel.

Letting go, White Canary let the woman drop like a puppet whose strings had been cut. She shook the melted, sticky mask off her hand, then looked up.

I wonder how Oliver's doing?

The thought was just complete when the truck slewed sideways, throwing her against the railing. She caught herself, staying on her feet even though her legs still weren't entirely steady.

I guess he's doing alright.

The three net arrows hit almost simultaneously, lodging in the front left tire of the big rig. The arrows deployed their payloads—high-tensile cable netting that zipped out and anchored in multiple overlapping points, some in the tire, some in the truck body, some in the street, most of them wrapping the tire and becoming a steel tangle around the axle.

The sheer weight and momentum of the big rig almost carried it through, but something snapped with a warbling *twang* and the truck cut sharply left, swerving up onto the wide median between the two sides of the highway, and then coming to a shuddering stop. The driver's-side door opened and a Skull fell out, tumbling onto his back, hands scrabbling at his waistband for some weapon.

The last net arrow from the quiver struck the ground between his legs and launched its payload. Instantly he was wrapped tight from shoulders to ankles, unable to move, all in the second it took Green Arrow to drop down from the roof of the tractor trailer.

"Well, that was fun."

Oliver slung his bow up over his shoulder and walked toward Sara, who leaned on the trailer's rear set of tires. He couldn't help but smile.

"Thank you for the help."

"Anytime." Her smile matched his. "Well, anytime I'm in town."

"Speaking of which…"

She held her arms out. "I'm in town."

"Anything I should worry about?" he asked.

She shook her head, blond hair moving just above her shoulders. "I'm in Star City for a bit and thought, 'I'll go home, see Dad, maybe help take down some regular old human criminals for a change.'"

"You're still with the Legends?"

She nodded.

"Last time I saw you it was aliens."

She raised her hands, palms out. "I didn't bring any with me."

"You know that stuff still weirds me out."

"I know it does." She bumped him with her shoulder. "That's why you can't be part of my team."

"I did fine with the aliens."

"We don't do much aliens. Dinosaurs a surprising amount, but not many aliens."

His smile widened. "It's really good to see you."

"I didn't know I could be such a bright spot for you."

"It's been…" His mind flashed back, filling with images.

Explosions reflected on water.

The slow leak of blood from the neat hole in Adrian Chase's skull.

The feel of his son, William, sobbing in his arms.

He pushed those things down.

"It's been a really tough couple of months."

She looked at him—not speaking—with the gaze of someone who had known him longer than almost anyone left alive. She studied him with that keen, tactical mind of hers, trying to read him from the history they shared. He saw her jaw tighten as she almost asked for more, then relax as she changed her mind.

"So, you want to call in the cops to pick up these Skulls, and then call it a night? I bet we can dislodge my bike. It'll get us back to the Arrowcave."

His face tightened. "I hate that."

"What do you call it? The Bunker?"

"Actually…"

She laughed. "Of course you do."

"Will your bike still run? You crashed it into a moving tractor trailer."

"It got shot, too." She waved her hand, dismissing both. "It'll be fine. It's not Waverider issue but it's a tough bike."

3

He wanted to touch it.

The urge made his fingers feel slightly electrified, as if microwires had been implanted, running alongside the nerves in them, firing infinitesimal bursts of electrons and protons from knuckles to fingertips. He ignored the sensation, keeping his hands flat on the desk, not feeling the blotter beneath them.

It sat behind the stapler, between the phone and the cup of pens, exactly where he'd found it on his first day back in the office. It sat where, any of the numerous times a day he reached for any of those objects, he could pick it up as if it were just another envelope. Just a regular piece of mail you would find on the mayor's desk. Perhaps a memo from a subordinate, a notice of some pending meeting, or even a letter complaining about the terrible job he was doing.

He wished it was any of those.

The side facing up, clearly visible, was plain—no

markings to interrupt the clean field of the cream-colored, heavyweight card stock that made the envelope. Yet he knew what was on the other side. Two symbols, meticulously drawn by a steady hand, a hand steady enough to perform surgery.

Or butchery.

Two symbols. Meant for him to interpret.

A green triangle with an X over it, and a simple series of curved lines that met in three points. A primitive representation of fire.

He kept his mind still as his body as he stared at it, ignoring the tension in his shoulders.

Ignoring the memory of fire blossoming along the coast of Lian Yu.

Ignoring the men in his office.

Ignoring the image of Adrian Chase and his half-smile of sardonic superiority. The heavy feeling of dread that sat low in his belly as he stared.

"Mayor Queen!"

The voice pulled him from where his mind had been, tugging from the side. He turned his head to look at the man to the left of his desk. Standing, holding a folder stuffed so thick it barely held the papers inside it, corners and edges jutting from the top.

The man took a step back, pulling the thick sheaf of paper to his chest like a shield against what he saw in Oliver's eyes. He didn't speak for a moment, wavering between staying where he was and taking another step back, to ease away from the mayor as a rabbit eases away from the gaze of a wolf.

Oliver took a deep breath, letting it slip slowly out of his nostrils, trying to center himself. He didn't smile. In fact, until he pulled himself back completely, his smile would only scare the man more. So he focused on who the man was, trying to dredge up a name.

Tatum. Walter Tatum, Director of Parks and Recreation.

"I'm sorry, Mr. Tatum," he said calmly. "My mind drifted a bit, and I missed that last part."

Tatum jumped a little at the sound of his name, still looking as if he might be prey, and his boss the predator. He kept his eyes averted when he spoke.

"Yes, Mr. Mayor," he said quickly. "This is actually very important."

"I'm sure it is, Mr. Tatum."

There was movement to the right as Quentin Lance, his deputy mayor, stepped forward. Rene Ramirez sat in a chair by the door. Even in a suit and tie Rene couldn't entirely relax. He seemed somehow coiled for action, as if ready to jump to violence like his vigilante alter ego, Wild Dog.

"Mr. Tatum here was just going over the details for the city's big Blues Festival next month," Lance said. "It's going to be quite event." At that, Oliver turned his attention back to Walter Tatum.

"As I was saying…" Tatum said, emboldened. He moved to set the overstuffed folder on Oliver's desk, then thought better of it and maintained his grip. "We have Starling Garden set aside, and I have secured both Lightnin' Muskgrove *and* Shonty Jones to reunite, along with Papa Legbone and the Hoodoo Social Club. They will headline, and I expect…"

Oliver glanced at the envelope again.

Instantly Lance and Rene were both in motion. Lance put a reassuring hand on Tatum's shoulder, and Rene took him by the arm, much like a bouncer. He didn't apply pressure, but the potential was there. Tatum trailed off, and glanced at them with confusion written across his features.

"Give the Mayor a moment, if you don't mind," Lance said. "He has a lot on his plate, you know."

"But, I need to…"

"Come on, you don't mind." Now Rene applied a little pressure. "Do you?"

Tatum opened his mouth as if to reply, then closed it again. With Rene guiding him he began walking toward the door, the overstuffed folder pinned between his body and the arm Rene held.

"I guess," he said finally.

"I'm sure the arrangements are fine, Mr. Tatum," Oliver called to him. "I have complete faith in you."

Tatum nodded awkwardly, still being led away. As they reached the door, he spoke to Rene in a low voice. "He hasn't been right since the kidnapping, has he?"

"He'll be fine, don't worry about him." Rene squeezed a little harder. Sweat popped in a layer over Tatum's forehead. Hearing every word, Oliver watched as Rene opened the door and hustled the man through to the outer office.

As the door clicked shut, Lance turned to Oliver.

"What the *hell* was that?"

Oliver pushed his chair back. "Nothing."

"I know a blues show isn't the most exciting topic—"

"I like the blues."

Lance cocked his head sideways. "You do?" he asked, surprise plain in his voice.

Oliver nodded. "I have all of Papa Legbone on vinyl, even his solo records."

"I'd have pegged you for a techno-metal-whatever guy," Quentin said. "Something… aggressive."

"I do like that. Doesn't mean I *only* like that."

"People have layers, I guess."

"Papa Legbone lived through being shot by his stepfather at the age of ten, a sawmill accident that nearly drowned him, an ex-wife who stabbed him in the face, and another who tried to set him on fire," Oliver replied. "He lost his left leg in a prison riot while serving time for assault when a fan caught Legbone with his wife after a show."

"That's a lot of life for one guy to live."

"The point is, his music is plenty aggressive."

"I've never listened to him."

"I'll put a mix together for you."

"Eh," Lance turned his face away. "Maybe not."

Oliver frowned.

"They play the blues in bars a lot," Lance said.

"Ah." The one syllable from Oliver was spoken low, but full of understanding.

"That's my problem, though," Lance said before Oliver could say another word. "Let's talk about yours."

"I don't have a problem."

Lance pointed at the envelope. "*That* is a problem."

"No, *that* is a splinter under my skin." Oliver shook his head. "It's an annoyance."

Lance moved to the corner of the desk where the envelope sat. His hand hovered over it.

"Want me to throw it away?"

"No."

"Want me to open it?"

"No."

"So, we just let this thing sit here, distracting you from your job, preventing you from getting Star City back to normal."

Oliver didn't respond.

"Look," Lance said, "I get it, you've always held onto things that make you feel bad."

"I appreciate the free psychoanalysis," Oliver said wryly.

"No, you don't."

"No, I don't."

"But I'm not wrong."

"I just want to move on from Chase, and all he did to us," Oliver replied. "Put it in the past, and heal."

"And yet this stays here."

They looked at each other. Neither man blinked.

The door to the office opened. Sara Lance stepped inside.

"Am I interrupting?" she asked. "The intense guy outside—I don't know his regular name—said to come in."

Quentin straightened sharply, surprise lighting his face. "Baby girl." Arms open, he crossed the space, embracing his daughter in a fierce hug. As Oliver watched them, his chest felt tight. After a moment Quentin pulled back, holding Sara by the shoulders.

"Let me look at you," he said, but she shrugged his hands away with a smile, reaching up to touch his face.

"Forget that, let me look at *you*."

They smiled at each other, and Sara jostled her father. "Actually, you look pretty good, like you're keeping yourself fed."

"I didn't know you were coming to town."

Sara looked past him, arching an eyebrow at Oliver. "You didn't tell him?"

"And miss this reunion?" Oliver shook his head. "It's good to watch your father smile."

"Hey." Quentin arched his eyebrow, just like his daughter, and pointed. "We're not done talking about this."

Oliver sighed. "We are for today." He moved around the desk. "You two have a lot of catching up to do, and I... have somewhere I need to go." He patted Lance's shoulder, kissed Sara on the cheek, and left the room.

* * *

"Everything okay?" Sara asked as the door shut.

"To tell the truth…" Lance took a deep breath, and let it out in a long sigh. "It's been a really hard couple of months."

"I keep hearing that."

4

"You *can* touch her, you know."

The voice was soft, the vowels slightly curved, but there was an authoritative edge to it. Before Oliver could turn, a dark-haired woman in a white coat came all the way into the room. He hadn't heard her over the rasp and shush of the ventilator and the hum and beeps of the various monitors attached to his sister, Thea, who lay, pale and frail, in the hospital bed.

"Go ahead," Dr. Schwartz said. "Hold her hand, stroke her hair." She made an encouraging wave in his direction. "Contact has been shown to help coma patients."

"I don't want to hurt her by accident."

She looked at him for a long moment. "I believe when you hurt someone, it is always very deliberate." It was a stone thrown in the well of his mind, rippling through remembrances of all the pain dealt at his hands. By dint of long practice, he kept it off his face.

"Not always."

"Your sister is made of stern stuff, Mr. Queen," the doctor continued. "She survived injuries that would kill others. She can withstand having you hold her hand."

Tentatively, being as careful as if he were disarming a bomb, Oliver lifted Thea's fingers and placed them in his. The pads were calloused from a thousand arrows he had shot. Thick and tough and nerveless, but in his palm, in the sensitive creases that cut across it, he could feel the flutter of her pulse and the bird-like weight of her slender bones.

"It feels so small," he said.

"Nevertheless, it won't break."

He couldn't take his eyes off her hand in his. To do so would mean looking at her, seeing her, completely. She looked so... not lifeless, he was far too familiar with death to make that mistake, but *hollow*, as if the spark—the wild fey spirit that made Thea the stubborn, *infuriating*, caring, fiercely loving person that was so much like their mother, *so much like him*—had gone elsewhere, leaving her body unattended.

Come back, Speedy. He pushed the thought out to her, trying to force it down to her through the connection of her hand in his.

Thea didn't move, didn't even twitch.

The shallow pulse did not waver or change.

Wherever she was, it was far away. He pulled a hard sigh through his nostrils and looked up to find Dr. Schwartz watching him carefully. After a moment she spoke.

"I know it doesn't appear so, but her physical condition *is* improving."

"When will she wake up?"

"That I don't know," the doctor admitted, adding, "I'm sorry."

"Is there anyone else we can consult?"

Dr. Schwartz frowned. "I've consulted with Dr. Price out of Blüdhaven and Dr. Oakroot from Midway, two of the top experts on this coast. And no doubt you are aware of the upgrades we've made to our facility, all possible through donations from your family. Your sister is receiving the best care she can."

"I wasn't questioning your—"

"Shush." She put her hand up to interrupt him. "I know. You're grasping for answers. I understand. I have been in your position."

He considered her words. "If that's true, I *am* sorry."

"Mr. Queen, you know that I am aware of your... night job."

He waited for her to continue.

"A man like you, both an active politician and a..." She let the word *vigilante* slip away unsaid. "Well, you are used to being able to tackle problems head-on, to solve them, to handle things and make them right."

He gave a slight nod of his head.

"Well, this isn't that sort of problem," she said. "As much as you might wish otherwise, this is something that is beyond your ability to fix."

"It's my fault she is here."

"You did not do this to her."

You're wrong.

The thought burned through his brain, a bullet shot from a gun and plowing its way across his cerebellum. Thea lay here, hurt, because of his actions, because of his very existence. Because of things he did, Adrian Chase had taken Thea to Lian Yu as a hostage. She was only there because she was his sister, a person Chase could use to manipulate him—and finally a person Chase could use to hurt him.

Images came, flashing against the back of his mind's eye. A chain of flames covering the island, black smoke roiling through the blast fields, his loved ones burned and hurt. Thea lying on the ground, bleeding and unconscious.

Dr. Schwartz moved around Thea's bed, coming close enough to lay a hand on his shoulder.

"You're doing what you can, here and now," she said. "Hold your sister's hand, Mr. Queen." With those words and a strong squeeze on his shoulder, she left him alone with the hum and beep of the machines and the silence of his sister.

"Why is this damn door down?"

Raylan turned as his supervisor, Crenshaw, came up the stairwell. He wasn't surprised at the man's appearance on the scene, he'd heard him huffing and puffing from two floors down.

Crenshaw used the safety rail to haul his bulk up onto the landing. The big man wore the same uniform as Raylan. Same polyester-blend gray slacks and blue button-up shirt with a DEARDEN TOWER SECURITY patch over the left breast. The fabric on Crenshaw's had turned dark in the pits despite the abundant air conditioning.

"You going to make it?" Raylan asked.

Crenshaw waved away his mild concern, staring at the flat slab of steel that blocked off the doorway.

"This thing shouldn't be down."

"No, it shouldn't."

"You know when this door is down, it kicks the kill switches on the elevators."

"I don't think they're kill switches."

"Elevators don't work," Crenshaw snorted. "Sounds like a kill switch to me."

Maybe we should leave that to the engineers, Raylan thought, but he said, "No alarms are going."

"Well, thank God for that. If they were, we'd be crawling with all kinds of cops and EMTs and other people all freaked out."

A loud *click* sounded, and the door began to slide up as if it had been oiled. Both men jumped, their hands going to the service revolvers on their hips.

The door opened to reveal a slender man with a head full of wiry red hair. Coveralls hung off him as he stood with his hand on a rolling dolly, empty but for a paint can with a wire handle. A tool belt hung at an angle off his hips, handles jutting and wires spooling from yawning pockets. He tilted his head, studying them.

"Why, hello gents! Top of the morning... no, *evening* to you."

"Who are you?" Crenshaw asked.

"No one of consequence, now that this door is repaired."

"Repaired?" Raylan asked. "We didn't have a repair order."

"Gentlemen," the man said, palms outstretched, "I get it that you didn't expect me, but honestly, how would I even be up this high unless someone in your department had cleared it?" He stared at the security guards, eyes wide and innocent.

"Who gave you access?" Crenshaw demanded.

The man shrugged. "I just go where I'm told. You know how it is. Bosses, right?"

The security guards chuckled at that, both easing their stances, hands dropping from their guns. Their supervisor *was* a huge pain in the neck, Raylan mused to himself. "What's that bucket of paint for?" he asked.

"Touch up. You try and you try but something always gets nicked."

Raylan nodded his empathy, and the man offered a quick salute.

Enough with these two, Alex Faust thought to himself. *I'm wasting time.*

"Well, I must be on my way," he said cheerfully. "Have a safe night, gentlemen."

As the two security guards nodded their goodbyes, as clueless as ever, he rolled the dolly to the elevator and stepped on.

And like that, he was gone.

5

Her hands moved on two separate keyboards, each set of fingers typing as she looked into the middle distance between two monitors, eyes flicking slightly to the left and the right, left then right.

Left then right.

Left right, left right.

leftright, leftrightleftrightleftright...

Processing information and acting on it immediately. View. Process. File. No hesitation, hesitation was for the weak. And in the realm of the cyber, Felicity Smoak had deleted all such weakness, long ago. When she worked like this her hyperactive mind, the mind that constantly ran from side to side, considering everything, from every angle, became streamlined and seamless. Wherever her focus landed, it was laser thin.

"What are you working on?"

Felicity jumped, startled, breaking the rhythm of her work.

"Jeez, you're like a cat," she exclaimed. "Like a ninja cat. With a cloak of invisibility."

"Sorry," he said. "I didn't mean to startle you."

"Yeah, well, mister, I'm going to put a bell on you when you aren't in costume."

"I've just been visiting Thea."

"How is—"

"No news." He shook his head slowly. "I came by to reload my quiver."

"Curtis did that for you earlier."

Oliver frowned.

"You know he does it right each time." Felicity stood, leaning on the steel desk. "He's obsessive like that."

"I know."

"And you know you're going to double-check his work, no matter what."

It took him a moment to respond.

"I am."

"So why the frowny face?"

Oliver looked at his reflection in a swing-line mirror attached to the corner of the desk. He had no idea what it was for, but he was sure it had a purpose. This was Felicity's world, and everything lived there for a purpose. She probably used it to read some super-secret backward-written hacker code.

For him it was just a convenient mirror. "This is just my face."

"It's a subtle frown."

He grunted in response.

"See?" She softened the word with a smile. "Subtlety at its finest."

He stared at her, blue eyes still sharp as his arrows, pricking her and drawing blood from her heart. She didn't flinch, didn't turn away, even though the directness of his gaze pushed at her like a force field. Words unsaid stopped in her throat, threatening to choke her.

This was Oliver.

Her Oliver.

Not my *Oliver*, she mused. *Not for a long while now.* Her resolve failed, eyes dropping as she turned back to the monitors on the desk. Her fingers began flying.

"Did you go out alone last night, and put a bunch of…" She leaned closer to the monitor, reading the words on it. "…'skull-masked criminals' in Starling General?"

"I wasn't alone."

Her forehead creased. "Who did you take with you? Because I'm pretty sure I have everyone accounted for last night."

"Sara's in town. She lent a hand."

"Ah, *her* I did not account for." Felicity leaned forward, voice tight with excitement. "Are there aliens? Last time she was in town there were aliens."

"She assured me it was just a visit, with no aliens."

"Ah, well," Felicity sighed, a bit disappointed. "Aliens are cool."

Oliver gave her a look that was less subtle.

"Well, you know, aliens are weird and super creepy,"

she added quickly, "except for Kara, of course—she was cool, and not weird. Okay, weird, but not *weird*-weird." She stammered as Oliver continued with his look. "Hey, but you did get 'skull-masked criminals,' which I know you prefer." A thought rushed into her head. "Wait, did you tangle with the Spooky Crew? Are they back?"

"These were different. I call them Skulls."

"The report I found said they were moving large amounts of drugs, and there was a stolen car ring and an eighteen-wheeler. Was this the operation that's been moving drugs through Star City? Or are there two operations? Maybe it's these guys *and* the Spooky Crew—but that can't be it, those guys were small fry. They couldn't grow into a major criminal operation with a big rig and dozens of members. Or could they? I'll look into it."

"I'm sure you'll track it down. No one can hide from the Ghost Fox Goddess."

"No, they can't," she said. "Wait, are you making fun of me?"

"Lightly teasing, perhaps. I'd never make fun of you." The way he stood, looking at her, made her feel very, well, *paid-attention-to*. She glanced over at the monitor, determined to keep it professional. She wouldn't talk about it. Not *it*.

"There was another thing last night," she said. "A known drug dealer found dead in Starling Park."

"Over-sampling his own product?"

"No, he was bludgeoned to death."

"Was he a Skull?"

"A who?" Felicity frowned. "Oh, yeah—no, not one of the drug dealers you and Sara put down. This was an unrelated drug dealer." She paused, then asked, "Do we have a new vigilante in town?"

"Could this be Vigilante himself?"

"The guy with the ski goggles and the machine guns?"

"Yes, that one."

"Not likely. He tended to shoot people, rather than hit them to death."

"Still, we can't rule it out. Where has he been?"

"Hell if I know," Felicity said. "Maybe he won a trip on a scratch-off. I mean, he had to have a real life, somewhere out there. Nobody just sits around watching crappy B-movies until they decide to put on a ski outfit, arm themselves, and go and be a pain in our ass. Maybe he collects stamps, along with his guns. Hey!" She stuck her finger into the air as a point occurred to her. "Here's a crazy thought—maybe he's been on a ski trip."

Oliver's mouth twitched into a small smile.

"What?" Felicity asked.

"One of the things I enjoy most in this world, Felicity Smoak, is watching you think out loud."

Her face warmed from her collar to her hairline. As much as she liked the way her brain worked, there was always the small, niggling fear tugging at the frayed edge in the back that her fast talking secretly bothered those around her. That they simply tolerated it at best. To have Oliver word his compliment the way he had… well, it *did* things to her.

And it set her mind back on the trail of the thoughts she'd had since the island. Lian Yu. Not the nightmare parts—not the explosions and the devastation—but the parts of things she wanted to say to Oliver, *needed* to say to Oliver, but hadn't.

"Do you mean that?" she asked.

"You know I do."

She took a deep breath and launched into it.

"Since we got back and got settled, as settled as we ever get around here, I wanted to talk about us and I know, I know, 'us' isn't an us but it's still a thing to talk about." She took a gulp of air. "I'm not crazy, there is a thing here, there's *always* a thing here, and I want to talk about that thing that is here, but with all the stuff from Chase, and Thea in the hospital, and William, and you off on solo patrols and all the rest, it just doesn't seem right that I'm worried about the 'us' that isn't an us." She paused, then kept going.

"It seems petty of me and I hate being petty and so I wait and I wait and I wait for the time to be right, for there to be a break or a lull or some moment where I won't be a selfish person for wanting to talk about a relationship that I ended. But the time never comes, the moment is never right, there's always a reminder or a new crisis or a thing that gets in the way, and I wonder, always wonder if I need to keep waiting, has it been long enough?

"How far out from what we went through should I wait? I mean, what would Emily Post say is the proper waiting period after someone's sister has been brutally injured, and his baby-mama has been killed?" Her hand flew to her mouth. "Oh God, baby-mama sounds dismissive, I didn't mean it to be that way."

Oliver said nothing, but the smile was gone from his mouth.

"See? Wrong time." Felicity looked down at the floor.

Oliver sighed. "Things are... *complicated* for me right now."

"I know that. Believe me."

"I'm still trying to get the Mayor's office back in line."

"I know."

"And Thea..."

"I know."

"And William needs my attention."

"Oliver!" Felicity put her hands up to stop him from talking. "I *know*, believe me, I know."

"When things calm down..."

"Will that happen?"

"It will," he reassured her. "William will get settled, soon enough."

"That will only happen if you find a way to connect with him."

"I'm trying."

"By being here, checking your equipment, instead of being home with him?"

The words hit the air between them, making it a cracked and brittle thing. They stared at each other over her accusation. Felicity's mouth became a hard line. Oliver leaned forward, about to say something.

The computer behind Felicity began blaring a low siren of warning.

"That would be the sound of something happening that is not this." Felicity turned, dropping into the chair and sliding closer to the monitor on the left. She cut the alarm with a quick strike of her fingers to the keyboard.

Oliver moved up, looking over her shoulder.

The monitors each held different information. One was a street map of some part of downtown Star City. In the center of the screen a red dot pulsed, glowing rings rippling outward like a target. Another had a stream of text flowing too fast for him to read, but he caught some words that ticked off in his mind.

Fire.

Emergency.

Explosion.

A third monitor, further off to the left, held a news report with a logo running underneath, the video feed revealing a skyscraper with black smoke pouring from windows midway up its height. Anxiety rose into a hard bubble behind his breastbone, scrabbling inside it like a living thing. After a long second watching the sooty smoke billow, he realized why this building looked familiar.

It was Dearden Tower.

Built by his father as a dedication to his sister Thea, and bearing her middle name, it was a property he had spent months visiting, going with his father to inspect it while it was under construction. His young mind had always been awed that his father would build such an enormous thing to honor the sister who hadn't yet been born.

It's going to be the safest building in the world, his father would say to him every visit. Now it was one of the properties he no longer held, but it still held him.

"Call the team—including Sara," he said sharply. "We converge on the location." He turned, moving away from the command platform toward his locker, where he would suit up.

Felicity watched him go.

"Good job, Smoak," she muttered. "Real smooth."

Yet she was already at work. Her fingers flashed, sending out the signals to the rest of Team Arrow.

6

They stood just behind the parapet of the Weisinger Building, silently watching the scene below. Across from them rose Dearden Tower. Black smoke roiled out broken windows on the tenth, eleventh, and twelfth floors. Flames broke the sooty darkness inside the floors, great licks of orange furling and curling as if the tongues of some consuming beast.

"Fire," Rene said, his Wild Dog hockey mask pushed up on top of his head. "Why did it have to be fire?"

None of them responded.

Oliver glanced down the line.

Diggle's face was hard set, creased under his gleaming Spartan helmet and looking down at the fire with steady eyes. His jaw bulged with tension, the small tic under his left eye fluttering almost imperceptibly. Oliver only saw it because he knew to look for it.

Dinah Drake's gaze was just as flinty, eyes narrowed under her mask. Both of her hands were clenched fists.

Always more demonstrative than the rest of Team Arrow, Curtis rubbed his face, long slender fingers stroking his jaw. His breathing came in small jerks and sweat ran along the edge of the T-shaped mask he wore on his face. Oliver knew the nervous motions were a way to cope with the anxiety the fire caused.

Rene swayed slightly and turned his head, cracking his neck to relieve tension. Every one of Oliver's team had been on Lian Yu when the bombs had detonated. He didn't know exactly what it had been like—he was on the boat with Chase's corpse and his trembling son—but he could see that they were all affected. Yes, they were strong. If someone didn't know them well enough, they wouldn't see the anxiety that laid across all of them like a yoke of razor wire, heavy and cutting.

Sara stood at the end of the line, and she leaned forward, meeting his gaze.

"Is everything okay?"

"It's been a rough couple of months." Rene spoke from beside her, eyes still pinned on the flame-filled windows. She rolled her eyes, but if he saw it, he didn't react.

"This is what we do, people," Oliver said. "We got dressed up for a reason." His words cut off any comment Sara might have made.

Motion filled a window two stories up from the smoke and fire as four people inside pressed against the pane. Despite the distance, the raw panic was plain on their faces, made grotesque by the shadows and flickering firelight.

"We good, Boss." Rene pulled his mask down over his face, his voice changing as it settled in place. "We good." Oliver nodded, feeling a small knot of pride at his people's bravery lodged in the hollow of his throat.

"Overwatch, give us the situation."

"First responders can't get above the ninth floor to rescue people stuck on ten through fourteen." Felicity's voice was in all their ears, crystal clear over the Palmertech comm system they all wore. *"The stairwells are blocked by something. There's a crew trying, but they're making no progress."*

"We can see people from here. How many need rescue?"

"Reliable numbers are hard to acquire, but there may be as many as twenty people on the floors above the fire. A rescue helicopter has been called, but it's not close and concern over the radio is that the fire and smoke will spread to the top floors before anyone can be rescued."

"No one has come to the roof of the building."

Curtis spoke up. "Those doors are probably blocked, too."

Oliver reached up to the quiver, drawing an arrow. "Spartan and Wild Dog, take the roof and get that door open so people can get to that 'copter when it arrives. Mister Terrific is with me, and we tackle the lower obstructions so the firefighters can get in and do their job. White Canary and Black Canary, gather the people on the upper floors and get them to that roof.

"Whoever did this is likely long gone," he added, "but be ready, just in case."

"How do we get from here to there?" Spartan asked.

"Leave that to me," Green Arrow said, firing the first grappling-hook arrow across the gap between buildings.

Spartan reached down, fingers closing around Wild Dog's arm, and hauled him up onto the Dearden Tower roof. Straightening and pulling his guns, Wild Dog nodded his thanks.

"I don't like hanging out in space like that."

Spartan shrugged, his gun also in hand. "Jump out of a few airplanes, and it'll feel like a cakewalk."

"I'll put that on my to-do list."

The area they stood on was flat, covered mostly in black tar, but they could see a patio area covered with mezzanine tiles and scattered planters with tropical shrubbery, placed around wrought-iron chairs and tables. To the left, under a pergola covered with some flowering vines, stood both a fully stocked bar and an elaborate gas grill. In the center jutted a shed-style building of cinder blocks with a steel door. Except for the door, it had been painted in bright colors appropriate for a southwestern adobe. The door was an unrelieved square of unadorned steel.

They moved toward it, Wild Dog matching Spartan's pace even though there was a substantial difference in their stride. Dull thuds reverberated from the steel door as if it were some strange percussion instrument being played from the other side. Spartan turned the volume up on his voice amplifier, and leaned close to the door.

"Hey!" he boomed. "We're here to help." The percussion stopped, leaving the noise of the sirens sounding thin and brittle from far below, and the whistling of the wind over the rooftop they stood on.

"The door is stuck." The voice was male, sounding as if it came from underwater. "I can't get it open and there's a lot of smoke and heat."

"Are you alone?"

A chorus of noises sounded, Spartan's sharp hearing picking out several distinct voices. They swelled for a second before falling off. Then they were replaced by the male voice from earlier.

"There's a group of us from Whisken Holdings and a few other offices. Maybe eleven or twelve of us."

"What's your name?"

"Darrell Grizzle."

"We're going to get you out of there, Darrell," Spartan shouted. "There's a chopper on the way." He turned the voice modulator back down to normal.

"This thing's been welded shut." Wild Dog pointed along the edges where the door sat inside a frame of the same color and material. Along the gap lay a thick weld, like a fat caterpillar that didn't end—one long wavy roll that looked like syrupy steel poured into the space between door and frame.

It was a heavy-duty seam.

Unbreakable.

Spartan looked at Wild Dog. "We have to do something."

Rene turned, taking in the entirety of the rooftop patio.

"I have an idea."

Black Canary propped her feet against the window, and kept her eyes fixed on her reflection. While speeding across the chasm between the buildings, her brain had begun to swirl. Zip-lining was one thing—racing into an inferno was something else entirely. Awareness of what lay ahead sat heavy in the pit of her stomach.

Eyes forward, seeing only herself and her partner while ignoring the clutching panic that climbed the vertebrae of her spine. The wind shear off the building pushed ferociously against her, making it difficult to keep steady. White Canary pressed against her, mouth close to her ear.

"Watch your eyes."

Before zip-lining to the burning building, they had discussed how they were getting inside, but it still took her a second to react and tuck her face into her shoulder. A big swaying push and a loud *THROONNGG* sound that vibrated through her soles and across the front of her body.

Give, she thought. *Just give.*

Three more times it happened.

Sway, *THROONNGG*, and vibration through her body like a shock. Each time the swaying arced further, the vibration more violent.

A sharply brittle crash followed the third *THROONNGG* and in one jerk of motion she fell. Her feet hit hard, jolting through her shins and knees, and her hip banged into something with bruising force. She gasped, and heat filled her lungs from the sharp intake of breath. Opening her eyes, she found herself in a room, kneeling on broken glass. Recovering her equilibrium, she quickly detached herself from the cable that still trailed out the window.

White Canary propped beside her with the grace of a ballerina. The blonde hero grinned at her, making the dimple in her chin even more pronounced. She followed Dinah's example and unhooked herself.

"Mister Terrific was right," she said. "The heat created enough backdraft to pull us and most of that glass right inside."

"He's usually right," she said wryly, gathering her resolve. "It can be very annoying."

"I've got a teammate like that." White Canary began moving forward. "Come on, let's see what you've got."

Dinah followed, White Canary becoming just a pale gleam of blond hair and pearl-gray leather in the sooty haze of the room. She moved faster to catch up, passing through the room full of cubicles just a step behind. The smoke that filled the air smelled like burning cotton candy and left an oily film on her skin.

Chemical fire. Anger settled in her bones, that someone had done this on purpose, this terrorist act. Then they found the first group of people.

"*That* was different," Curtis Holt said.

Green Arrow unclipped from the cable, giving him a hard look. Heat and smoke rushed past them, being sucked out the opening where a window had once been.

"I've hang-glided, parachuted, and zip-lined, but I've never done it into a burning building." Mister Terrific dropped the clip from his costume. He saw the look coming from under Green Arrow's hood, directed at him. "I'm just saying, it was an experience."

"Think about it on your own time," Green Arrow growled. "We have work to do." He turned on his heel, moving into the flames. Mister Terrific followed, closing his mouth to keep the sooty smoke out of his lungs as much as possible.

"Overwatch, why aren't the sprinklers working?" The voice in Holt's ear belonged to Green Arrow.

"*According to everything I see, they are,*" Overwatch replied.

"They aren't. See what you can do."

"*On it.*"

The office they moved through had been demolished. Desks and chairs overturned, flames licking around them. The ceiling tiles that weren't fallen or reduced to so much confetti had been scorched black and the carpet crunched, brittle and hard underfoot, melted in great swaths through the middle.

Mister Terrific scanned everything as he followed, taking in what he could through the acrid smoke that made his eyes water. As the tears ran over the T-mask that adhered to his face, his engineer mind worked overtime.

The scorch marks and the angles in which the destruction paths lay indicated an explosion. The flames that traced the walls and decorations—still burning on anything they could—were a darker orange, amber at their core. The smoke that rolled past felt oily against his skin, like a petrol fire, but didn't sting. Breathing was hard but not a genuine struggle, so the flame wasn't eating all the oxygen in the room. Sweat ran freely down his back, and he wanted to shrug off the tight-fitting Kevlar-reinforced leather jacket to cool off. Still, the heat wasn't so intense he felt any danger to his lungs and their delicate linings. The back of his throat itched in a mentholated sensation, and his mouth filled with the taste of burnt sugar.

His brain listed fourteen chemical combinations that would create an explosion of this level, then result in a fire with smoke of those characteristics. None of them occurred naturally in modern construction, and none of them was powerful enough to do any structural damage to a building like this.

Using his long stride, he closed the gap with Green Arrow.

"This was intentional."

Green Arrow stopped under a glowing EMERGENCY EXIT sign.

"What do you mean?"

"This fire was made in a lab, by someone. It won't do any damage to this building."

"The floor is blocked off." Green Arrow pointed at the steel door in front of them. "The building isn't the target."

"Oh."

"Overwatch, where are the firefighters blocked?"

Felicity's voice sounded. *"One floor below you."*

"Why can't they come up?" Mister Terrific asked.

"The isolation doors," Green Arrow said.

"Got it in one guess," Overwatch said. *"The one between nine and ten isn't opening."*

"Isolation doors?" Mister Terrific coughed.

Green Arrow turned to him. "Every fifth floor has an isolation door installed," he said, "designed to be impenetrable and fireproof, to act as barriers in extreme situations. My father was especially proud that he'd included them."

"Extreme situations like this one?" Terrific asked.

"It was so each set of floors could act as a panic room of sorts. There was a lot of fear of terrorist attacks back then."

"Sounds completely reasonable, not crazy at all." Mister Terrific coughed again, the smoke drying his throat.

"In hindsight, it might have been a bad idea for a fire," Oliver admitted.

"There must have been some safety factor," Holt said. "Why can't fire and rescue get through?"

"They're reporting that their override code doesn't work," Overwatch answered, *"and they're still working on getting the heavy cutting gear up the stairs. They have an electronic locksmith on the crew, but the door is too hot to touch and he can't work in Nomex gloves."*

"It's hot? Is there fire on our side of it?"

"Not that I can see from here, but on the floors above you, yes. I'm running a diagnostic on the door itself through the buildings systems, but there's no fire, I repeat, no fire, on your side of the isolation door."

Green Arrow pushed through into the stairwell.

"Then let's go knock down a door."

"You think this will work?"

Wild Dog let the propane tanks taken from the grill and the tiki bar drop to the tile with a dull *thunk thunk* sound.

"I don't know, Hoss," he said, "but I know that this…" He tapped the wall of the building beside the steel door. "…is cinder block, and it's easier to get through than that door—but what we brought ain't enough to do the job. We gonna need something with more kick than our guns."

Spartan nodded. "I understand that, but will *this* work?"

"That's a question for Curtis, but he ain't here, so

let's see. It might not do anything more than make the wall weaker." Wild Dog put the tanks together in front of the wall, one on top of the other.

"How are you going to light those things? A bullet will just let the gas escape."

Wild Dog pulled a black rectangle of plastic from a utility pocket on his pants.

"What is that?" Spartan asked.

Rene wedged the device into the handle of the front tank and pulled a zip tie tight around it. The zip tie compressed a button that caused the device to click and arc a blue spark of electricity between two contact points. The tie held the button down, making the device cycle in a *click-click-click-click*.

"That's the ignition switch I yanked out of the grill," Wild Dog said as he began moving away. Spartan followed, and about forty feet out, near the parapet at the edge, they stopped. Wild Dog pointed at the tanks.

"Now, shoot just under that and the gas should light on that ignition."

Spartan stared at the tiny spot. The margin of error was slim—nearly nonexistent. An inch or two off and the gas would simply leak out, never reaching the spark from the ignition. It was a precision shot. He'd made similar ones many times as a soldier, even more on the practice range.

He squeezed his hand together, the muscles tight around his knuckles and finger bones.

"This was your idea," he said. "You take the shot."

* * *

They found four people on the twelfth floor, and added them to the civilians from the tenth and eleventh. Herding the frightened civilians between them, they led them up, working their way to the roof.

"Be careful," Black Canary called out. "Fire is unpredictable."

Without turning around, White Canary raised her hand in a thumbs-up. The man in front of her sobbed into a hoodie he held in a wad over his face. The smoke had thinned with each floor they'd passed, but it still hung in the air with the shimmering heat. This floor, however, appeared flame free.

"I can't." The man in front of her stopped walking, shaking his head. "I can't," he said again.

Black Canary reached toward him. "Only a little further, sir."

"No!" the man screamed hoarsely. "I can't go further!"

"Sir!"

The man's face twisted ugly. "You masked freaks are leading us to the fire! I won't go!" He turned, grabbing the door they were passing, turning the knob with a violent jerk. The wisp of smoke curled up over the man's knuckles as he screamed in pain.

Abruptly the door was sucked in, dragging the man forward. Black Canary snagged his shoulder, yanking back. The man's hand came off the handle, leaving skin stuck to it like meat cooked in an unoiled pan.

The door yawned open, a black maw of swirling smoke. Black Canary pushed the man away as the opening belched out a fireball large enough to burn them all to ashes.

7

The heat radiating off the door baked through the thin leather gloves he wore.

That wasn't right.

The door was just as he remembered—a flat unadorned steel slab in a two-inch steel track, no knobs, no handles of any kind. He would draw on it with chalk while his father worked, overseeing the men who performed the physical labor of raising a skyscraper, forcing beams of steel and slabs of concrete to do as they willed and defy gravity.

This door had a flame-retardant core. It *wouldn't* burn.

"Overwatch, where are the first responders?"

"*On the other side of the isolation door,*" she replied.

"Then there's no fire making this hot," Mister Terrific said.

"No, there's not," Green Arrow grumbled.

"What is it, then?"

"*I can answer that now,*" Felicity said over their

comms. *"The good thing about a state-of-the-art building is that they generate lots of real-time information about what's happening."*

"Enlighten us, please," Oliver said brusquely.

"The door has a massive electrical charge running through it, and it's acting like an overloaded capacitor, holding the heat you feel."

"Then cut the power."

"That was my first instinct, too." Felicity's voice came in and out slightly, and he pictured her doing what she normally did on the comms, rolling around in her chair and talking with her entire body. *"But the security measures in the building would require either a physical interference at the main grid in the basement, or shutting down three city blocks—one of which includes a hospital, and another has a terminal disease hospice.*

"So no can do," she concluded.

"We'll have to figure something out here."

"If I come up with a solution I'll chime in."

Green Arrow turned to Mister Terrific and growled, "Figure something out."

"Oh." The taller man stepped back. "You mean right now?"

"Yes."

Mister Terrific's mouth opened, then closed—as if he wanted to say something, then thought better of it.

"You chose the name Mister Terrific for a reason," Green Arrow said, putting a hard hand on his companion's shoulder, eyes fierce through the emerald mask. "You haven't failed to live up to it yet."

Mister Terrific nodded at the reassurance, yet, despite the heat sweat there, a chill ran up his spine.

Something tore in her throat. A shear of hot, wet pain told her that something vital to the operation of her voice had violently come loose.

Still Dinah Drake screamed.

Black dots crept at the edges of the fire that was her world, the hungry fire, the beast, the eater of flesh. The inferno had been unleashed when the panicked civilian had flung open the door that had held it back. The fire, starved for oxygen, raged out in a wave seeking to consume them. Black Canary had done the only thing she could.

Open her mouth, and scream with all her might.

The sonic force shunted around a hard knot of agony, pushed out with sheer will, slamming into the consuming fire like a ringing hammer, holding it at bay. Her scream pounded inside her skull, the feedback from it curdling her stomach. Something trickled down the back of her throat, something that tasted like hot, wet pennies.

She spasmed, wanting to cough.

At a small drop in sonic force, the fire surged toward her, eating its way closer. She smelled the singe of her own hair and ignored it even as it tried to crawl in and join the tickle cough that threatened to make her throat clench, cutting off her canary cry.

She screamed harder. Dropped to her knees, not feeling them bang on the floor. The fire looked even larger from here, a hovering force of absolute destruction, pressed against her cry with a physical weight. It was bright, so bright and hot.

Through the haze of her vision came movement.

She was pulled sideways, leather jacket pulling tight across her shoulders and chest like a lasso. Her muscles creaked as she fought and the voice thundered in her head.

Got to stand my ground! If I fail, the others will be burned alive.

She surged against the pull, sonic scream wavering, making the fire pulse toward her. Then everything turned upside down, and started spinning. Her throat closed, canary scream ending as if it had been chopped in two by an ax. Her legs were singed even through the thick material of her costume as the flame poured itself into the space where she had been.

Dinah hit the ground with a hard jolt, any pain from it driven out by the shock of not being burned. White Canary loomed over her, blond hair hanging low enough to tickle against her skin. The other hero smiled widely.

"Good job. You got skills."

Black Canary pushed herself up, throat too raw to say *thank you*, so she nodded, then looked around. They were in the stairwell, the people they had been herding to safety huddled along the rail to her left.

"You good?" White Canary asked.

She nodded again, not trusting her voice. She'd never pushed that hard, not even against Black Siren on Lian Yu.

Sara stood and reached down. Dinah took the hand and let herself be pulled to her feet. She noticed the strength in White Canary's pull.

No wonder she was able to pick me up and carry me.

"Get up," White Canary said to the civilians who had dropped to the floor. She moved close to the man who had panicked, looming over him. "What's your name?"

The man swallowed. "Brad."

"Listen up, *Bradley*, did you see what she just did to save your skin? That was amazing. She held *fire* back with just her voice." She leaned in close, her face nearly touching his, not snarling but speaking low through her teeth. "Can you do that, Bradley?"

"No." Bradley wouldn't look at her.

"Then from now on, until you are safely out of this building, how about you follow our orders and trust us?"

He nodded, eyes still down.

White Canary turned away and winked at her as she mounted the first steps up. "I'll walk point from here, so you take it easy for a bit."

Black Canary touched her fingertips to her mask in salute.

Sara smiled and began marching up the stairs, the civilians following her like sheep. Her voice came again, but this time through the comms as well as echoing in the stairwell. The effect was eerily disjointed.

"The fire's spreading fast," she said, sounding calm despite their situation. "I hope you guys have that door on the roof open."

The comms in their masks didn't click or hum, but White Canary's voice was suddenly there in their ears, strangely calm for the words she said.

"The fire's spreading fast. I hope you guys have that door on the roof open."

Spartan looked down at Wild Dog. Rene knelt, arms braced on a wrought-iron chair, the semiautomatic pistol in his hands extended toward the two propane tanks.

"Take the shot."

Wild Dog pushed his mask up, sweat running down his face. He swiped the sleeve of his jersey over his eyes to clear them.

"Hot up here."

"I've got one, too," Spartan said. "Take the shot."

Wild Dog tilted his head, looking down his arm, across the sights of the pistol, to the small square just above the sparking ignition.

"Take the—"

The gun kicked as his finger squeezed, spitting a bullet across the rooftop patio. It struck the tank before the *crack* of it breaking the sound barrier reached their ears.

For a long moment, nothing happened. Then there was a blade of hot blue flame as the ignition sparked into the propane, then nothing as it sucked back into the tank.

Wild Dog and Spartan looked at each other.

The tanks exploded in a blast of flying metal and blue flame.

"How much longer?"

Mister Terrific looked down from where he hung by a pipe, and swallowed. Green Arrow intimidated him. He wasn't sure why. He'd never been anything but supportive—well, except when he'd tried pushing the entire team away from joining up. But the team was solid now, solid as osmium. None of them would betray Green Arrow.

Not again...

"How. *Long?*"

The question broke into his thought pattern. He carefully twisted the nozzle between his fingers and dropped back down to the floor.

"Now."

Green Arrow nodded. "Okay, what's my part?"

"Oh, it's easy for you." Curtis moved toward the isolation door, motioning for Green Arrow to follow. "I'm going to use the T-Spheres to send an electric surge through that—" He pointed to the sprinkler system. "—which should activate all the sprinkler heads. They're all aimed at the door. When the door is coated in water, it will rapidly cool this side, causing it to—"

"Cold water in a hot pan." Green Arrow cut him off.

"Yeah, thermal shock." Mister Terrific reached toward his face, stopping himself before he could adjust glasses that weren't there.

"The cold water will make the door warp," Green Arrow said. "I'm familiar."

"Okay, when the water hits the door I need you to put explosive arrows here—" He pointed to the upper right corner. "—here—" Lower right corner. "—and here." The center of the door.

"I can do that."

"At the same time."

Green Arrow looked at the door and nodded. "I can do that." He touched the comms. "Overwatch, tell fire and rescue to move back around the corner of the last stairwell."

"*Will do,*" Felicity said.

"Tell them it will be loud," Mister Terrific added.

"*Will do.*"

They moved back to the turn of the stairwell, to have cover from the backlash the explosive arrows would create. Mister Terrific reached under his jacket, pulling out the two silver spheres, each a little smaller than a man's fist. A stylized "T" was inset in each shiny surface. He tossed them gently into the air and they rose with a barely audible hum.

"They'll do what you want them to?" Green Arrow asked.

Mister Terrific smiled. "Yes, it's actually intriguing, I use a series of—"

Green Arrow gave him a look from under the emerald hood.

Mister Terrific stopped talking.

"Tell me about it later," Arrow said. "No, don't tell me later, tell Overwatch later. She'll love to hear how it works."

"She already knows," Terrific replied. "She helped me work out the guidance system."

"I'm sure it's fascinating."

"It is." Mister Terrific's mouth was a hard line, his feelings bruised.

"It's just not my forte."

"I know."

"Let it be enough that I'm impressed."

Mister Terrific nodded. The T-Spheres rose in the air, moving toward the ceiling. They circled the electronic switch box before inching forward until their sleek metal sides almost touched the iron pipe.

"Get ready."

Green Arrow turned, pulling a three-part arrow from his quiver and notching it in the bow. He looked down its length, mind calculating the distance and angles—some of it conscious, but most of it happening in the instinctual area of his mind, honed to sharpness by years of living on an island where it was live or die by the shot you made or failed.

Lian Yu.

He pushed that from his mind. No time for it. He needed calm, the water, no ripples, no waves, just the smooth placid surface of his mind so he could make the shot. Squinting down the arrow, he rolled his thumb, just ever so slightly, on the notch of the arrow, micro-adjusting the angle of the fletching.

A buzzing *crack* sounded above him, followed by a gurgle and then the spray of dirty water that shot in an arc from where he stood. The water hit the door, sending steam roiling into the air. Still he focused on the target.

"Wait for it to bend," Mister Terrific said.

The steam parted under the onslaught of the water.

An image appeared on the door.

A green triangle, covered with a red X, and surrounded with a series of lines meant to represent primitive flames. It was only there for an instant before rinsing away.

The door creased in a sudden jerk, as if a giant fist had struck it.

"*Allons-y!*" Mister Terrific cried.

Green Arrow released the projectile. The triple arrow crossed the space, splitting into three, each piece striking the marks set by Mister Terrific. On impact all three exploded with a wave of concussive force that kicked back to the space where the two heroes stood. They braced against the impact.

As the steam and smoke cleared they found the door slewed off the track, ready to be dragged out of the way. Mister Terrific reached out to clap Green Arrow on the shoulder, stopping before he actually touched the Emerald Archer. His arm fell but his smile stayed.

"I never get tired of seeing you make those shots!"

Green Arrow didn't reply.

"Careful, ma'am." Spartan pulled a woman through the blackened hole in the concrete wall. She nodded, holding his arms.

"Thank you, thank you so much," she said shakily before moving toward the group of people Wild Dog had gathered on the other side of the rooftop. The plan had worked. Not perfectly—they'd had to use one of the wrought-iron chairs to make the hole big enough for people to actually fit through, and the tile had been destroyed around the blast site, becoming a treacherous field of slippery broken stone. Nevertheless, mission accomplished.

He turned to find White Canary crawling free, Black Canary right behind her, both of them singed and covered in soot. Black Canary's lower half was scorched, part of one leg burned.

"Are you okay?" he asked her.

She nodded in response, lifting a thumbs-up.

"She really sang down there." White Canary put her hand on Black Canary's shoulder. "So her voice is shot, but she's a little badass."

Black Canary touched her lips with her right hand, pulling it away in a downward motion in Sara's direction.

"Is that sign language for thank you?"

Black Canary nodded.

White Canary laughed, "One of the two signs I know. The other one isn't polite."

"I'm glad you two are out," Spartan said. "The helicopter will be here in a few minutes." He paused and looked around. "Any word from Green Arrow or Mister Terrific?"

"Mister Terrific?" White Canary's eyebrows creased. "Really?"

"He's a big fan of yours." Wild Dog walked up. "Everybody's situated until the chopper gets here." Behind him the civilians sat or lay on the roof. They were soot-stained and haggard but mostly uninjured aside from a few burns here and there.

"We got lucky here today," Spartan said.

"None of this was luck." The voice came behind them. Green Arrow stepped out through the hole in the wall, Mister Terrific behind him. "This was a deliberate attack."

The team fell silent.

8

"Mayor Queen!"

Oliver stopped, one hand on the door to his office, as the sharp sound of his name and title broke through the single-minded focus that had ridden him since returning from the fires in Dearden Tower. Walter Tatum stood, rising from the chair in the waiting area outside his office.

"Could I have a word?"

Oliver took a centering breath before speaking. "I'm really in a rush this morning, Mr.... ah, Tatum. Can it wait?"

"I'm sorry, but it can't." Tatum stepped closer, his Adam's apple bobbing with nervousness. Oliver took his hand off the door and turned to face his visitor. He didn't speak, just stood, watching, waiting for the other man to start.

"As director of Parks and Recreation, I don't feel as if you take my office seriously."

Oliver let the accusation sit for a moment.

"Why would you think that?"

"It's not just you—I don't think *anyone* takes it seriously," Tatum replied. "Not since that damned show was on television. Thank god it was finally canceled."

"I assure you, Mr. Tatum, I don't watch television."

"Really?"

"I don't have time for it."

Tatum grunted his surprise. "How do you unwind from the stress of being mayor?"

By dressing as a vigilante, carrying a bow and arrow, and bringing criminals to justice.

"That's personal, Mr. Tatum."

"I'm sorry."

"Is there anything else?"

"We still need to go over the plans for the Blues Festival."

Oliver reached out, causing Tatum to flinch slightly at the motion. Ignoring that, he put his hand on the bureaucrat's shoulder.

"I've looked over your proposal, and approved it," he said calmly. "Just stay in your budget and do whatever you wish. It's a good, thorough plan and I trust you with it."

"You do?"

"Implicitly."

Walter Tatum blinked rapidly. "I don't know what to say." His eyes went watery under his glasses.

"There's nothing *to* say, Mr. Tatum." Oliver smiled

widely. "I am sure that with you at the helm, the Star City Blues Festival will be a smashing success." He stepped back, smile still in place, moving toward his office door again. "Now I have other things that need to be handled."

He was inside his office with the door shut before Walter Tatum could respond.

The lock clicked and his entire body tensed back to rigid lines, the smile gone and replaced with a hard-set jaw and a crease between his eyes. He was across the room and behind the desk in four long, purposeful strides, knocking the chair out of the way with his hip.

It was still there.

Still behind the stapler, between the phone and the cup of pens.

The envelope.

He watched it as he would watch a cobra coiled and ready to strike. It felt just as venomous. A seed of doubt began to grow in the back of his mind, though. Had he really seen what he thought he saw on the isolation door? Could it have been a trick of the light? His mind stuck on a loop—the image of a green triangle, a red X, and the symbol of fire? Had it been projected by his brain?

Could he have made it up?

He turned the envelope over.

A green triangle, a red X, and the symbol for fire.

It had been there. And it had something to do with this envelope.

The paper rustled under calloused fingertips as he dug under the flap and tore it open. Once the package had been breached he upended it and gave it a shake. A slim silver rectangle clattered to the desk.

He watched it for a long moment, not breathing, waiting for something—*anything*—to happen.

Nothing did.

Pulling the chair around he sat and picked the object up. It was a USB drive. He inserted it into the port on his computer, and it automatically opened to one file—a video clip with a simple title.

OLIVER

The mouse hovered over the icon a long time before he clicked.

"Well, I guess I'm dead."

It took all of Oliver's control not to close the video.

Adrian Chase sat behind his desk in the office of the district attorney, smiling at the camera. That smug, sinister grin Oliver had seen too much of in his life. When he'd learned Chase was Prometheus. When Chase had tortured him. When Chase had taunted him in prison before breaking out.

When Chase had shot himself in the head.

And here he was again.

"I bet you thought you were done with me, didn't you?" Chase leaned closer to the camera. "But you need to understand that I am *never* going away. I've marked you. Exposed you for your true nature, and you will never be rid of me. I'm in your DNA. In your blood. I am knit into your skin."

The words lashed at Oliver.

"I wonder who died on Lian Yu." Adrian stroked his chin, contemplating. "Was it someone you can live without? One of 'Team Arrow,' a soldier, someone who 'knew the risks'? You know you can think that, but it's not true. They didn't know your history. They trusted you to lead them to a good fight, one with honor, but really they were all just pawns to your ego. I wonder if they realized that, just as they passed from this world. If I see them I'll ask." Adrian smiled. "But *you* know—and that's the important part."

They all chose to be vigilantes.

He tried to reassure himself, still listening.

"Maybe it was someone you can't live without," Chase continued. "As you're watching this, are Thea or Felicity gone? Why is it you brought them into your murder spree, Oliver? The women you love the most. Do you actually hate them? Are you so broken that your love and your hate are one and the same? Is it them in particular? You killed my wife. Your mother is dead because of you. Now, have you killed Felicity? Is Thea dead because of you?"

The image of Thea, small and frail, surrounded by machines and tubes and the cool, stale, recycled air of the hospital room, filled his mind. He shut it down and kept listening. Chase moved from behind the desk, walking over to the camera until his face filled the screen.

"I hope they all experienced my gift, so they don't have to see you as the man you are." Chase chuckled. Oliver's knuckles creaked as his hand clenched into fists.

"Speaking of gifts," Chase said. "I've left one for you. I suspect that's why you finally watched this video. My guess is that you stubbornly refused to give me voice... until you couldn't avoid it any longer."

Oliver hated how Chase seemed to know him, even from the grave.

"Just for you, my beautiful Oliver, I've set someone on your trail with enough money to perform his particular brand of art. He's a showman—that's how I convicted him the first time—but of course, his case got overturned after I was arrested. He's still around though, and hates you almost as much as I do. He's going to use my money to pay you some special attention, all on my behalf." Another low chuckle. "He'll bring the house down.

"You've seen his handiwork by now. Remember, as you try to do what you can, that every time he makes art it's you who will be responsible. And every time—" Adrian stood, his face completely filling the screen. "—I want you to remember Lian Yu."

9

"Are we sure this guy is dead?"

Oliver stood, arms crossed and leaning against a rail as he waited on Felicity to finish. She was so intent on her task, it was as if the rest of them weren't even there. He didn't look over at Rene as he responded to his question.

"He's dead."

"Okay, Hoss, he doesn't seem so dead."

"Rene's right," Curtis said, stepping in stubbornly. "He sounds like he made that video yesterday."

Oliver pushed himself off the rail, the one that surrounded the raised computer dais in the center of the Bunker. He kept his voice calm, but only barely, and he couldn't keep the bitterness out of it.

"I saw him blow his brains out. My son, William, still has nightmares about stepping over Chase's corpse to get off the boat. So, when I tell you he's dead, I know what I'm talking about."

"Okay, let's calm down." Diggle stepped forward, hands moving Curtis back. "Chase put us through hell—"

"Literally," Dinah interrupted. Her voice had returned after an evening drinking a hot toddy of whiskey, honey, cinnamon, and ginger followed by a morning of drinking chamomile tea laced with Gingko Extract. It was still a bit hoarse, deeper than normal due to the soreness at the bottom of her larynx. She wouldn't be able to full-force canary cry yet, but she was on the mend.

Diggle shot her a look. "But we came through it, and the team is still together."

"What team are we on?" Sara climbed the steps to join them on the dais.

"Team Arrow," Curtis replied.

White Canary nodded and moved to stand by him. "I'm a big fan," he said as he put his hand out to shake, smiling as she took it.

"Mister Terrific?"

"Yes, Curtis," he said. "It's impressive, everything you do."

"I'm just doing what we're all doing," she said. "But, thank you." She leaned in, lowering her voice, "So, what are we waiting for?"

Curtis did the same, grinning at the conspiratorial nature of the conversation. "Felicity is…"

"I've got it!" Felicity cried out, spinning in her chair. "Alex Faust."

Sara smiled and shared a nod with Curtis. She'd

forgotten the energy of being in the room with Felicity and Oliver. The rest of the team added to it, but she could watch those two and their chemistry all day. Her time with Oliver left her with a love for him that would always be inside her, a strange sisterly affection with a hum of romance underneath. She'd never had anything like it with anyone else, but then again, she'd never had the history she had with Oliver. The wild affair when he dated her sister Laurel, which both thrilled and guilted her, especially since Laurel was gone. The time spent together in this vigilante life, his hand in her resurrection—it was the fabric of a connection unlike any other.

Even with that, the chemistry between Felicity and Oliver could light up a building.

And Felicity was smoking—*Smoking?*—hot, especially when she was in her mile-a-minute-I'm-giving-you-all-the-information mode.

"Who the hell is Alex Faust?" Oliver asked.

Felicity adjusted her glasses. "Chase gave us clues in his speech, and since he is—was—a manipulative, deliberate sonnuvagun, I took his information at face value and did a records search, looking for any convictions of people with explosives backgrounds. I came up with three. Three options of people who were familiar with or experts in the use of heavy ordnance, who Chase succeeded in convicting, but were subsequently released once he was exposed for being a psycho.

"Thomas Nadir Thompkins," she said, ticking the name off with one finger, "convicted of terrorist acts using sticks of actual dynamite. Apparently he took his initials seriously.

"Stanley Labowski," she continued, "also a terrorist, but more of an anarchist, fond of using grenades. And Alex Faust," she said, ticking off the third finger, "locked up for murder via building demolition."

"Sounds like we have three suspects," Dinah said.

"The first guy, TNT—" Felicity shook her head, ponytail swinging snappily. "I can't believe I'm using that code name."

"Cisco would be proud," Oliver said.

She ignored him. "—TNT is currently serving time in a Texas prison for attempting to blow up a national monument, and Labowski is so very dead after the Gotham PD stopped him from blowing up Gotham City Hall. So Alex Faust is our guy—the only one MIA and unaccounted for."

"What's his story?" Oliver asked.

"Gimme a minute." Felicity spun her chair back to the computer screen behind her and began reading. "Apparently, Alex Faust is insane."

"We know that," Diggle said. "He blows things up for fun."

"Not just for fun," Felicity said. "Apparently he was the lead expert on a controlled demolition team, working for Brick Droppers, Inc.—no, I did not just make that up—when he... oh." Her voice trailed off to nothing.

Oliver moved beside her and his hand dropped gently on her shoulder as he leaned down to read what had stopped her.

"What?" Rene grunted.

Oliver took a deep breath and stood straight. It was a long moment before he turned and spoke.

"In the setup to demolish a condemned high-rise, someone didn't do due diligence, and a group of children snuck inside to play. They were in there when Faust detonated the charges, collapsing the building and killing them all."

"That's awful," Dinah said.

"What are you not saying?" Diggle asked.

Oliver didn't answer. Felicity got out of her chair and stood next to him, her hip on his, just barely touching.

Curtis looked from Oliver to Diggle and back.

"Ummm, what's going on here?"

"Oliver isn't telling us something," Sara said. "He always gets that squint in his left eye when he doesn't want to tell you something."

Curtis, Rene, and Dinah all leaned forward slightly, studying their leader's face.

"Three of the children were Faust's," Oliver said. "It broke him, and he began using his skills to wreak havoc."

"Damn." Diggle and Rene said it at the same time, likely both thinking of their own children. Oliver straightened to take back control of the floor.

"It's tragic, but we can't let it matter. We can't allow ourselves the luxury of sympathy. He almost killed a lot of people at Dearden Tower, and he has to be stopped before he hurts a lot more. If Chase chose him as a weapon, then something big is on the horizon. It's up to us to stop it."

"We'll all do our job, Hoss, but…"

"No 'buts,'" Oliver snapped, slashing the air with his hand. "We take him down. Priority number one." He looked from face to face, waiting for each of them to nod or give some other hint of agreement. Satisfied, he continued. "Felicity, I want everything on Faust. Dig as deep as possible and find me any information that could point to where he'll strike next."

Felicity nodded. "On it. I'll look for some connection that links him to you as mayor, Oliver, or Green Arrow. Since Chase still is pulling the strings, I'll bet there is one."

"Good idea," Oliver said. "Diggle, go see if Lyla will let you shake A.R.G.U.S. for information. She has some resources we don't."

"Any excuse to see my wife," Diggle said.

"Rene, take Curtis to the street and kick the dirt until something comes to light."

"Wouldn't I be better helping Felicity?" Curtis frowned.

"She's got it—go and learn with Rene."

"C'mon, man." Rene jerked his head toward the armory. "Let's go suit up and I'll teach you how to get information." The two men, as much difference between their heights as there was between their approaches, stepped off the dais. Rene was in the lead.

"Sara," Oliver said, and then he stopped.

"Yes."

"If you're going to be around, I'd like your help on this."

"I'm a Legend, Oliver. I have a timeship, so I can be around anytime." *Even take time off work at Sink, Shower, & Stuff*, she mused.

"I don't want to ask too much."

"Enough," Sara said, smiling. "I'm enjoying it."

Oliver nodded. "Then use any contacts you have to look for information."

"I can go down some alleys the others can't."

"Thank you."

She tossed him a quick salute, smiling as she did.

"What's for me?" Dinah asked.

Oliver turned to look her straight in the face. "Mine your police contacts, and see if you can find anything."

"No problem." She turned to walk away.

"Dinah, wait," Oliver said. "I've got something I'd like to show you."

She turned back.

Oliver stepped off the dais, followed closely by Dinah. They walked over to the end of the armory where the costumes hung in tall cylinders. One on the end stood closed, the outside a map of smooth lines and small lights.

Sara put her elbows on the rail of the dais, leaning forward and watching closely. Oliver turned, making sure he had Dinah's undivided attention. He spoke, his words low enough that only she could hear. She looked at the cylinder, awe raw on her face.

Oliver touched a switch and the cylinder rotated, opening to reveal its contents. When he spoke, Sara could hear him again.

"I thought it was time you stopped getting shot at in just a leather jacket," he said, gesturing. Inside was a sleek tactical suit—boots, pants, jerkin, gauntlets, and a mask that looked like the one Dinah wore currently. Yet somehow, through some magic of design, the uniform looked even tougher, almost mean in profile.

Intimidating.

The entire suit looks intimidating, Sara thought.

It was sleek, with mesh-covered plates form-fitted over striking and defensive surfaces like the forearms and the shins. Buckles and straps reinforced the joints and quilted Kevlar covered vital areas like the kidneys. Her eye followed it all, analyzing the structure of it. It was the perfect compromise of protection and mobility. It had a style designed to intimidate anyone she went up against, and to instill confidence in anyone she tried to help.

Dinah's mind went back to the man in the burning building. *Bradley, that was his name.* Maybe if she'd been wearing this costume, he would have remained calm and followed orders.

Oliver moved, just slightly, and she realized he

was waiting on her to say something.

"Are you sure?"

"You're the Black Canary," he said.

"I'm not Laurel or Sar—"

"No, you're not," he said, cutting her off. "But you are a vital part of this team, and a worthy carrier of the title. You're a symbol to the criminals and their victims."

The weight of the legacy fell on her. She hadn't known Laurel Lance, but she'd been working more with her father, Quentin Lance, who opened up about his daughter from time to time. Especially after their run-in with Black Siren—the Earth-2 version of Laurel—and she saw how the mention of Laurel affected Oliver and Felicity.

Yet this was *her* costume. Her *uniform*.

When she'd come to Star City, she'd only done so to get revenge on Sonus for killing Vince, her partner. She'd been a vigilante, traveling the highways, fighting crime with her skills and her sonic cry. There had been a freedom in that. No one to care for, no one to lose. There had been times when part of her wanted to walk out, to hit the road again, to go back to having nothing to lose.

She looked Oliver in the eye.

"I'll do everything I can to live up to the legacy."

"You already have." Oliver smiled. He looked past her and she suddenly felt that tingle between her shoulders that meant someone was watching. She turned to find Sara Lance watching. The White Canary,

Laurel's sister, and the first person to be Black Canary. Sara nodded.

Dinah couldn't wait to wear the uniform.

"She'll do well—already *has* been doing well."

Sara turned to find Felicity there. "I saw her in action yesterday at that building fire," she replied. "She's got skills."

"You're okay with this?"

Sara let the thought slide over her. "I am. She's good, and it's not like Laurel can be Black Canary."

Felicity's look grew intense, to the point it was almost uncomfortable.

"What?" Sara asked.

"Ummm, you should really talk to your father."

"Why is that?"

"Because you should," Oliver said, joining them on the dais. "He should be the one to talk about Laurel being gone. You could both use it."

"I'm fine, actually," Sara said. Her mind turned back to her conversation with Laurel—in the afterlife through the Spear of Destiny.

"Then it could be good for him."

Oliver reached out and put his hand on Felicity's arm, fingers landing gently on her wrist. "I have to go check on William. Keep tabs on everyone."

"Will do." She looked down at Oliver's hand, staying on her wrist. It was a casual touch but felt more… intimate than that. He leaned in close, voice low.

"I want to finish our conversation, as well."

She nodded, her throat tight, and glanced at Sara, who watched them with her eyebrow cocked and a slanted smile on her face.

"Thank you for helping," Oliver said to her and then walked off.

After he was far enough away, Sara turned and stared pointedly at Felicity.

"Oh…" Felicity sounded flustered, but she was smiling. "Wipe that grin off your face."

1 0

She met him at the door, her things bundled in her arms.

"I can't handle him, Mr. Queen," she said. "I quit."

"The agency said you were trained to work with children." He stood in the doorway, blocking her escape attempt. She shook her head, a frazzled curl falling to roll along her brow.

"Not him. Not enough."

"Shondra, please," he said, arms out in supplication. "He's a ten-year-old who just lost his mother—have compassion."

"I can't do therapy with him."

"He has a therapist," Oliver protested. "I need someone to be here with him while I work."

"Mr. Queen, please don't make me feel bad about this."

Yet he *wanted* to make her feel bad about it. The protectiveness he felt toward William surged inside him. He wanted to lash out, to berate this woman who had insulted his flesh and blood. At the thought, he closed down those emotions.

She hadn't insulted William.

She was just leaving.

"Of course." He stepped aside, holding the door. "I'll make sure you are paid for today."

Shondra watched him for a moment, waiting for more argument. Oliver returned her gaze with a blank expression. So she shrugged her backpack onto her shoulder and walked out, not looking back.

Oliver shut the door behind her and turned, looking around the apartment. With the childminder gone he was alone, William probably in his room. The apartment seemed to hang around him, loose at its joints as if it could collapse and fall apart at any moment. It was a nice apartment, a place Felicity had found for them, spacious enough for two people who were still strangers.

The thought sent a pang through him and the regret for all the missed years seared his heart. He moved through the space, around the couch, heading toward his son's bedroom. He could face criminals with guns and not have as much tension as he had just walking toward a room.

He passed an abstract painting on the wall. It had been there when he took the apartment, part of the staging he'd purchased. It was a nice piece of art, a Holmquist, and he appreciated it aesthetically, but it held no connection to him. It was just art on the wall—he owned it, but it wasn't "his."

Sometimes he felt that way about everything but being the Green Arrow.

Stopping outside William's shut door, he listened. No noise came through. He knocked softly and reached for the knob, turning it and opening the door. William sat on his bed, reading, the covers crumpled and off on the floor. He didn't look up as Oliver entered, just stared at the book on his knees.

He looked small, hunched over the book. The emotions inside Oliver roiled around each other. Concern, pride, a need to protect, and guilt—all coated in a layer of fear. Fear of failure, fear of rejection, fear that William would hate him, first for abandoning him and then for letting his mother be killed.

"Hello, William," he said, and instantly he regretted it. *Crap, what was that? "Hello, William," like I'm talking to an adult I've just met.* "Hey." He moved to sit on the end of the bed. Two action figures—the Flash and Captain Cold—lay there. He picked them up, setting them aside as he sat. He looked sharply around the room. On the floor, half under the edge of the dresser, lay the Green Arrow action figure.

William didn't move, other than turning the page.

"What are you reading, son?"

William didn't respond.

Oliver reached out, moving slowly, waiting for his son to flinch. Gently he touched the corner of the book, lifting it just enough to read the title. *My Side of the Mountain* by Jean Craighead George.

"I've read that book."

His mind flashed back to the years in exile on Lian Yu, living off the land, hunting, foraging, scavenging. Harsher, uglier than the survival shown in the book—but then again, Lian Yu wasn't a children's book.

William didn't look up.

"Do you like it?"

William shrugged, but kept his head down.

"Have you gotten to the part with the falcon?"

William twisted, drawing his knees up and turning to face away from his father. He pulled the book up closer to his face. As he did, Oliver's chest felt like it had been filled with cement. He watched the son he didn't know, but loved so much it hurt in a way he didn't know things could hurt.

Slowly he stood, "I'll go make dinner. If you need me, I'm here."

William didn't respond.

1 1

"You about ready?" the driver asked.

The man in the back of the van didn't look up, just kept pushing bullets into the curved magazine between his knees. "I'd have been ready if One-Eyed Joey here had done his job."

"Hey!" Joey said from the bench across from the speaker. "I'm not your butler."

"I go on a job I expect *everyone* to be professional." The man shoved the magazine into the assault rifle across his lap and pulled back the bolt.

"Professionals check their own equipment, Chavis." The driver slid out of the seat, joining them in the back of the panel van and picking up a shotgun. "Joey got the guns and the ammo, you do the rest."

"Look, Mick," Chavis said, and he narrowed his eyes. "I don't like you two. I'm an idiot for signing on to be a part of this crew."

"This is your audition." Mick began pulling things

out of the bag on the floor between them. "You're not a part 'til you pull this off."

"I'm from Blüdhaven," Chavis said. "Knocking over a nightclub will be a piece of cake. Hell, with credit cards and e-tickets, it's hard to get decent cash from a place like that."

"Yo, it's a *big* nightclub," Joey said, and he laughed. "Blüdhaven ain't got nothin' on Star City."

"You don't even know Blüdhaven."

"Knock it off, you two." Mick handed Chavis a wad of cloth. Chavis shook it out, holding it up in the dim light. It was a slipover hood, the face of it painted with a wide red X below the eyeholes.

"What's this?"

"You gotta have a gimmick in Star City, if you want attention."

"We're criminals—why would we want attention?"

"Look, Chavis, you got a good rep, quick with a gun and not a coward." Mick leaned in. "Here we got players who do big things. You want the real money, the real power, you get their attention and they bring you into their operations. That's what the gimmick is for."

"Your gimmick is a bloody X on your face?"

Mick pulled his mask on. "We're the X Gang, and we'll cross you off the list," he said, words muffled. "Now mask up."

Chavis shook his head. "I should've stayed in Blüdhaven."

* * *

"Hurry up, old man!" Mick screamed over the music that throbbed around them. He pressed the muzzle of his shotgun against the back of the security guard who sat in a chair in front of him. He had his hands raised and his eyes closed, trembling lips moving in a silent prayer to someone who might or might not be listening.

"I'm trying, I'm trying." The man's hands shook as he shoved wads of crumpled money from the counting table into the bag.

"Don't drop any of those bills!" Joey rammed the muzzle of his rifle into the man's ribs, making him jerk sideways. "We want them all."

Chavis shook his head. The bass line of the music from inside the club pounded against his temples and the mask made him sweat and his face itch. The X on the front of it had been done with spray paint and the harsh chemical burn of it was all he could smell. He looked left and right, keeping watch for anyone coming from the concert in the arena. Some kind of jam band was on the stage, all drums and guitar and heavy bass. He hated that kind of music, hippie music, but it made for a light security staff and a lot of money in the box office.

Money the man was done shoving into the bag.

"Here, take it." He pushed it away as if it were on fire.

Joey giggled and grabbed it, swinging his rifle up and clipping the man across the temple with the muzzle. The thin skin over the man's brow split wide, blood rushing down over his eye as he stumbled from the blow.

"That's for not moving faster." Joey moved around the table to join Mick as the man wiped blood from his eye and stood straight.

"Please," the man said. "Take the money and go."

Chavis shook his head again.

"Before we do," Mick racked the slide on his shotgun, the metal-on-metal clack cutting over the deep throb of the music. "You've been crossed out by the X Gang."

The man stood there, hands raised, one palm bloody.

"Say the name!" Mick screamed.

"The X Gang!" the man cried. "The X Gang!"

"Hey," Chavis reached his hand toward Mick. "We got the cash. Let's go…"

Mick swung the shotgun toward him.

Chavis jerked his rifle up on instinct. The two of them stood, fingers on the triggers, staring at each other though the eyeholes of their emblazoned hoods.

Joey giggled.

The security guard wept.

I'm going to have to shoot this idiot, Chavis thought.

"We gotta spread the rep," Mick growled.

Joey screamed when the first bullet struck him in the thigh.

Chavis slammed his back against the alley wall. He couldn't breathe, his chest feeling like iron bands had clamped down and been cinched around him. He could only sip the air. Through the pounding in his ears he heard himself. It sounded like he was crying.

Salt tasted on his upper lip. It could've been sweat. Could've been tears.

In his head all he saw was One-Eyed Joey bleeding out on the ground, the puddle under him spreading in a rush, streams of thick syrupy crimson pulsing from between his fingers.

And Mick.

Mick took one high in the chest, a bullet that hit him like a sledgehammer hit concrete it intended to pulverize. He watched as Mick flipped backward, picked up off his feet and spun head over heels before gravity slammed him to the ground. Whatever sound he made as he landed, it was drowned out by the thunder of the gunshot so concussive it breezed across his chest when it hit.

He had run then, run as fast as he could, following Blüdhaven rules.

"Masks on the scene, get gone, get clean." So the song went.

Blüdhaven had vigilantes, just like Star City. You didn't stay while they were on the scene. Especially when you watched them drop two of your three-man crew.

I thought they used arrows in Star City? he thought. *I hate this town.*

What was that sound?

He looked around the corner.

Nothing, just a dirty alleyway, trash piled and strewn across it.

Lucky I didn't break my neck.

He slumped against the wall.

Maybe I got away.

Cameras! He jerked up, eyes searching the alley for any sign of a camera. In Blüdhaven, that was how the masks tracked you. They saw you on camera and next thing you knew, *bam*, you were busted.

There, on the corner of the building, a dull red light. A security camera. He had to move.

Rolling left, he pushed off the wall with his shoulder, sucking in air to—

WHAM!

Something hit him in the temple. He stumbled, dropping to one knee. Pain pulsed from his ear across the backs of his eyes. His head felt swollen, mushy on the inside, his entire brain rattled. His vision went blurry, everything skewed, the colors all wrong. Nevertheless, he could see a dark shape that stood between him and the light above.

The figure was tall and wore a green hood. It leaned down toward him, the space where the face would be just a shadow in the blackness. Noises came from the hood, but his ears rang like epileptic church bells and he couldn't hear anything but them.

He tried to talk, but his swollen head wouldn't let his brain connect with his mouth. There was a flash of darkness and sharp pain jolted from his face.

He'd been slapped. The green hooded figure had slapped him across the face.

He knelt, rocking from the blow, but it cleared his head a little bit. He raised shaking, empty hands. He was caught, he'd go to jail. No big thing—he'd be back on the street in forty-eight hours and back in Blüdhaven in another four beyond that.

"I surrender."

The hooded figure pulled out a pistol, the sodium-yellow lights in the alley gleaming along its barrel.

"Tell me what I want to know." The voice was amplified, booming and thunderous, rattling his skull.

What? What the hell does he want to know? Chavis tried to find the knowledge in the soup his mind had become. The hooded figure moved the gun to the other hand, holding it by the barrel now. He raised it, Chavis's eyes tracking it, as it moved up and back to the furthest arc of the vigilante's arm. Just past it, up on the wall, he could see the steady red dot of the still-watching camera.

He was still focused on it as the gun fell, but he stopped seeing it as the pistol-whipping began.

Oliver looked up as Lance stepped into his office, shutting the door quickly behind him. He set aside the report he had been reading. The look on Lance's face said he wanted to discuss something, and that it wouldn't wait. He waited for him to start.

Lance pulled up a chair.

"We need to put someone in Thea's place."

Oliver leaned back in his chair. "You think so?"

"Look," Lance said, "I don't mean to bring up anything painful. You know I love that kid, but she did a helluva job keeping up with you and making sure you see everyone you need to without making anyone suspicious of where you go when you do your 'other work.'" He shook his head. "I can't keep up with it all, not and do the job you ask me to do."

"Thea isn't just my family, Quentin, she's an excellent chief of staff. It's not like we can replace her by calling an employment agency."

Lance blew air out of his mouth. "You don't know the half of it. I'm taking calls and trying to juggle people for you. Man, they get upset if you mess up their time with the mayor." His hands went up in surrender. "I just can't do it."

"Then let's move Rene up."

Lance stared at him for a long moment. "You *did* hear the part where I said people are hard to handle?"

"I did."

Lance shook his head. "I don't think so."

"He'll be fine."

"Yeah, but will everyone else?"

Oliver's cell phone vibrated on the desk by his hand. A glance showed that it was Felicity texting. He picked up the phone.

"Let's give him a chance."

FAUST LOCATION UNLOCKED.
TRANSMIT OR F2F?

"We have to finish this later," he said, fingers already typing.

MOBILIZE THE TEAM

Lance didn't even try to keep the irritation from his face.

1 3

The water lapping against the hull of the boat was black and looked slick in the sparse light of the riverfront. It wasn't the biggest ship in the harbor—a mid-sized freighter one-third the size of the one on which he perched—but it would have at least five levels and countless nooks and crannies for enemies to hide in. This was going to be a hard mission. They would have to hit fast and drop as many as they could to keep from being overwhelmed.

Men and women carrying guns moved around the dock and the boat, not being subtle. He studied their movements and found no indication of military training. Not even the precision he had seen in the Skulls. These criminals simply wore dark clothes, no uniforms to make them easily recognizable to each other, no masks to conceal identity, just a bunch of thugs walking around "protecting" the dock. There were only four of them on the deck, none of them guarding the two gangplanks that were the only way someone could get on or off.

Amateurs.

But a lot of them. Just with the ones below him, they were outnumbered ten to one, and most of them were armed with more than a bow and some arrows. With that thought he shifted the quiver on his back and kept watching, and waiting.

"Spartan in position." Diggle's voice was clear in the comms.

His eyes shifted to the far side of the boat where Spartan would be hiding in the shadows, waiting on the signal. He couldn't see him, but knew he was there.

"Black Canary in position."

He twitched a smile at the sound of pride in Dinah's voice. She had been a good addition to the team. Even though he was a little wary of meta-humans, he found that having one on his side could be a good thing. As a result, when Rory—Ragman—left and Dinah came along, he'd been comfortable asking her to join the fight.

He looked to where she was supposed to be, spotting her on top of a stack of crates on the deck of their target. She blended into the darkness, thanks in part to her new tactical suit. He only saw her because he had the higher vantage point, and knew where to look.

"Mister Terrific checking in."

He didn't look for Curtis. He would be way on the other side of the ship, somewhere out of sight. *Hopefully* out of sight. Holt had come far since joining the team, applying natural athleticism to combat skills, training under the guidance of the more seasoned members. He was the weakest fighter on Team Arrow, but more than able to handle the level of thugs they were dealing with this night.

His stealth skills were hit or miss, though.

Maybe Sara could work with him while she was here. She would be able to teach him more than anyone else about stealth and camouflage. Thinking about her caused him to look where she was supposed to be, and he caught a glimmer of something light coming over the rail of the ship near the bow. It was just the faintest flicker of not-dark against the night. He didn't know how she could blend in like that, wearing white leather and having blond hair. League of Assassins training was the only explanation.

"*White Canary in position,*" she said, her voice a whisper. Then the comms went silent as everyone waited.

"Any word from Wild Dog?" he asked.

"*He responded,*" Felicity said. "*But nothing since.*"

"He had that thing," Curtis said. "Maybe he got delayed."

Oliver shifted his weight, changing position to ease the bulk of the loaded quiver on his back, considering how the plan could be adjusted if he wound up a man short.

"*I'm here,*" Rene snarled across the comms, his voice in a lower register than normal, simmering with anger. "*Ready to put the hurt on some bad guys.*"

Green Arrow stood from the shadow of the stacked tractor-trailer containers and drew his first arrow. He didn't say anything over the comms, but simply let fly.

The two explosions lit the night from the left, throwing orange firelight up over her. She crouched lower, in case anyone was looking in her direction, but all the crooks below her were running to the rail to see what the ruckus was. A few started down the gangplank on her end of the ship. She could hear their boots clanging on the metal stairs, even over the chorus of their shouts.

Her heart raced, a thrill chasing through her veins on a stream of adrenaline. The explosions were jarring, the sound and light of them, trying to toss her mind back to Lian Yu and the hell into which it had exploded. She'd barely escaped with her life alongside the others.

But they *had* escaped.

Dinah pushed all that away, focusing on the here and the now, applying to the situation a mindfulness that only came with combat training. She wasn't on Lian Yu, she was here, on this ship, in her new costume. She felt invincible, the new suit fitting her as if it were custom made—which it probably was.

Black Canary.

She'd been called the name, but now, in this suit, she felt… well, she felt like a superhero. Gripping her bō staff tightly, she waited for the signal to begin.

Another explosion rattled the ship, vibrating into

her joints even up on the stack of wooden crates on which she perched. After the boom of it was a screech of metal.

The signal.

Up and over, she dropped from the top of the crates, giving just a brief glance up to see Green Arrow zip-lining across the space from the huge Japanese freighter he'd been on to the deck of the ship the rest of the team occupied. Her boots hit the deck, and immediately she had to duck to keep a thug from caving her skull in with a crowbar. As she dropped low the metal bar hit the crate with a thud. She used the momentum of her drop to swing the bō staff in a low arc that connected with the man's ankle. It snapped under the blow and the man fell.

She pulled back to hit him across the temple to stop him from screaming, but he passed out cold.

Movement to her left made her jerk around.

A flash of light, and she spun away.

The gun fired in the woman's muscular hand, spitting muzzle flash just inches below her chin. The bullet missed her, singeing its way through a wave of her hair and lodging in the crate as well, but it was high enough that the flash took some of her night vision, solid dark eating the bottom edges of what she could see. She stepped back into the woman's reach, getting inside the firing range, and locked her arm over her opponent's outstretched one to keep the gun pointed behind her.

The woman snarled and lunged, her forehead crashing into Black Canary's, making her diminished vision flare white with sharp, jolting pain. She dropped her bõ staff, knees nearly buckling. The woman jerked her arm, trying to free her gun hand. Dinah clamped down tighter and threw herself at the woman's chest. Pressed closely against her she could see—mostly—enough to twist and slam the hard point of her elbow into the woman's chin. That close she heard teeth clack, even over all the chaos around them.

Blood sprayed up onto the thug's cheeks, her lip split from the elbow strike, eyes rolling up. Black Canary let her go and stepped back, making room, then bent to retrieve her bõ staff. Two quick strikes, one to the forearm to make the gun clatter to the deck, and the other across her temple to drive her down, as well.

The thug dropped like she'd been shot.

Black Canary stepped over and moved to the gangplank, watchful for any other attackers. Reaching it, she jerked the lever to raise the plank into sailing position, satisfied when she heard the hydraulics kick in. A glance over the rail showed the end of the gangplank rising, already a few feet off the dock.

A thug about midway down hung onto the railing as it rose, unsure of what to do even as the sections of it began to fold into themselves, including the one on which he stood. Black Canary watched until he dove off and fell along the ship's hull to splash into the black water below.

Vision back to normal, she turned to find the rest of the team.

Wild Dog thumbed the magazine release, reloading as the empty fell away. Still moving forward he began to fire at the group of thugs still standing. A handful lay on the ground, already out of commission from his first attack. His mind was a wire strung taut, all his rage at life and lawyers and court systems compressed into a line so fine it could have sliced flesh, if it were real. It was a focus he let ride him, turning him into an efficient machine.

Two of the goons fired at him, machine guns chattering bullets in his direction. The wire thrummed, vibrating behind his eyes, as he turned toward them, not moving for cover, just lining them up in his sights and pulling his own trigger. The two of them seized and twirled, dropping to join their associates.

Three more thugs ran, and on autopilot he popped off in their direction, not even aiming consciously, his eye, his mind, and his gun all one continuous circuit of efficiency. Two of them stumbled and fell, hitting the deck hard. The third turned the corner around a stack of pallets laden with boxes.

Drop the empty clip.

Pop a new one in.

Thumb the slide release.

Wild Dog began to follow after the runaway thug.

Mister Terrific spun, his feet leaving the deck and twisting in the air to avoid the length of chain whistling at the end of a massive thug's hand. He flipped over it as it cut the air where his kidney had just been, and landed on his heels.

He stayed low, crouched, as the hulking thug swung the chain in an arc around his head and brought it down in a figure eight. Curtis leapt back, hands coming out from under his jacket.

Holding his T-Spheres.

He released them and they zoomed forward, driving themselves into the thug's stomach with enough force to lift him off the deck and drop him on his knees. It took them a moment to push their way back out of his bulk.

"Stay down," Curtis said. "I don't want to hurt you more."

The thug nodded, staying on his knees but lifting his hands up in supplication, his head hanging low as he sucked air.

That was easy.

Mister Terrific pulled a zip tie out of his pocket and stepped forward, reaching for the man's outstretched hands. He had it looped around one wrist when the thug turned his hand and grabbed Curtis's sleeve. Before he could pull back the thug launched himself forward, wrapping his arms around Mister Terrific's torso and lifting him off the ground. Doing so left him off balance, however. Mister Terrific drove his foot into the crease of the man's hip and shoved, making him stumble backward. As they dropped down Curtis rolled, toppling the thug all the way to the ground.

But he didn't let go.

Suddenly the vigilante found himself pinned beneath a thug who outweighed him by twice his bulk. He bucked, using his shoulders and hips to bridge up, but the bigger man shoved him down again, driving the air out his lungs. Before he could bridge once more to try and breathe, there were meaty hands around his throat.

Mister Terrific dug his fingers under the edges of the thug's hands, trying to pull them off his windpipe. The pressure on his larynx increased and a line of pain cut across his esophagus, as if the cartilage inside had creased, folding in on itself.

His head pounded from a lack of oxygen.

He reached up, tapping the thug on the side of his face.

The criminal shrugged his hand away and snarled, "No tapping out in this wrestling match."

Mister Terrific pulled down on the fingers, loosening them just enough to gasp, "Wasn't... tapping... out..."

Before the thug could respond the T-Spheres slammed into his head. He jerked straight, going stiff, muscles locking up as his eyes rolled back in his head. Mister Terrific pushed him off, the big man falling sideways, unconscious. He stood, swallowing vigorously to try and clear the hard, painful lump there. He made the signal to call the T-Spheres back to his hand and put them away, massaging his neck with the fingers of his other hand.

Catching a glimpse of Wild Dog's jersey, he began following it across the maze of crates.

White Canary dropped down next to Spartan, landing with no noise. Her arrival made the circle of thugs around him stop suddenly. Her costume almost gleamed in the shifty darkness of the boat, making her look like a vengeful angel touching down. She gave him a grin and jerked her head in the direction of the gang of thugs that had pinned him into the corner. A smear of something dark ran along her jawline. He didn't see any active bleeding, so he assumed it wasn't blood.

At least not hers.

"Want an assist?" she asked, pulling out a pair of nunchaku. Somewhere off to the side there was another explosion and the sound of grinding metal, but if she noticed it, she gave no hint.

His hands felt swollen, tight laced with a deep ache in the joints and tendons. He'd caught a few punches in the brawl and landed a few of his own, so they hurt even through the padded jacket of his uniform. His helmet had saved him from a particularly crushing blow from an opponent who had gotten behind him earlier.

He wasn't about to go down but...

"Oh, yeah," Spartan said, raising his fists. "Let's mop these guys up."

As one they stepped forward, training and experience making them angle their backs to each other, dividing the bad guys between them like a knife through an air balloon.

He caught the first one with a punch he slipped under the thug's gun arm. His fist flared with some pain, but it was worth it to see the criminal drop. His follow-through was a wheel kick that landed his heavy boot into the back of another attacker, sending him stumbling to the ground. He grabbed the thug's shoulder, bracing himself as he snap-kicked the gun from a third criminal, this one a woman with short-cropped red hair.

As he slammed his elbow into the skull of the thug he held, the redhead landed on his back, throwing a wiry arm around his throat beneath his helmet, holding him in a choke. He pulled his shoulders up, driving the bottom edge of the helmet into the muscles of her arm. She howled in pain, loud in his ears, but didn't let go. He spun on his heel, making her legs flail out. Stopping suddenly slammed her into his back, one leg out to his side.

Latching onto that he jerked up, bracing his elbow against the knee, applying joint-separating pressure.

That made her let go.

As she slid off his back he hauled up on the leg he had captured, increasing her momentum. She bounced off the ground, limp and unconscious. Her dead weight dragged at him and he let go to keep from being pulled to the ground.

He stumbled, stopping himself on one of the crates. Looking up, he caught sight of White Canary in action. She was a blur of movement, driving her way through the criminals who seemed to be standing still by comparison. The nunchaku whirled around her, too fast to see in the dim light, but their effect was immediate.

Whirr and *smack*, and a thug hit the ground as if dropped from a height.

Whirr and *smack*, and another one crumpled like a stack of cardboard boxes.

Spin, *whirr*, and *smack*, and one more bent in half to be taken out by a spinning wheel kick that landed on the back of his neck. She wasn't just Sara Lance anymore. Not the same person he had known for years, and fought beside in the past. She wasn't simply a vigilante—not like him, not just a soldier in the fight for right.

She had become poetry of violence, a song of brutal efficiency.

She was the White Canary.

Damn, he thought, *she's a superhero.*

The thought brought him no feeling of inadequacy, simply awe at what someone he considered an ally— and even a friend—had become. He knew the League of Assassins had trained her. He knew she'd been through the Lazarus Pit, brought back from death. He knew she'd spent the last bit traveling through time alongside the Legends.

He was still impressed.

As the last thug lay moaning at her feet she shook her hair out of her eyes and gave him another reckless grin.

"Let's go find the others and join their fun."

1 4

The deck of the ship rushed up at him as he slid down the zip line, shooting arrows into the dock and herding the criminals who had yet to board the ship. Close enough, he released his grip and dropped. Right onto the back of a thug who had his rifle aimed at Black Canary.

He hit solidly, all his weight and momentum driving through the bottom of his boots, transferring it into the thug like a wrecking ball. The machine gun chattered out, bullets flying up into the night sky. The man didn't stand up as the Green Arrow rolled away and onto his feet.

Spinning, he dismissed that one, then drew and notched an arrow. He located another target, a figure moving quickly across the deck, and fired. The arrow streaked across. He already had another arrow notched and ready when it struck down its target.

He fired four more, clearing the area in front of him.

Into the comms he said, "Green Arrow in position, converge."

Moving over to the rail, he glanced down. The gangplank below was a twist of scorched metal courtesy of the explosive arrow he'd fired at it before zip-lining down from his perch. The one on the other end had been drawn up by Black Canary and hung folded at the top of the ship's hull.

The ship was cut off. All the henchmen on the docks had been removed from the equation. The rest of his team were moving steadily toward him. Now all they had to do was clear the lower decks. As they gathered around him, he spoke into the comms.

"Overwatch, any idea how many we could be dealing with down below?"

"The ship hull is too dense to get any type of satellite imaging, except that a lot of heat is being generated in the cargo hold," Felicity said. *"Judging from the schematic, you can get to it just two decks down."*

He nodded, even though Felicity couldn't see it from the Bunker, then spoke to Team Arrow as he began moving toward the hatch.

"Alex Faust is priority number one," he growled. "We find him and take him down, no matter what. Teams of two."

They all nodded, falling into step after him as Felicity began giving directions over the comms. Abruptly the ship's motors revved, the deck vibrating under their feet.

"Is that the engine?" Mister Terrific asked.

They stopped moving, boots and shins absorbing the oscillation caused by the boat's motor. The vessel lurched sideways, and slowly began chugging away from the dock.

"I think someone is on to us," White Canary said.

"What do you think their first clue was?" Wild Dog replied sarcastically.

Green Arrow spoke, voice stern. "Doesn't matter. Faust is the objective. If he's expecting us it means he'll probably be easier to find." He began moving toward the below-decks hatch, Team Arrow on his heels.

"You should be coming up on the cargo bay hatch."

"We see it, Overwatch," Green Arrow answered. The hatch was shut, a lever lock in place. He stopped, raising his hand to signal the rest of the team to stop as well. There was no window in the door, just a welded metal slab. They'd made their way to this point unhindered, not encountering any resistance.

The trap was obvious.

For the briefest moment he considered turning around, just leaving. Ordering the team to evacuate, walking away to confront his target another time when it was on his terms, not Faust's.

To be smarter.

Or luckier.

To avoid another Lian Yu.

William.

Adrian Chase had put Faust on his trail. Chase knew his identity, knew about William. If he had told Faust... the ramifications could be fatal to his son, and to those he cared for most.

He would protect William, at whatever cost.

"Be ready for anything." His murmur carried to everyone through the comms. He put his hand on the lever and opened the door.

"Well, it certainly took you long enough."

The voice came from a dark so thick it felt like pressure against their skins. A dim light entered through the open hatch, but it could only diffuse, not disperse, the inky blackness. It was too weak, not enough. The team fanned out behind him, covering his back. He pulled an arrow from his quiver, notching it into the bow in his hand.

"Faust!" he bellowed, voice amplified by the distorter. "I know you're here. Show yourself!"

"Oh, I'll show myself." The voice thrummed off the metal walls, warping into a psychotic melody. "After all, we are nothing more than what we choose to reveal."

"He's quoting Sylvia Plath?" Wild Dog muttered.

"You know Sylvia Plath?" Black Canary asked.

"I've got the soul of a poet."

Before Green Arrow could tell them to be focused

there was a *buzz* and a *click*, and light flooded the room they were in. Klieg lights had been strung along the top of the cargo hold and now they blazed down like the eyes of some sun god. He squinted up into their glare, then turned his eyes down before his vision could go spotty. Even with the top half of the cargo hold lost to shadow, the room loomed around them. Its walls rose twenty feet up, braced with steel beams. They had been scrubbed and scraped by whatever things had been transported in this hold, and now they were more rust than paint. A steel catwalk surrounded the room midway up the wall, connecting additional hatches like the one through which they'd entered. A dozen or more ropes hung to the floor, scattered through the cargo hold.

On the other side of the vast space stood a man.

Middling height and awkwardly thin, he seemed to be loosely knitted together in the mud-colored suit that hung off him. Frizzy hair spilled over one side of his clean-shaven face. Even this far away his smile could be seen. He leaned casually against a rough wooden table, and there was a suitcase-sized mechanical device on it. Beside him stood a stack of orange plastic bricks piled to the same height as the table. Behind him was a wall of similar bricks that stood ten foot high and stretched nearly across the width of the hold.

"As you can see," Alex Faust said, indicating the plastic bricks, "it would be best if you hooligans refrain from shooting any bullets, or even arrows, in this direction."

"Semtex," Spartan said. "It's stable. Bullets and arrows don't set it off."

"You are correct about Semtex," the man replied, "but do you think I'd be here if I used plain old, *boring* Semtex? Certainly not without doing a little doctoring of my own." He giggled and the sound rippled along the steel walls. "Does that seem like the kind of person Prometheus would leave in charge?"

Exchanging glances, Spartan and Wild Dog lowered their guns.

As they looked to him for guidance, Oliver's hands itched to draw his bow and put an arrow feathers-deep in Faust. But he couldn't stop picturing Chase, pulling the trigger of the gun he held to his own temple, and then hearing the first of a chain of explosions that might mean everyone he cared about was dead.

Everyone but the son he held in his arms.

He hesitated.

"I know what you're thinking." Faust cocked his head, looking at him. "And you're right. I might have a dead man switch. It wouldn't be out of character." He sighed, swinging his arms around dramatically. "But you don't really know my character, now do you?"

"We know the character of the man who put you up to this."

"Does that make you more or less certain of how I'll act?"

"Screw this," Wild Dog growled. "What's to stop us from just going over there and delivering a beat down to this psycho?"

Faust pointed toward the darkness above the lights. "They are." As one the hanging ropes began shaking as men in black tactical gear rappeled to the floor, filling the space between them and Faust. Green Arrow did a quick head count.

They were outnumbered three to one.

"Have fun!" Faust called. "I'd stay and watch, but I really need to go." He patted the device on the table. "Don't get so caught up in dancing that you forget about Betsy here." He flipped a switch, causing a red light to begin blinking. Then he turned and slipped around the end of the wall of doctored Semtex.

Oliver slung the bow over his back, speaking over the comms so everyone heard him. "They don't have guns, so Faust must be telling the truth. No shooting, not even away from the explosives. If there was just one ricochet…" He didn't need to finish the thought.

Spartan and Wild Dog looked at each other.

"Ah, hell," Spartan said, holstering his pistol.

Dinah stepped forward, twisting outside the man's attempt to grab her. As she passed him, she fired a punch to his temple. He stumbled. She drove the end of her bõ staff into the back of his knee and leaned, her body weight making the joint crumple and fold.

He went down to all fours with a cry of pain that she silenced with a quick strike to his neck.

Something heavy struck her back, just to the left of her spine and above her kidney. It knocked her forward and left her gasping for air as her diaphragm spasmed. She hopped to keep from tripping on the henchman she'd just knocked out, spinning around to see who had struck her.

Another opponent had his fists raised, poised like a boxer, coming toward her with short, crab-like steps. He was thick, cables of muscle laid under the skin of his forearms, a square plug of violence. His left eye pulled up at the corner, lifted by a wad of scar tissue where his eyebrow should've ended. He *was* a boxer, at least a brawler, so he would know how to use the power in his physique for maximum damage.

She was grateful for her new suit. If she'd been wearing just her old jacket, he would have hospitalized her with that blow. As it was she straightened, facing him.

"Ah, girlie," the boxer said, raising his voice to be heard over the din of the fighting that rose around them. "I came straight over here when I spotted you."

She swallowed down her canary cry, forcing herself to hold it in. She didn't know how stable the explosives in the room might be, and couldn't take the chance of setting them off, no matter how much she wanted to blast the lewd grin off the man's face. At the thought, though, she smiled as he stepped closer to her.

She'd just have to knock off that grin the old-fashioned way.

"You glad to see me, girlie? I'm glad to—"

Dinah slid the bõ staff through her lead hand, driving with her hips to put as much torque behind it as she could. The staff flew straight out, moving faster than could be seen, and crashed into the boxer's mouth, knocking teeth out in a spray of blood. He cried out and crashed to his knees as if his feet had been cut out from beneath him. Overknuckled hands clasped his mouth, blood running off their bottom edge to drip on his chest.

Black Canary stepped forward. "You glad to see *me*, girlie?"

Her boot caught him in the stomach, just under the breastbone. He went pale and fell to the ground.

She was already moving to the next target.

Spartan jerked up, applying pressure on the throat of the henchman he had in a headlock. The man's hands scrabbled at Diggle's jacket, but he was relentless and within a few seconds the man went limp.

There was a satisfying thud as he let him drop.

Another henchman, a tall lanky specimen, swung an ax at him. He turned into the swing, reaching out and grabbing the henchman's shirt. His fingers rolled into the ripstop cloth, pain shooting along the tendons due to the pressure. Using the hold as leverage, he fired a flurry of elbow strikes at the man's head. Ax-man jerked away and the strikes barely grazed him, mostly landing on his shoulders. The henchman lashed out with the ax, striking Diggle with the flat of it. It wasn't a solid blow, but still it made a hard throb of pain across his side. He let go, taking two steps back. Ax-man shifted the ax in his hands, raising the blade as if to begin chopping Spartan down to size.

Diggle watched the ax rise, struggling to draw breath. That ax head was going to split his skull, and he couldn't get enough oxygen to move.

Goodbye, Lyla and little John. I love you.

With the ax raised up over his head, the ax-man jerked three times, then went stiff. His hands opened and the ax slipped around through his claw-like fingers, to strike his own face. His eyes rolled up and he fell forward, crashing on top of his weapon.

White Canary was there.

She stepped forward, helping him up. Spartan glanced at the fallen henchman and saw three shuriken jutting from the man's back.

"Black lotus gum," Sara said. "Knocks out the biggest and the baddest in under a minute."

Spartan grunted, "Good trick."

"League of Assassins, baby," she grinned.

"Thanks for the assist," he said. "Sorry I needed it."

"You got hit with an ax—it could happen to any of us."

She ducked left, another henchman's ax whistling

past where her head had been. Spartan stepped forward and put an uppercut into the man's jaw, sending with it every bit of anger he held. The henchman fell like a tree in a hurricane wind.

Now his hand throbbed with pain to the elbow.

"Not all of us," he said.

She gave him a quick push. "So we're even—stop being grumpy." She turned away and began to fight again. Diggle shook his hand out and did the same.

"Oliver."

He knew the voice on the comms was for his ears only, since Felicity used his name. He drove a palm strike into the chest of the henchman who was charging him, hand tensed to make it like a thing of iron. The henchman stopped short as the shock of the blow jolted through his body, disrupting the functions of his nervous system. Raising his fist over his head, Oliver dropped a devastating back-fist to the suprascapular nerve cluster between the man's neck and shoulder. The flechettes stored along the back of his gauntlet added weight and rigidity to the strike.

The henchman fell face forward.

"Go," he said, tracking another target.

"We have a problem."

"I don't have time to play twenty questions, so tell me." He moved toward a henchman coming up behind Wild Dog.

"The boat you're on is changing course, and is heading toward Cape Dixon."

He remembered Cape Dixon, a small outcropping into the water, not truly large enough for the term "cape," and nearly all of it was wide sandy beaches. This time of night it should be deserted.

The henchman reached him, swinging knuckles covered in brass. He slipped the punch, driving his knuckle into the ulna nerve in the man's inner bicep.

"What's the problem?"

"Rangerettes Midnight Jamboree," Felicity said. *"There are three hundred girls camping on that beach."*

Damn. He landed a back-fist but it just skimmed off the henchman's shoulder.

"How long—" He grunted, swinging again. "—till we get there?"

"Thirteen minutes."

The henchman caught him a stiff shot to the cheek that made his eyes water. Training turned into instinct and he latched onto the man's wrist with iron fingers and yanked, pulling his assailant off balance. He grabbed him around the waist and spun him into the air, driving him to the floor. Then he turned to look for Curtis, and found him a few feet away.

Mister Terrific dropped low and did a sweeping kick, knocking the legs out from under an opponent built like a cement mixer. The man crashed to the floor on his back, the breath forced out of him. Curtis scrambled over, putting his knee on the henchman's neck, pressing against the carotid artery. He kept the pressure on until the man's eyes rolled up into his head and he went still.

Suddenly Green Arrow was next to him, flipping a henchman up and slamming him down so hard Curtis felt the steel floor under him vibrate. He stood as Oliver stepped over and put a hand on his shoulder.

"*Overwatch and Mister Terrific.*" Green Arrow's voice echoed through the comms. "*Disarm that device.*" Oliver gave him a push toward the table and simultaneously pulled a flechette from the back of his glove and flung it at an advancing henchman.

"*On it,*" Felicity said.

Mister Terrific nodded, even though Green Arrow had turned away.

"*Wild Dog, watch Mister Terrific's back. If he can't stop that bomb, we're all dead.*"

"*On my way, Hoss,*" Wild Dog said.

Green Arrow spun, driving his heel deep in the stomach of an attacker, folding the man in half.

"*Spartan, go after Faust, Black Canary assist. Be careful of booby traps.*"

Spartan and Black Canary didn't respond, simply following orders by moving toward the gap through which Faust had slipped. As they did, White Canary swung on one of the dangling ropes, wrapping her legs around a henchman's head. She flung herself forward, snapping him around and off his feet, driving him to the steel floor.

She stood. He didn't.

Sara moved next to Arrow. "I guess you and I are mopping clean-up."

"I know how much you like housekeeping." He clenched his fists, watching henchmen gather themselves to attack. Many were moaning on the floor, out of the fight, but there were enough to be a problem. He'd divided the team to their strengths. He and Sara were the best hand-to-hand fighters, and Wild Dog held position as runner-up due to his sheer ferocity. Curtis was without a doubt the best chance they had for defusing the bomb, especially backed by Felicity in the Bunker. Diggle's marksmanship made him best suited to run down Faust.

Felicity clicked her mouse furiously. Her voice went over the comms to Curtis and Rene.

"Guys, let me know when you're in position."

It drove her crazy to only have access to voice, but there were no cameras on site, and no way for any satellite to pick them up through the hull of a moving freighter. Though blind, she'd have to make it work.

She took another swig of coffee that had gone cold, oily, and bitter. Her face twisted but she kept staring at the screens in front of her, fervently wishing she could just see what was happening.

* * *

Mister Terrific loped across the cargo hold, using his long legs to eat the distance. A henchman lunged at him and he twisted away, causing the man to stumble past him. He glanced back to find Wild Dog already on the assailant.

Wild Dog slammed into the man, using his momentum to drive his hockey mask into the guy's nose. Blood gushed, sluicing off the hard plastic of the mask to run onto the jersey in spatters of crimson. Rene looked down at it, shaking his head.

"Oh, hell no, you done it now." He launched in, driving fists into his target's torso. The henchman gasped, turning the blood sheeting his mouth into a weird bubble between his lips. Wild Dog reached back, knuckles just inches from the floor, and launched his fist like a rocket sled on rails, torquing at the hips to drive his fist with every ounce of power he could summon into the soft spot he'd created.

The man crumpled under that last blow.

Wild Dog turned, facing outward, and backed his way toward Mister Terrific, fists raised in front of his bloodstained jersey. "Stop that bomb," he called over his shoulder. "I've got you covered. I can't go out dirty like this."

Another man plowed into him and he went down swinging elbows and fists. Mister Terrific hesitated, but moved on, trusting Wild Dog's ability to fight.

1 5

Orange emergency lights lined the curved corridor, casting everything in strange shadows. Spartan was in the lead by just a few feet, gun up and at the ready now that they were far enough away from the explosives. Black Canary stayed close, and neither of them spoke. The rubber soles of their boots made no noise on the metal floor, even though they were moving quickly.

They could hear Faust ahead of them, running just out of sight. The sound was echoed by something behind them. Black Canary hesitated, slowing her steps, and sub-vocalized, her voice so low it barely carried past her lips.

"I'll catch up."

The comms link picked it up. Spartan nodded broadly so she could see the motion, but he didn't stride. She slipped into one of the shadows between lights, her costume blending with the darkness.

Spartan disappeared around the bend of the corridor.

The noise from behind them continued to draw closer.

She gripped her bõ staff tighter.

After only a few moments two henchmen appeared from around the bend. They were cut from the same cloth—same height, same athletic build, same stride that indicated some form of military training. They moved like Spartan and were nearly his size. They even held matching batons in their right hands.

She held her breath as they marched by, passing her without a sideways glance even though she could have touched the one closest to her without stretching. Then she stepped out, took a deep breath…

…and screamed.

Both of them stumbled, knocked forward by the sheer force of the sound waves. The henchman on the left dropped his baton and fell to his knees, hands clamping over his ears. Her cry made the metal walls vibrate, the air between them shimmering as the ripples reverberated off them.

The henchman on the right stopped moving, bracing himself against the blast of her cry. He held onto his baton, his hands remaining down.

A twinge of pain cut deep to the left of her esophagus, a small reminder of pushing her voice against the fire. She stopped screaming, and as the echoes of her cry faded, they were replaced by the weeping of the man who had fallen. He was lying on his side in the fetal position, hands clapped over bleeding ears.

The right henchman turned to face her.

Why didn't he go down?

He raised his left hand and his fingers began to dance, spelling out words.

For a moment, a split second, she was taken aback by the concept of a deaf henchman. There was no reason he couldn't be deaf *and* be a criminal. She knew from her career as a cop that all kinds of people went the wrong way, and in this case it certainly made him effective against her. Still, she had never considered the possibility.

Her mind swirled until he swung the club at her head.

Dinah jerked her staff up in a block, and the impact tore it out of her hands. Her opponent followed with a hard front kick aimed at her stomach, but she twisted and caught it on her hip. The blow skidded across her back a few inches, pain radiating under her skin.

Bruise, she thought.

Using the momentum from the impact she spun into a high heel kick, aiming to break his jaw. He bobbed back, though, her boot barely grazing his chin, not enough even to daze him. She came around and back on both feet, hands up in fists.

The baton thudded against her arm.

Her Kevlar-reinforced jacket saved her a broken bone, but a shock of pain ran down her arm and into her fingertips, and they lost their strength.

The henchman drew back and swung again.

She dove under, the baton whistling through the space where her head had been, tucking in and rolling back up to her feet. Holding the other henchman's baton.

Her teeth clenched tight behind a grin she didn't want to suppress. She was a stick fighter. She spent more training time working with a full bõ staff, preferring to use both hands, generating power at each end of the hardwood weapon by using the length of it as a lever with her as the fulcrum, turning her strength into crushing force.

But she had started with shorter sticks. The baton in her hand was spring steel and collapsible, an ASP like she had carried before she made detective. It was lighter than the rattan batons she used in escrima, but the steel had much less give.

In anyone else's hands it was a bludgeon.

In her hands?

It was a bonecrusher.

The henchman shared her grin and shifted, adjusting his body into the lowered stance of a trained fighter. He raised his empty hand between them and beckoned her to engage.

She swiped out with the baton, flicking it at his outstretched hand. He pulled back quickly and she missed. He wagged a finger and clucked his tongue at her. And then he attacked.

First came a downward swing at her skull. Her baton came up, redirecting the motion and opening up his arms so she could jab in with the end of her baton, shooting for the little tab of bone at the bottom of his sternum. Snap it off, and breathing would become a hitching pain with every gulp of air. Again he swept down, baton smashing into hers with a *clang* that vibrated into her fingers. She twisted, letting the impact drive her blow downward. The tip of her ASP cracked the side of his knee, good and solid at the juncture of his anterior cruciate ligament. He stumbled, slewing sideways as his knee crumpled.

She let loose a canary cry.

The henchman couldn't hear it, but the force of the sound waves pushed him further off balance. She stepped in, swallowing the cry as she raised the baton. He raised an arm to block her, but one swing knocked it aside. The next drove into the place where his neck became shoulder, creasing deep in the juncture beside the trapezius. She watched his eyes roll back as the nerve cluster there short-circuited.

He was done. A quick glance and she saw his partner was also still down. She kicked his baton, sending it clattering down the hallway, and tossed the one in her hand away after it. The feeling had mostly returned in her other hand as she picked up her bō staff and left the henchmen behind to follow after Spartan.

He swept around, leg out, taking down a henchman who landed on his shoulders and skull. Mostly skull.

The spinning leg sweep took him into a roll that

brought him to his feet again. He shoulder-checked a large guy who tried to grab him, knocking him sideways. Stretching, he swung a fist at a third henchman but overreached and missed. That henchman threw himself at Green Arrow, driving him back.

Green Arrow pulled a flechette from the back of his glove. He drove it down and the scalpel-sharp blade slipped easily into the meat of the henchman's arm. Instantly blood coated his fingertips, adding to the iron-and-salt scent of the air.

The henchman rolled, bellowing and pulling away from him. His flailing elbow caught Green Arrow in the mouth. Pain shot through Green Arrow's face, from his chin to the back of his skull, just one solid bolt of hurt. His teeth clacked, biting his tongue deep enough to draw blood that filled his mouth all hot and tinny-tasting. His eyes watered from the blow and his brain went animal and wild.

His eyes narrowed and he focused, finding the henchman pulling the flechette from his arm. Arrow spit his own blood onto the floor between them. The henchman tried throwing the flechette back at him, thin, sharp steel spinning through the space between them, still coated in blood.

Green Arrow caught it in midair.

He flung it downward, and it flew like an arrow, sinking hilt-deep into the henchman's boot. The man opened his mouth to howl, but Green Arrow was already on him. He swung three short jabs, driving with his shoulder, torquing with his hips. His fists sank in, as solid as a lumberjack chopping down a tree. He was so deep in the pocket of the henchman's reach that he felt the man's breath on his cheek as each blow folded the henchman more and more, until he was bent completely at the waist.

Oliver stepped back and the henchman dropped to the floor in a boneless heap.

Fists up, Green Arrow pivoted, ready for the next one.

"What does it look like?"

"Um," Mister Terrific said, looking down at the inside of the device on the table. "It looks like a psycho built this."

"What do you mean?" Felicity asked through the comms.

"Oh, sorry, hold on a moment." He pulled out his T-Spheres, tossing them up. They hovered above him, one scanning the device, the other filming. "You should have live feeds now."

"Ah, got them."

Mister Terrific waited for her to study her screens.

"Wait…" Her voice drew out the word. *"Is that a Hamilton 308 bomb timer device?"*

"It is."

"And an acid battery relay?"

"Yep."

"*And a cell phone detonator?*"

"Yep."

"*Wow, an old flip-style burner phone,*" Felicity muttered. "*Way to go hipster retro style there.*"

Mister Terrific waited for her to get to the rest.

"*What is that plate thing there?*" she asked.

"That is a pressure switch, circa World War Two."

"*German?*"

He shook his head before remembering she couldn't see the motion, since the T-Sphere was focused on the device and not on him.

"British. From a limpet bomb, I believe," he said. "I mean I know it is, 'cause I wrote a paper on them in World History in the eleventh grade."

"*Those old bombs they used to magnetically adhere to the undersides of boats?*"

"The same."

"*Whoa,*" Felicity said. "*And I thought the flip phone was retro.*"

"He wired all of them together," Curtis responded. "Like I said, psycho."

"*So if one goes they all go?*"

"Looks like…" Something nagged at him.

"*What's wrong?*" Felicity asked. "*I can hear something is wrong.*"

"Where is the clock?"

"*Don't you see it?*"

"No, there is no clock." His face itched under his mask. "You don't put this much work into something like this unless there's a countdown. That's one of the things psychos want most, to have everyone watching closely as they get blown up."

"I've read Faust's file. He does things for show. He will *have a clock."*

"There's not one here. I'm looking at digital interfacing with analog hooked up to mechanical, and none of it has a timer."

One of the klieg lights overhead blinked out.

Mister Terrific looked around. Green Arrow, White Canary, and Wild Dog still fought Faust's thugs. Darkness ate the section of the hold where the light had shone down.

A red dot appeared on the front of the device.

"I think we may have found our timer."

Another klieg went out.

1 6

"What happened to the lights?"

White Canary turned, hip tossing a thug to the ground. He bounced hard off the steel and tumbled away. The move put her close enough to Wild Dog to ask the question.

"Don't know," he grunted, kicking out at a henchman he'd just knocked down to all fours. His boot clipped the bad guy on the jaw, the impact shuddering up Wild Dog's shin to his knee. "But I don't like it." He put his hands to his mouth and called out to Mister Terrific. "Hey, Hoss! How's it coming?"

Mister Terrific waved his hand but kept his head down, looking inside the device Faust had left behind on the table.

Wild Dog turned back to her. "He's got it though."

White Canary grabbed his jersey, pulling him sideways as she pivoted and lashed out with a kick that took the legs out from under an assailant who had tried to drive a long-bladed knife into Wild Dog's back. The henchman slammed face-first to the steel floor. The knife spun away toward the dark spot in the cargo hold.

"I'm sure he does," she said with a crooked grin.

Wild Dog shouldered her to the side, stepping in front of the guy trying to zap her with a wide Taser. Rene clamped his hand on the henchman's wrist and jerked the hand holding the weapon, shoving the crackling electrodes up under the man's beard. His fingers squeezed the other man's hand, depressing the trigger and sending electricity up into the bad guy's jaw. The man's boots jittered on the floor as his body locked in a convulsion.

He was out before Wild Dog let off the button.

Another light went out overhead.

"Still don't like it," Rene said.

Spartan gave the man a short chop, driving the grip of his pistol between the guy's shoulder blades. The blow wasn't hard enough to do any real damage, but it was enough to send him tumbling down the metal stairs Spartan had just climbed.

Diggle watched him bang his way down and sprawl at the bottom, and used the moments to catch his breath. Running up stairs like that was hard. His thighs burned and his lungs felt shallow from it, as if they couldn't take in enough air. A band of tightness ran across his chest.

Shaking it off, he kept climbing, chasing after Faust.

Pulling himself up over the last step he found himself on a deck. Ahead he could see Faust undoing the rigging on a motorized lifeboat. He raised his gun and fast walked across the open space.

"Freeze!"

Faust stopped, hands remaining on the block-and-tackle pulley system used for lowering the boat. He looked over at Spartan, hair falling across his face.

"But, I'm almost finished," he said. "A task only half started is a task undone." He began working on the release of the boat, even though he kept watching the oncoming enemy.

"I *will* shoot you." Spartan's hand was tight on the pistol.

"I believe you," Faust said. "I truly do, but I have this thing in my head, it's a timekeeper, a tick and a tock and *clickety clack* that never stops, never stops, never stops, it just keeps going a click and a tick a second. Even when I sleep it's there."

"I don't care." The muscles of his shoulders started to burn, deep in the fibers of them, the same hot sensation that came after a long workout.

The boat dropped half an inch.

"Oh, you should," Faust said. "Because of it I know we don't have much time left, and I'd much rather be shot than stay for the inferno this boat is about to become."

"That's not going to happen." The first micro-tremor ran down his tricep like a trickle of hot pain. He tightened his grip on the pistol.

"It will," Faust replied. "It is inevitable. You don't have anyone who can decipher the ignition I built for this occasion." He stepped into the boat, one foot in it, the other on the deck.

The gun in Spartan's hand rocked left then right as the micro-tremor slid down into his forearm. The carpal tunnel swelled shut and his fingers went nerveless and wooden.

He pulled the trigger.

Faust dropped into the boat, disappearing from sight.

Spartan lowered the gun, holding it close to his body to steady his convulsing arm.

Faust sat up. He reached above him, grabbing the end of the release rope on the block-and-tackle pulley. He grinned widely and waved as he yanked the release. The boat fell away.

Sprinting as best he could, Spartan reached the rail as the lifeboat splashed to the water below. Faust hit the ignition switch for the outboard motor and it fired to life with a throaty chugging. In seconds the lifeboat pulled away from the ship and disappeared in the dark.

Spartan holstered his pistol and turned.

Black Canary ran up from the stairs.

"He got away," Diggle said.

Three klieg lights burned overhead.

Green Arrow hit the comms. "The lights are tied into the bombs?"

"We think they are the countdown," Felicity's voice said.

White Canary and Wild Dog stood a few feet away. Henchmen lay around them moaning. He moved over to them.

"You two need to get out of here," he ordered. "In case the bomb doesn't get disarmed."

"What about them?" White Canary motioned to the floor full of downed henchmen.

"Corral them up to the deck and off the boat. They can carry their own."

"Man," Wild Dog said. "First we kick their asses, now we save their asses."

"Wild Dog—" Green Arrow growled, the warning deep in his voice.

Rene threw his hands up. "I know, we're heroes. I get it."

"Come on, hero." White Canary jerked her head to the side. "Let's get these doggies rollin'." They began pulling henchmen up to their feet, pushing them to the door of the cargo hold. Green Arrow watched them for a second, then turned toward Mister Terrific.

Mister Terrific didn't look, even though he felt Green Arrow walk up like a high-pressure front. The man projected intensity twenty-four seven, but when he was in costume the intensity became nearly overwhelming, as if the hooded figure could bend the universe through sheer force of will.

Which was ridiculous. Physics didn't work that way.

But if it did…

"Where are we at?" Green Arrow asked.

"Um, nowhere," Curtis replied. "I mean, we're on a boat with a *lot* of explosives, but—"

"Not talking to you."

"Oh."

Felicity's voice came over their comms. *"At present speed, you hit the cape in four minutes and thirty-seven seconds."*

"How much explosive is this?"

No one said anything.

Mister Terrific twitched. "Oh, you mean me?" he said. "Right." He scanned the stacks, tallying mentally. "Assuming standard weight and consistency of—"

"How much?" Green Arrow growled.

"Looks like approximately six tons."

"Overwatch?"

"One sec," Felicity said. Time stretched as she calculated. *"That much explosive will turn the ship into shrapnel. Anything past two minutes from now and there will be injuries. Probably twenty-five percent at that point. Every second after, multiply by ten percent 'til you reach one hundred."*

Green Arrow stood for a second, weighing the information.

"I can keep working," Mister Terrific said. "I'll get this."

Green Arrow pointed to the center of the device. "Is that the pressure switch from a limpet bomb?"

"How did—"

"*Yes.*" Felicity cut off Mister Terrific's question.

"That will detonate?"

"*Yes.*"

He motioned Mister Terrific toward the open cargo hold door. The room was clear save for them. "Let's go." He touched the comms, sending his voice out to the entire team. "Everybody off the boat and get as far from it as you can. Go now—we'll catch up."

Another klieg light snuffed out as they ran across the room.

They cleared the last doorway, moving out onto the empty deck. Green Arrow kept moving, talking over the comms.

"Sound off."

Wild Dog's voice came over the comms. *"We're gone. All cleared except you two. We left a boat for you."*

"Ninety seconds to the threshold," Felicity's voice said.

Green Arrow reached the controls to the cargo bay and pushed the big green button there. A deep rumble started up as the wide metal bay doors began to slide open.

"What are you doing?" Mister Terrific asked.

"Making a path of least resistance."

"Ah, so the force of the explosion will go up instead

of out." Mister Terrific shook his head. "There's too much material down there. The ship is still going to be wrecked."

The cargo bay doors stopped moving, open all the way.

"Thirty seconds," Felicity said, voice tight with worry.

Green Arrow unslung his bow, drawing out an arrow. "How deep do we need to be in the water to survive?"

Mister Terrific's mind worked, calculating a hundred factors—exponential force, shear point for the ship's steel hull, system momentum change, the insulation of water, the release of force going upward now against the buoyancy of the ship, and more.

"Thirty seven and a half feet minimum."

Green Arrow nodded.

He notched the arrow and aimed down in the cargo hold, using the glow of the last klieg light to see his target.

He inhaled.

"Wait," Mister Terrific said. "You aren't—"

Exhaled.

The arrow flew.

Pivoting, the two vigilantes ran toward the rail and leapt, both of them flinging themselves out into the open air. They arced, falling, one with the grace of an Olympian, the other with the grace of a savage, splitting the water at the same time. Both kept their bodies streamlined, shooting into the murky depths.

Their momentum had just slowed when the thunder

rumbled under the water and light flooded down on them, even through the dark water, as the ship exploded and sent down a fiery rain of burning metal.

JULY 2017

1

She fiddled with the chopsticks in her hand, moving them between her fingers, rubbing them together, clicking the tips of them against her napkin.

Doing everything but eating the sushi on the plate in front of her.

"What's on your mind?" he asked. They were in the Bunker, and the rest of the team was off and away, leaving just the two of them working late.

She jumped at his question. "What? Oh, nothing."

His eyebrows lowered. "Felicity."

She glanced up, and then back down at her plate. "I'm always uncomfortable with chopsticks. I mean, I know how to use them." Her mouth quirked and her eyes went sideways as a thought occurred to her. "Actually, I know how to use them to take someone out if we were attacked."

"I know." He almost smiled. "I taught you that."

"Did you know that in Japan they don't use chopsticks to eat sushi?"

"I did know that."

"They don't use them to take people out, either."

Now he did smile. "That's not true. Where do you think I learned how to do it?"

She looked at him with narrowed eyes. "I'm not sure you're actually joking."

"I am," he said. "I learned the chopstick technique in Russia."

"Let me get this straight, Oliver Queen." She leaned forward, lowering her voice. "You're telling me the criminal underworld in Russia eats *sushi*?"

He leaned forward, lowering his voice to match hers.

"They love it. Sushi and vodka."

She sat back and made a face. "Ugh, now you've ruined it for me."

He laughed loudly and smiled widely, enjoying the banter. It had been far too long since he and Felicity had dinner alone. Most meals were captured things, food eaten between other activities, not something to be enjoyed.

This, tonight, felt strange in its normality.

"Would you like to order something else?" he asked.

She shook her head. "No, but I will *not* be having any vodka." She placed her chopsticks on the napkin. "And I am eating this the traditional way." She picked up a piece of sushi between her fingers, and popped it into her mouth.

"Why, Miss Smoak, I think you have that technique down."

"Thank you very much, Mr. Queen."

"Please, no need to be so formal. Call me Mayor Queen."

The laugh burst out of her, taking her whole face.

"You truly are stunning," he said.

The seriousness of his tone stopped her short. The mood between them shifted, going from light and cheer-filled to something, not exactly darker, but weighted with potential. Her hands touched her dress, fluttering under the intensity of his gaze.

"It's new."

"Not the dress," he said flatly. "It is lovely, but I meant what I said. *You* are stunning."

Her cheeks grew warm but she held his gaze, unable to turn from it, unwilling to break that connection.

"You clean up pretty good yourself."

The Bunker fell away, leaving nothing but the two of them and their history together. The tangled and complicated story of *them* that tied the two together and kept them apart, things that had been done, things that had been said, things that had been forgiven, and things that didn't need to be. Tonight they were something neither of them had experienced before.

They say the words "once in a lifetime" so easily, he thought.

"Oliver," she murmured, her voice filled with affection.

"Felicity."

The sharp chime of his phone split the moment

like an ax through bone. The magic siphoned away as he reached for it, leaving them both awkward and emotionally raw. Unable to resist, he read the text.

She watched his face and recognized the look on it.

"What's wrong?"

"I'm sorry, I have to go." He drew away, the moment completely gone. "It's William."

She met him at the door with her things bundled in her arms.

"I mean it this time, Mr. Queen. I am done. Don't even try to talk me out of it. It won't work this time."

Behind her the apartment was a wreck. His eyes picked out the path of violence. It started on the couch and moved around the living room, into the kitchen, down the hall where he couldn't see it anymore. Pictures on the wall were askew, things knocked off tables and shelves. A shoe lay on the floor by the table, a book near the kitchen counter. The rug had been kicked up and now lay in a bundle instead of being flat on the floor.

"Is William okay?"

The three words came out as a threat.

Shondra took a step back.

"He's fine, physically," she said. "But he still needs a lot of help."

Relief flooded him, washing through his chest like cold water. He didn't even realize how much tension had built inside him, like pressure in a glass bubble. So much that the thing containing it had begun to crack and splinter.

"I'll find him help." The door still open, he motioned toward the hall. "You may go."

"I won't be back." She said it with defiance and slight anger mixed, he thought, with embarrassment. He was the mayor, there was no reason to be scared of the mayor.

"No, you won't." Oliver guided her with a sweep of his hand. She stepped over the threshold and turned, mouth open to say something.

He shut the door firmly in her face.

She was gone from his mind the second he stepped away from the door. He shook off his suit jacket, laying it over the end of the couch, then stepped over a broken plate containing the remains of someone's—probably William's—dinner mixed with shards of shattered porcelain. Squaring his shoulders he moved toward his son's room.

The door was shut again.

He knocked softly and turned the knob. Pushing the door open gently, he tensed, waiting for some thrown projectile to smash against it.

Nothing happened.

The door opened to a room that looked almost normal. Based on the rest of the apartment, he had anticipated some destruction. William's room looked just as it had when he'd left this morning, the bed slightly more rumpled, a few action figures and other assorted things in different places but, on first glance, fundamentally the same.

His son was nowhere to be seen.

"William." He stepped into the room, eyes scanning.

His voice was the only sound. The covers on the bed revealed that William wasn't under there. The closet door yawed open, showing the jumble of shoes and boxes that lived there at the moment. There wasn't enough room in there, unless William could fold himself into a tiny square that didn't breathe.

He leaned over, peering into the small gap between the matched set of dressers. William could fit there, hidden almost perfectly.

It was empty.

A noise from outside the room made him step back into the hall.

It wasn't a sob, not strong enough for that, not sharp enough for that. It was smaller, quicker. A hitch of breath, a brief—so brief—little strangle of noise. Frowning, he moved down the hall to the bathroom. It was a small room, all white tile with a blue accent that surrounded the sink, toilet, and tub. The shower curtain was closed, but it moved, just slightly, and there was a dark shadow inside it.

What should I do? he thought.

If only he'd brought Felicity with him. She was awkward with people sometimes, but her good-heartedness would've shone through, would have set William at ease.

Oliver didn't have a good heart to shine through. He had made himself a vessel of violence, of vengeance. But a traumatized boy, his traumatized son, couldn't be dealt with using fists and arrows and brutality.

He wished for Thea.

His sister would've had William comfortable in moments. But Thea wasn't here, couldn't be here.

He was.

He was here with his son.

Oliver knelt on the tile next to the shower. He didn't say anything, simply stayed, letting his presence fill the space, waiting to see if William would acknowledge it. After many long moments, the form shifted inside the tub, moving just enough to make the vinyl curtain rustle.

"When I was your age I used to have a space in the kitchen." He lowered his face closer to the shower curtain, his voice even, almost monotone, as he tried to speak gently. "A cupboard that everyone had forgotten about. When I found it the only things inside were dozens of jars of something that looked like mint jelly and two dented cans with no labels. It was small, not much bigger than I was." He swallowed his discomfort, not knowing where his confession was going, just working off feeling. "It was dark but I liked that. It was my place. I was safe there because no one could find me—they didn't know where I was. It was my hiding place."

"I'm not hiding." William's voice was quiet, but the bitterness still cut through.

Gently, Oliver nudged the curtain open. William lay in the bottom of the tub on his back, eyes closed. His hair was plastered to his forehead with dampness, but otherwise he looked as if he were simply sleeping.

"What are you doing then?"

It took a long time for William to answer.

"Being alone."

He didn't open his eyes.

2

The whiskey splashed into the tumbler. There was no ice or water to break it up, just a fall of deep amber that filled the glass two-thirds full. He set the bottle down and lifted the drink.

The fumes of it took his breath slightly, filling his mouth with the taste before he even took a sip.

The doorbell chimed.

He set the glass down, the whiskey untasted.

Moving quickly, before the doorbell could chime again, he crossed the room and opened the door. John Diggle stood there.

"John," he said in greeting, stepping back to let his friend inside.

Diggle looked him up and down, taking in Oliver's rumpled sleeves and creased pants, then glancing around the still disheveled apartment.

"Rough night?"

"I just got William to bed."

The newcomer didn't even glance at his watch. He knew exactly how late it was.

"Well, turn the television on to channel fifty-two, the evening is about to get worse."

Oliver sighed, stepped over, and picked up the whiskey. He raised it. "I have a feeling I'm going to need this. Would you like me to pour you one?"

Diggle just shook his head.

Oliver took a pull from the glass, the dark liquid lighting the back of his throat with heat. It splashed down into his empty stomach, his half-finished sushi dinner long departed from his system, and began to work immediately.

Topping the glass, he left the bottle open on the bar and went to the couch. Diggle had already found the remote and sat perched on the edge of the couch with the television on. Oliver sank into the cushions as Diggle found the right channel and anchorwoman Bethany Snow filled the screen. Tonight she wore a sharp blue suit that made her hair seem more blond than normal, and she wore an expression more stern than usual. She was mid-sentence as Diggle unmuted the television.

"—we live in this city with vigilantes as a fact of life. Unlike the bright and shiny Flash in Central City, ours operate in the shadows. Most of the time they seem to make a difference. However, their means and methods are always questionable.

"Should we allow these people to interfere in police

investigations just because they have costumes? Worse, what happens if they decide to go rogue and become criminals? Would the police be willing to stop them, and would they even have the means? Are we simply biding our time until we are in danger from the very people some look to as heroes?

"Channel fifty-two has this exclusive video, obtained just tonight, showing the Green Arrow crossing the line." She leaned in to the camera. "Before we roll I have to warn you, this footage may be unsettling for many viewers. It depicts a brutal attack. Yes, the victim is a criminal who had just been part of an armed robbery attempt moments before this was recorded. That aside, this footage contains violence that is difficult to watch. If you have young children in the room, you may want to send them out now."

Oliver looked over at Diggle, who nodded back to the television.

The footage began, silent, a grainy image of a door in an alleyway. From the left side of the screen a young man stumbled into the frame, coming around a corner. He crouched against the wall for a long moment before glancing around rapidly. This stopped as his face turned toward the camera. He moved to stand when from the left side a dark figure, moving in a blur, crashed into him, driving him to the ground.

The figure bent, lifting the man before slapping him with a wide swing of his right hand. The young man raised his hands in supplication to the hooded figure who loomed over him, then turned back to the camera.

The young man was begging for mercy.

The hooded figure pulled a gun from a holster he wore on his side. Oliver leaned forward, the half-full glass of whiskey forgotten in his hand.

The hooded person swung the gun high, reaching far behind him for the maximum amount of force. He held the gun back, shoulders moving in a way that Oliver recognized as the body mechanics of yelling. He had a moment to wonder what the hooded figure had screamed before the beating began.

Over and over and over again the gun rose and fell, coming back up a little darker each time.

For the last few minutes of the beating the young man lay motionless on the ground, long unconscious and unable to fight off his attacker. Appearing to be satisfied, the hooded figure wiped his gun on the young man's shirt, holstered it, and moved off camera.

Bethany Snow's face came back on screen. Diggle muted the sound before she could speak, then he turned toward Oliver.

"That wasn't me," Oliver said.

"I know," Diggle said. "I've trained with you enough by now to recognize your moves. Lyla turned me on to this, so I came over to give you a heads up."

"Does A.R.G.U.S. know who it is?"

"She asked me the same thing. Looks like you have a copycat."

Oliver took another drink. This time the alcohol

tasted bad in his mouth. He made a face and set it down on the table.

Have to remember to pour that out before William wakes up, he thought. "Could it be one of Faust's operatives? Perhaps someone else Chase has set up for me to deal with?"

Diggle considered both possibilities. "I'd strike the Chase angle just because that psycho already showed he'll let you know—even from the grave—when he is messing with you." Diggle shook his head, "Man, that guy."

Oliver knew exactly what he meant. It was difficult to grasp how meticulously evil Adrian Chase had turned out to be. Keeping secret his identity as Prometheus, while working alongside them as Adrian Chase. Burrowing his way into all aspects of Team Arrow, turning people he, Oliver, had taken under his wing and using them to betray the team. Uncovering his secret son. Even now, dead by his own hand, he still tormented Oliver and Star City.

Adrian Chase was a nightmare in human form. Pure psychotic obsessive evil personified.

"Back on track," Diggle said. "We've gone up against Faust twice now, with the fire at Dearden Tower and then on that ship. He had some muscle working for him, but nobody like this. This guy is completely different. He looks low-key, more like a lone wolf vigilante."

"You think he's purposely copying me?"

"Did you not hear the 'lone wolf vigilante' part?"

"I'm not a lone wolf."

"I'm your friend, and on your team. Trust me, you're still a lone wolf at your core."

Oliver said nothing. Even this far in, he still found it tempting at times to default to his original modus operandi. To working alone. Every time he worked with Team Arrow, it took a conscious effort. Being solo had been ground into him during his time on Lian Yu, where he could only rely on himself.

It was more complicated than self-reliance, though. He'd seen too much bloodshed, too many people hurt and killed—too much mourning caused by his mission in life—to be entirely comfortable having other people do what he did.

Even the man sitting next to him.

John Diggle had proven himself a warrior long before Oliver ever met him and brought him into the fold, serving in the army with distinctions for valor in combat. He'd listened to the stories Diggle told late in the night. John had also proven time and again that Oliver could rely on him, trust him with his life and the lives of those he loved. Yet Oliver still had to fight the temptation to cut him out when things got bad.

John had a family, Lyla and John junior. If anything happened to him because Oliver included him in a mission...

The guilt wouldn't destroy him—his heart was too closed off, too calloused for that—but it would drive him further from his tenuous connection with humanity, push him back over into the killer he always could become again. He was never far from that, really, but if Diggle was killed, he might well embrace it.

Just like Adrian Chase had said.

"—get out there and find him." Diggle was talking, but he hadn't been listening.

"I'm sorry, John, what was that?"

Diggle looked at him. "You okay?"

"I'm fine."

Diggle turned his head, giving Oliver the side-eye.

"Really, I'm fine, I just have a lot on my mind."

"Oliver, you *always* have a lot on your mind."

"Then you should be used to it."

"Was that a joke?"

"May have been," Oliver replied without changing his expression. "You were saying—"

"I said maybe we should hit the streets, and find this copycat of yours."

"I agree."

"Gotta wonder if he might even be a good addition to the team."

The words made Oliver clench his jaw. "I don't think so."

"I'll admit that what we saw in that footage was pretty brutal," Diggle pressed, "but really, we've both done just as bad. Judging from the reports, this guy took down three armed criminals. That's impressive by any measure."

Oliver didn't say anything in response, but the

tension across his shoulders made him shift on the couch. He glanced at the glass of whiskey, but left it where it was.

"The team is fine as it stands," he said.

"We lost Ragman and Artemis. We could replace them."

"The team. Is *fine*."

"We could always use another shooter."

"I've got you and Rene. Shooters are covered."

"I'm former military, Oliver, you always need more shooters."

Oliver gave his friend a hard look.

Diggle raised his hands. "I'm just saying, with this Faust still out there, and the fact that the bad guys just keep coming, we could bring this guy in, see if he's a match, and then train him if he is. It could be a good thing."

Oliver forced himself to consider it. "I don't like the idea," he said, "but we should find this copycat and see what side he's on. That may give you your answer."

Diggle let it stand.

It was as close as he would get to an agreement.

3

No one questioned her as she walked down the hallway. Beige walls, pastel artwork in blond wood frames, and tile on the floor a pale eggshell-and-sage-green speckle turned off-white from the cast of the fluorescent lights above. Everything seemed bland, muted, designed to keep people calm in uncalm times.

Until she reached the uniformed Star City police officer reading a magazine outside room 623 of Starling General. He was lanky, stretched tall, all knees and shoulders in the chair he sat in. He had the sleek otter build of a swimmer. He stood out, his dark blue SCPD uniform a harsh contrast as it ate the light.

He didn't stand as she approached, but he did give her the once up and down, his eyes flinty, checking to see if she was a threat. He seemed to dismiss the notion, then gave her another up and down look over, this time with a cocky grin and a sparkle in his eye.

She shrugged as she drew near, moving the hem of

her short-cropped leather jacket.

Exposing her badge.

The cocky grin disappeared as he jumped to his feet.

She raised her hand, reassuring him. "It's alright, Officer—"

"Kannan, ma'am."

"Drake, Dinah." Her hand went out between them. It took a moment for him to reach out and shake it, and when he did it only lasted a second. She noted that he didn't give his first name as she had.

"I'm here to ask our suspect a few questions," she said.

"I thought he was the victim of a crime?" Officer Kannan scratched the bottom edge of his jaw. "He took a real beating from the Arrow."

"I think they call him Green Arrow now."

"Green Arrow, Blue Arrow, Purple Arrow," he said, his voice harsh. "It don't matter what they call him."

Great, she thought, *this guy doesn't like vigilantes.*

Then again, neither had she once.

Before she became one.

"We have two eyewitnesses who put him as part of a crew called 'the X gang,'" she replied. "They tried to rob the Cashmere Club. He's not just some civilian who got jumped."

"He looks like he should be dead," Kannan said. "Nobody should've lived through a beating like that."

"I'll see that when I go in."

Officer Kannan nodded. "You want me to keep my

place? 'Cause I could go take care of some business."

"Go stretch your legs, do your business, get some air and some coffee." She waved him off. "I'll handle this for the next half-hour, so be back before then."

"Thank you, ma'am." He touched his fingertips to his brow in a salute.

Dinah watched him walk down the hall, pausing to check the nurses' station. She allowed a tiny smile when all the nurses ignored him completely, and he kept going.

Once he'd rounded the corner, she pushed the door open.

"Tell me if this hurts, and how much."

The doctor's thumb pressed deep alongside the thick scar, digging underneath it. Diggle watched it happen but there was no sensation, not even pressure. The area felt numb, as if it had been anesthetized. That sent his mind back to some of the things Oliver had shown him about pressure points. There was a nerve bundle where the doctor was applying pressure. He should have had pain shooting all the way up into his neck, making his jaw clench and his eyes water as the muscle chain spasmed.

Instead he felt nothing.

"Now, don't be stoic, Mr. Diggle," she said. "I need honest feedback to this, that'll get us nowhere."

"I'm not being stoic, Doc." He took a deep breath,

trying to clear some of the bitterness out of his voice. "Nothing is happening."

Dr. Schwartz moved her hands, using her fingertips to feel along the edge of the scar. "I know it can be frustrating, Mr. Diggle."

"That's not as comforting as you think it is."

"Have your symptoms gotten worse?"

"That's why I'm here," Diggle said.

"What are you experiencing? Besides frustration, that is."

"I can't feel my hand," he said. "It's like it's asleep all the time, and sometimes it goes into spasms, and I can't control it at all." The very thought made him grimace.

"Have you noticed any triggers to the spasms?"

Only that it happens when I need to pull the trigger, he thought.

"It's random," he said instead.

Dr. Schwartz frowned and stepped back. "You know, neurological conditions that result from injury are almost impossible to pinpoint. Oftentimes the best thing we can do is observe the symptoms, and treat those as best we can. It can be a long process of elimination."

"Afraid that's not an option, Doctor," he said. "I need some kind of treatment to fix this now."

She sighed. "I know why you want to rush this, but don't you think you should use this as a reason to step back and allow yourself to heal?"

"That's not how it works, Doc."

"That's not how you *want* it to work, you mean."

He didn't respond, just stared at her. He wasn't going to argue the merits of what he did as Spartan. It was a thing that spoke for itself.

"Okay, Mr. Diggle, be stubborn." She picked up his chart and began writing. "For now, I'm going to raise your dose of Neurotin, and we're going to set up a regimen of aggressive e-stim treatments, alongside acupuncture."

"Still sounds like you're just treating the symptoms."

She dropped the clipboard down, giving him a hard look. "It's what we can do right now. There may be another option available to you because of your A.R.G.U.S. connections, but I'll have to make some calls before we can even discuss it."

"I don't want A.R.G.U.S. brought in on this. That's why I came to you."

"Do I have to tell you how many options you're cutting off by doing that?" she said, holding his eyes with hers. "I might not even be able to fix you."

Diggle chuckled. "I mean what I say. Honor my doctor–patient confidentiality."

Dr. Schwartz frowned deeply, but nodded her assent. "Then forget it," she said curtly. "Until I find out more, we do the e-stim, acupuncture, massage, and medicine regimen." She put his file down and stepped away. "For now, however, the best you can expect is improvement. You need to adjust your expectations."

He thought about her words, and they weighed heavy on him. He was unreliable in his current condition—and unreliable in the field was a way to get hurt.

To get someone else hurt.

He'd have to be vigilant to make sure that didn't happen.

"Can I put my shirt back on?"

"Yes, Mr. Diggle, you may put your shirt back on."

The room was dark, lit only by a low bank of lights from behind the bed. On it lay a man wrapped in bandages. Tubes ran to bags of fluids hanging from a tall stainless-steel IV rack. Wires connected to ECG electrodes wound together in a thick, multi-colored cable across the man's chest, trailing off to connect him to the machines that beeped and buzzed and hummed, tracking his vital statistics, watching over him even when he was alone in the room.

She moved to the side of the bed and spoke low, just loud enough to be heard over the machinery in the room.

"Chavis."

For a long second the man on the bed didn't stir, didn't move, and she was unsure if he had heard her through the thick layer of gauze swaddled around his head. This close, she could see a thin strip of stubbled skin just below the edge of the bandage, where they had shaved his head to do surgery.

Under the stubble the skin was bruised violet.

It matched the rest of his face.

Chavis looked like he was wearing a mask that had

been melted in an oven. His left eye was swollen shut and so purple it looked black, puffy and grape-skin thin, as if the smallest scratch or puncture would cause it to pop and gush. His bottom lip jutted out, chapped and split down the center and stitched back together with small clear sutures. Bruising continued on his chin, and she could see the right-angle check marks that indicated the bottom of a clip in a pistol grip.

His breathing was ragged, dragging in and out of his lungs. He wasn't on any type of respirator, but just struggled to capture oxygen. For a moment she almost said his name again, and then his head moved slightly and he made a small noise. She couldn't tell if he could see her through the swelling in his eye.

"Who?"

"Lieutenant Dinah Drake," she said. Looking at him, she felt bad about her harsh judgment, and understood the officer outside and his view of Chavis as a victim. This was a man who had suffered a horrendous beating, and he truly looked as if he should have died.

"I already talked to the cops," Chavis rasped.

"I have a few more questions though," she said.

"I don't know…"

"It won't take long, Chavis. I'll be out quick," she promised.

"Okay."

"Why were you targeted?"

"What? What do you mean?" he asked. The monitor connected to his heart began to beep faster.

"Why did the vigilante come after you? Do you know him?"

"Know?" Chavis pulled on the thin blanket draped across him, clearly growing agitated. "Why would I know the Arrow guy?"

"Green Arrow?" Dinah asked. "You think the Green Arrow did this to you?"

"Had the hood."

"But he pistol-whipped you."

"It was the Arrow guy." Chavis shook his head and moaned from the pain it caused. "I don't know him."

"But you're certain it was him."

"Who else? He's the Star City guy." Chavis shook his head as much as he could. "I should've stayed in Blüdhaven—at least there our masks have rules."

Dinah dropped the tone of her voice, using it to create a rapport with the man on the bed. She knew it might not work, that he might be too terrified after what happened to him, might be in too much pain or on too many drugs, for it to work.

"We're almost done here, Chavis," she said. "You have a little more in you for me?"

He considered it. His face turned more toward her and his eyes moved up and down.

"Yeah."

"On the footage we have, it looks like he was asking you something. What was it?"

"He kept asking about the drugs."

"Drugs? But you were performing armed robbery,

nothing to do with drugs."

"I know. I mean, I might smoke a little, but I don't mess with moving any weight like that."

Yes, you're just an armed robber.

"What did you tell him to make him stop assaulting you?" she asked.

"I gave up a dealer I know, someone big enough to put a stop to him."

"I need a name."

"Cross."

"Manny Cross?"

Chavis nodded weakly. "He runs the Skulls. He tried to recruit me when I came to Star City but I took a pass." Chavis closed his eyes, "I'm glad I did. This guy took a bunch of them out not long ago, but then he was still using the bow and arrow. Not like when he got me."

She could see he was fading, worn out from the pain and the meds. She gently patted his arm.

"Thank you for your help." She turned to leave.

"Lieutenant Drake?"

"Yes."

"He didn't stop beating me because I gave him the answer. He did it because he thought I was dead."

4

Some mornings it paid to get to work early.

Early being relative, since so much of fighting crime happened at night. Criminals and the cover of darkness and all that.

She'd been running various data spreads to try and pinpoint some kind of activity initiated by Faust. So far, he'd been a complete ghost. Someone hiding this long from her was unacceptable, and thus she had been coming into the Bunker early to adjust the parameters and to keep everything going smoothly.

In doing so, she'd discovered that Oliver was also using the early morning time.

To work out.

When he was really frustrated, he worked out harder than normal, driving himself to the edge of his ability, working his body until every muscle had been hit. Flexing and stretching until he glistened with sweat.

She sipped her coffee and watched.

He was on the salmon ladder.

She loved the salmon ladder.

Didn't care too much for actual salmon. It was fine and all—*why did everyone want to put lemon on fish?*—but their ladders were a sight to behold.

Oliver pulled himself up, cable-like muscles flexing, twisting under his skin. He swung and jerked, using sheer strength to power his way up to the next set of hooks. Once there he did a series of pull-ups on the bar.

It took a lot of core strength.

Core strength she could see with the bunching of his abs, the tautness of his hip flexors standing out like cables. Cables down which she had run her fingers not that long ago.

She took another sip of coffee.

At the top, he did a pull-up that turned into a full press, lifting himself halfway over the bar itself. He hung there, in space, a carving of all things masculine. The light fell on him from above, catching the highlight of each muscle and casting a deep ridge of shadow underneath them.

It took her a long moment to swallow her coffee.

She could tell when he spotted her because he dropped down, landing lightly like a cat and moving toward her. Still buzzing on the adrenaline generated by his exercise, his movements had a pantherish grace, all liquid power and languid motion.

She forgot about her coffee.

"Sorry," he said. "I didn't think anyone would be in this early."

"Oh, it's fine. I'm not complaining," she replied casually. *Really not complaining.*

He leaned close to her and picked up a towel that had been draped over the rail beside where she stood. He was so close she could feel the warmth pouring off his body, the heat of movement. It made her head go a little wonky for a moment.

He pulled back and began drying off, and she pulled herself back together. She watched him, paying attention. She loved his body, but it was Oliver's face that captured her every time. It was a strong face, one made for scowling—which intensified his eyes, but generally it held more than a trace she thought of as lost little boy.

This morning though, his features appeared haggard. The circles under his eyes were too dark, his stubble too solid, and his mouth was a hard line.

"You look like hell," she said.

He frowned. "Um... thanks?"

"I mean, you look fit," she said, and she bit her lip, stared at his abs, and muttered, "like really, *really* fit." She kept staring until he reached for another towel. The movement broke her concentration, making her look back up at his face. "You haven't been sleeping."

"How do you know that?"

"I know what you look like when you get a good night's sleep."

It took him a long moment to respond. "Yes, I suppose you do." The intensity of his look and the intimacy of his voice made the back of her neck warm.

"Um, why aren't you sleeping?"

"It's William."

"Was it bad the other night?"

"He's..." Oliver sighed and moved to lean on the console, near enough to touch her if he wanted. "He's been through a lot."

"I know how that feels." The moment the words were out of her mouth she wanted them back. "I mean, I can imagine how it feels, I don't *know* how it feels. I mean my mom is still alive. In fact, she's due to visit again soon, that won't be awkward or anything—" She stopped talking, and she could *feel* the mask of horror on her face. "Oh, god, I just made the death of your son's mother about me—I'm a horrible person. I suck. I am the worst."

"Felicity, it's okay. I understand."

Change the subject, she thought. "Is he getting better?"

"Some. He still has trouble sleeping. And he's angry."

Felicity made a face.

"What?" Oliver said.

"Well, he is your son."

"I *was* a lot like him at his age." His eyes drifted up and over her shoulder. "My parents didn't know what to do with me."

"Really?"

He nodded. "I almost got shipped away to military school."

"Oh, that would have gone over well. You do so well with authority."

"I don't have a problem with authority."

"As long as you're the authority," she finished with a smile. "What kept you from being sent away?"

"Raisa," he said firmly, definitively. "She was my nanny as a child, and my only true friend. My growing up wasn't exactly child-friendly."

"But Raisa made it better?"

"She saved me."

"And William is just like you were?"

"It's... frightening how much we're the same."

Felicity sighed and shrugged. "Sounds like you know what to do."

He considered it. "I wonder if Raisa would be willing to come help."

"If she's family, she will help your son." Felicity reached out and put her hand on his arm. "You should put your energy into helping William, and once he's better we can talk about that thing that we don't talk about because we need to talk about it." Her eyebrows pulled together tightly. "You do know what thing I'm talking about that we aren't talking about, right?"

"I do," he reassured her.

"Good!" She smiled. "Because I wasn't sure with all the talking, not talking about the thing." She pulled herself back on track. "But I'm here, not going anywhere, perfectly patient to talk about the not-talked-about-thing when William is better."

"Felicity Smoak—" Oliver leaned in and gave her a quick kiss on the cheek. "—you are too good to me."

He turned away.

"I am, you know," Felicity said quietly, her voice light and dreamy as she watched Oliver walk away.

He still hadn't put a shirt on.

Dinah pulled the door closed softly, not wanting to disturb Chavis's rest. Officer Kannan was back in his chair.

"Did you get anything good out of him?"

She had a flash of annoyance that he hadn't stood when she left the room. It was a disrespect of her rank and, she suspected, a disrespect of her gender. She put a note of his name in a mental file. There would come a time she would show him the error of his ways.

"I'll have it in my report," she said. "Oh, that's right, you won't have the right to read it." She stepped around him, and began walking away. Over her shoulder she added, "If I catch you slacking off on this detail, you'll be doing foot patrol in the Glades."

"Yes, ma'am," he muttered.

She turned the corner and moved past the nurses' station, dodging around bustling nurses and orderlies and gracefully making her way through the crowded hallway. She went through the doors that led to the elevators and saw a familiar sight.

"John?"

Diggle turned around, and he didn't look happy to see her.

"Oh yeah, Dinah," he said. "You were here to question that guy about the beating."

"I am," she said. "But why are you here?"

The elevator opened and they stepped inside.

"Just a basic check-up," he said. They both moved to the back of the elevator car, standing side by side but far enough apart that they wouldn't be in each other's way if anything were to happen. Other people joined them, showing no such awareness.

She leaned toward him, speaking from the side of her mouth.

"Are you sure everything's okay?"

The elevator chimed, the doors opened to a new floor, and people filed out two by two. John waited until they were alone in the elevator before responding.

"Everything is just fine," he said firmly. They both stepped off the elevator into the lobby and, after saying a quick goodbye, began moving in opposite directions.

5

The sun landed warm on her shoulders as she crossed the grass. Moving quickly, she used her long legs to eat up the distance as she crossed City Park. School was out for the summer, so the park was full of kids. Children running to and fro, playing ball, throwing Frisbee, some reading books, some sitting quietly by themselves, some feeding the ducks on the pond.

It was strange to walk past normal life. People who just were, and lived and didn't have to deal with violence. She couldn't remember what it was like to just go home at a normal hour and have dinner like normal people, to discuss what was on television that night, to go to bed early.

It had been a long time.

Instead her life was spent chasing criminals, fighting crime while wearing a mask, and interrogating men who had been beaten within an inch of their life. Dinah could see on the edge of things where her life would be something that might break other people. Normal people.

Yet she loved it.

It felt natural to her.

Situation normal, all screwed up, she thought, although she didn't hold onto it, just let it wash over her. Maybe it was the normal people doing normal things that caused her to contemplate her life as she walked across the quad, moving toward the marble steps of City Hall. Perhaps it was the dichotomy of the things she had done, in the light of such an average day for them.

If asked, she wouldn't say she *enjoyed* being a vigilante. That seemed wrong. There was a satisfaction in taking criminals off the streets, but she had done that just being a cop. It was the very reason she even became a cop.

Some criminals, however, the ones who went beyond the pale of normal villainy, they were a serious threat to the police and to the city itself. Some could potentially even destroy the world. Villains like that were the reason she had become a vigilante, and there was a part of her that would never give it up, never stop fighting those extraordinary kinds of evil.

Never stop being the Black Canary.

Sara Lance peeled out of the crowd and moved in next to her, matching her pace, walking with her toward City Hall. Like her, the blond crime fighter wore civilian clothes.

"Nice blouse," Dinah said.

"It's something I picked up while working." She looked Dinah over. "Well, someone surely has a serious face today."

"Just thinking random thoughts."

"Serious thoughts?"

"Somewhat. Nothing to worry over." Dinah waved her hand in dismissal. "I'm glad you could join me," she said. "I thought you had left us."

"Think nothing of it. I'll be with you till the end of this case."

"How does that even work?"

Sara chuckled. "It's better not to think about it too much."

The two of them reached the doors to City Hall. They were impressive, stretching twelve feet tall and made of oak and glass and polished steel. Dinah pulled one of them open and waved Sara through. They crossed the lobby together, walking past the security desk as Dinah flashed her badge.

"That's pretty handy," Sara said. "I might have to get one of those myself."

"Somehow, I didn't think you'd want to go through a weapons detector."

Sara grinned. "You flatter me."

They rounded a corner, walked down the hall, and saw two familiar faces.

"There's my daughter," Quentin Lance said.

He spread his arms and he and Sara hugged as Rene and Dinah looked on. Dinah caught Rene's eye.

"How are you doing?" she asked.

"As well as could be expected," he said.

"Don't be a pain in the neck," Lance chimed in. "He's doing great."

Rene shrugged. "I have to go finish this business, Hoss." Before anyone could respond he turned and walked away quickly.

"Is he okay?" Sara asked.

"Yeah, he's fine. It's just been a long day," Lance replied. He turned to Dinah and pointed to the door at the end of the hall. "Oliver is waiting for you."

"I'll go see him now." Dinah nodded, and lightly touched Sara's arm. "I'll see you soon." Sara nodded back and smiled. Then Dinah turned to Quentin and firmly gripped his arm.

"How're *you* doing?" There was concern in Dinah's voice. She didn't know if Sara had been told what happened on Lian Yu, what her father had been through there, so she didn't ask outright, but she felt the need to ask about his state of mind.

"I've been okay," he said.

"If you need to, call me."

"I will."

Once she was gone Sara turned to her father. "How about you take a girl out to get some coffee?"

There was a knock at the door, and Oliver looked up.

"Come in."

The door opened and Dinah stepped in. He set aside the file he was working on, folded his hands on the desk, and gave her his undivided attention.

"Is this a good time?"

"Of course," he replied. "Did you find out anything that will lead us to Faust?"

"I don't know that the beating had anything to do with Faust." She sat in the chair across from the desk, crossed her legs. "There was nothing that indicated his involvement."

"As… *manipulative* as Chase has proven to be, I have a hard time believing it could be a coincidence, happening so close to our recent encounter."

Dinah didn't speak for a moment. "It's a great big city full of crime, Oliver," she said finally. "You know we have a lot on our plate."

Oliver considered her words. Dinah would know more than he would about the everyday crime in Star City. She dealt with the common criminals in the streets, as well as the threats that the team faced from persons that were beyond the norm. This was why he valued her perspective. He sat back, moving his hands to his lap. He wasn't completely convinced, but he was willing to listen with an open mind.

"Please," he said. "Tell me what you think."

"Well, first of all, everyone thinks that you did this," she said, being brutally honest with him. Holding back would do him no good.

"I didn't."

"I know that. The victim and a lot of people on the force think that you did."

"The police think that this was me?"

She nodded. "Most of them actually don't have a problem with it. This guy was an armed robber, after all." Dinah felt a twinge of guilt over the assumptions she had made about Chavis, just because of his criminal past. After seeing him in that hospital bed, however, she couldn't think of him as anything but a victim of a vicious crime.

She came back to the conversation. "Support for Team Arrow is high among the rank and file."

"That's good to know."

"Don't be too comfortable with that though," she said. "They all still look at us as vigilantes, as a necessary evil, and their trust could be broken with next to no effort."

"Do you think that's what this new vigilante, this copycat, is trying to do?" he asked. "Undermine our standing with the authorities?"

She considered the possibility, shook her head, and dismissed it.

"According to the victim, this guy was looking for a drug dealer."

"A drug dealer?" Oliver said. "Might he be trying to start up the drug trade again?"

"The drug trade never went away," Dinah said.

"Not really. You disrupted it in a major way with that bust of the Skulls. Oh, god, is that really what we're calling them?"

Oliver just shrugged.

"Anyway, he seemed to be looking for the source of the drugs in town."

"Are drugs that hard to find in Star City?"

"Not on the street. The users can always find them, but the players, well, players are pretty well hidden." She shifted in her chair. "That's why I think this guy is going after a source, and he may have just found it."

"What does that mean?"

"Well, our victim gave up a big fish in the drug pond. He gave up Manny Cross."

"I don't know who that is." He looked angry with himself at the very idea.

"Cross is someone that we've had on the radar for a long time. He's got a high public profile, and covers his drug import business with his legitimate dealings. We've tried, but we haven't been able to touch him. It's a big operation and we drop a lot of his street-level operatives, but nobody gives up anything about Cross.

"What we *do* know," she continued, "is that he used to move drugs through the city using the harbor and the trucking industry. His focus seems to have changed, though, and now he's keeping the drugs *in* the city, and they're hitting the streets in a big way."

"Sounds like we need to put him on the list."

"I thought you already had. He's tied in with the

Skulls." She shook her head. "I still can't believe that's what we're calling them."

"Think of a better name, and we'll use that," he said. "But why did you think I'd already put them on the list?"

"Because of that incident with the car carrier."

"I knew the Skulls were active," he replied, "but I didn't know anything about Cross until you mentioned him. I wound up tangling with his crew by following a tip."

"Is that why you took White Canary for backup?"

Oliver chuckled. "You don't know Sara very well—she just showed up that night."

"I don't know her that well, but I do like her."

Oliver raised an eyebrow.

"Oh, not like that. I like that she's direct. Doesn't have any artifice."

"No, she has none of that," Oliver agreed. "Back to the beating of this guy, Chavis—if this copycat is going after Cross, we need to stop him quickly."

"Why?" Dinah asked.

"I don't understand the question," Oliver said.

Dinah leaned forward in her chair. "Look, I saw his handiwork up close. I don't know how good he is at investigating, but he took down three armed robbers and obviously has no problem doing what it takes. I say, let's concentrate on Faust and clear that book up, because the team could use the closure with Chase."

She leaned back again. "If this guy does any

damage to Cross, it only helps Star City."

"I don't like the idea of a loose cannon running around."

"Who do you hate the idea of more?" she asked. "A loose cannon aimed at a major drug dealer, or a psychotic explosives expert commissioned to create chaos and mayhem, all by a dead psychotic criminal mastermind who hated you?"

Oliver had no answer.

6

"Well, I must say they're very impressive specimens."

The tall man in the dark blue uniform didn't respond other than to tilt his head in a slight nod. He watched Alex Faust move between the rows of his men, all standing at attention. Faust was an odd-angled man and he moved with odd-angle motions, elbows out and hands extended, almost as if he were constantly moving things out of his way. He was the polar opposite of the men around whom he walked.

Thirty of them, a mixed bag of physical attributes, but all of them wearing the same sharp battledress uniforms in the same midnight-blue color. They formed five columns of six men each, all of their shoulders and spines ruler straight, their feet together in polished boots, and their arms down their sides. None of them would give a man like Faust any respect, had they met him in a bar or on the street. He was too odd, too strange, the complete opposite of discipline. If they weren't mercenaries then they would never allow him to inspect them like this.

But they were guns for hire.

And he was the man with the money.

"You say they're trained to the highest specifications?"

"My men are tip-top, sir."

"They work well under pressure?"

"They're all combat proven. Battle-tested to the core."

"Are they all veterans?" Faust kind of hopped around and moved back over by him.

"There's all kinds of battle, sir. Some of them have seen combat, others are ex-military from various places."

"And a lot of them are ex-convicts?"

"Some have gone up against the police, A.R.G.U.S., or the masks in town." Tall Man shrugged. "You don't have a problem with criminals, do you?"

"Of course not," Faust said, "but the kind of crime that I'm involved with requires a certain amount of… steadfastness. Since criminals are a cowardly and superstitious lot, I need to know that your men will do as they are ordered when things begin to explode."

"We are neither cowardly nor are we superstitious."

"It's just a saying."

"What assurances would satisfy you?"

Faust tapped his chin as he thought about it. "Which one is your best man?"

Without hesitation Tall Man's voice rang out, "El Tigre!"

Immediately from the ranks stepped a man slabbed with muscle. Even under the uniform it was obvious. Average height, he looked almost short, his proportions were so skewed, as if the amount of muscle he carried had compressed him with its weight. Even so, the tall man noted, he moved with the grace and ease of his namesake. Unreadable ink spilled down his python arms where they weren't covered by sleeves. Tattoos of matching quality spilled from his collar and up onto his throat.

"I asked for your best," Faust said. "Not your most intimidating."

"El Tigre did two tours in Afghanistan, where he accomplished forty-three confirmed kills and an additional thirty-six unconfirmed. He returned and served eight years in Iron Heights. Inside, he became the reigning shiv champion until—"

"Excuse me," Faust interrupted. "What is a 'shiv champion'?"

"Shivs are illegal knife-fighting matches held in the sub-basement levels at many supermax prisons. They take their name from the crude weapons made by prisoners."

"How exciting," Faust murmured. "How do you become the champion?"

"You kill people, and you don't die."

Faust studied the man. "Why are you El Tigre?"

El Tigre looked at Tall Man, who shrugged his permission to speak.

"I earned my name by giving other men stripes."

Faust nodded and turned. "I'm convinced."

"Then we have the contract," Tall Man said.

Faust reached into the pocket of his coat, pulling out a square object. "Not exactly," he said. "I'm convinced this is your best man." He tossed the square to El Tigre, who snatched it from the air with one quick move of a thick hand. A red light began flashing on the corner of the object. El Tigre looked at it impassively.

"What is that?" Tall Man asked.

"That?" Faust asked airily. "That is a bit of my homebrew explosive, a new formula I'm trying out. It should have a concussive radius of about three feet."

"Why is it flashing?"

"You said your men were steadfast when things went boom. I'm testing that resolve. Let's see how steadfast your best man is." Tall Man looked at Faust, gauging exactly how far he would take this. Faust watched El Tigre, his fingers steepled in front of him.

"Hold your position, soldier," Tall Man said to El Tigre. The mercenary nodded and resumed attention, the flashing object held by his side.

Seconds passed like minutes.

Faust leaned over, speaking to Tall Man from the side of his mouth.

"None of the others have moved."

"My men are disciplined." Tall Man couldn't keep the tension from his voice. "I don't want to lose my best one for no good purpose."

"The amount of money I am going to pay you is a fine purpose."

"Is your intention simply to buy cannon fodder?"

"You mean do I intend for all of your men to die?"

"That is my meaning."

Faust considered his answer. "I don't intend it, but soldiers die," he replied. "I am about dangerous business." He turned sharply to Tall Man. "I need to know that your men are also about dangerous business."

Tall Man extended his hand. "My soldier hasn't moved a muscle."

"Why, you are right." Faust walked over to El Tigre and studied him. The mercenary kept his eyes straight ahead. "Look at him, spine rigid, not even a tremble or a trickle of sweat to betray any nervousness he might have inside, from holding an armed explosive device." Faust plucked the object from El Tigre's hands. It continued flashing as Faust began casually tossing it into the air and catching it as if it were a simple tennis ball.

"So," Faust continued. "If El Tigre is your best, then who is your worst?"

"All my men are the best you can hire."

"Oh, come on!" Faust cried out. "We're so close now! Leadership is about cold calculation and harsh assessment, so just tell me, who here is the weak link in your chain?"

"Rickson!"

From the back of the ranks stepped a blocky man with bulging biceps and a blond crew cut. He moved up with precise steps to stand beside El Tigre.

"Rickson is a decorated combat veteran. He is a fine soldier, and I have no complaints with his performance. I would not have him here if he wasn't among the best of the best."

"He does have a chiseled jaw, doesn't he?" Faust stepped close to Rickson, looking up into the man's ice-blue eyes. "A real poster boy we have here." He slapped the bomb against Rickson's chest. It stuck to his shirt. Faust stepped back. The moment his hand left the object the red light began flashing in a staccato rhythm. Rickson's hands slapped at it, trying to dislodge it from his chest as Faust moved quickly away.

"Hold your position, soldier!" Tall Man shouted.

The light stopped blinking, burning steady and bright. Rickson's fingers were under the edge of the bomb, prying a corner off his shirt.

A flash of light and a blast of noise, and suddenly the upper half of Rickson became a red mist. Viscera and gore painted the right side of El Tigre and the row of soldiers behind him.

"I cannot, and will not, abide weak links," Faust said. Tall Man simply watched Rickson's legs collapse into a pile.

"The good news is, you and your men are hired." Faust clapped him on the shoulder. "We'll be working tomorrow night."

El Tigre stood motionless with his former brother-in-arms dripping off his expressionless face.

* * *

She watched her father blow on the steaming cup of coffee he held in his hands, as she sipped her Killer Frost, a white chocolate cold brew coffee over ice. It was Jitters' newest drink on their secret menu. A hyperactive teenager in line ahead of her had ordered one, and she figured anything that had a kid so hyped he was nearly *vibrating* had to be good. So she'd ordered one, then realized that a lot of the people inside the busy coffee shop had the distinctive drinks. There was a lot of vibrating going on.

It was sugary, but the flavor was nice and it was cool.

"I don't see how you can drink regular coffee on a summer afternoon."

"Hey," Quentin said. "There's air conditioning in here."

She smirked at his attempt at humor.

His face turned serious. "I drink a lot of coffee these days."

"That's good."

"Better than the other stuff I was drinking."

"I'm proud of you, Dad." She took another sip. "But I really want to talk about something else."

"Oh yeah? You don't want to just keep congratulating me for doing the bare minimum everyone else does, every day?"

She frowned at the bitterness in his voice. "Don't

put down your achievement, or I'll kick your ass."

"I wasn't." He recovered, and chuckled. "It was just a bad attempt at humor."

"I'll say." She watched him, considering whether she wanted to dig at his "humor." She knew a lot about avoiding feelings with bad humor and jokes that weren't really jokes. In fact, she'd learned it from him.

She decided to let it slide for the time being. He was sober and holding it together, as far as she could see, but she made a decision to keep checking in with Oliver from time to time, to make sure her dad was doing okay.

"So how's Dinah working out?" she asked, changing the subject.

"Dinah?" Quentin said. "Dinah's great. Solid cop, reliable, trustworthy. Smart as a whip. She's one of the good ones."

"And how's life outside the office?" she asked, "You can't spend every hour of the day worrying about the people around you—you need some time for yourself, too. Have you got any… you know, prospects?"

"Prospects?"

"Yeah, like someone you can hang around with in the real world."

"I'm too busy."

"C'mon, Dad, surely there's someone you at least have your eye on."

"Stop." He said the word firmly, almost harshly, and she pulled back. "It's not like that. Besides, I'm…"

He hesitated. "Well, I'm still hung up on Donna."

"Donna?"

"Donna Smoak."

"Felicity's mom?"

Quentin nodded and took a sip of his coffee to cover the embarrassment at discussing his love life, or lack thereof, with his daughter.

"Well," Sara smirked. "If Felicity is any indication, then way to go, Dad."

"According to Donna, Felicity takes after her dad, but Donna's a knockout."

"What happened with you two?"

"You know, this thing we all do," he replied. "It's too dangerous to have people close to you."

She did know. Most of her relationships were one-offs, little flings, not that she didn't care about them, but dating a civilian would be almost impossible. She looked at her father. He wasn't a vigilante. Yes, he was involved with, and a part of, Team Arrow. She knew he got directly involved in what they did, but he was still on the periphery.

Hell, if he could find some happiness, then he should go after it.

"You know, if you get another chance with her you should take it," she said.

"I can't."

She put her hand on his, getting his full attention. "I haven't seen that look in your eye…" She swallowed the words "since Mom," and instead said, "…in a long

time. I bet Felicity didn't get her fierceness from just
her dad. Bring her in, tell her what really happens here,
and let her decide if you two can be a thing."

"I can't do that."

"You could quit."

"What?"

"Walk away from this, if love is on the line."

He sat back, looking deep into his cup of coffee as
he considered her words.

"I don't think I can at this point."

"I understand," she said, and again, she did. She
wouldn't want to stop doing what she did. *Is that why
they call it a mission?* she wondered. *I always thought that
was cheesy, but I guess it applies.*

"Did you really want to ask about my dating life?"

His words pulled her out of her contemplation.
"No, not just that, at least. I wanted to talk about Dinah
becoming Black Canary."

Quentin's head jerked left then right, looking all
around to see if anyone had heard her. Dozens of people
surrounded them. All of them who were in groups,
even just pairs, were deep in their own conversations.
Anyone who was alone had ear buds and their phone,
listening to music or watching a video or connecting
over social media.

"Relax, Dad, nobody's paying attention."

"You never know in this town."

"Okay, relax, Dad. *I'm* paying attention and nobody
is listening to us."

"Okay." He sat back.

"Did you know Oliver made her the official replacement?"

"I did, and it's the right thing for him to do." He nodded. "I mean, you can't argue with the choice. She's the perfect fit, even has the canary cry and everything."

"He had her a uniform made."

"Oh." Quentin frowned, but only for a brief moment. "So she's even going to look the part."

"She does."

"That's good," he said. "That's right."

"I just want to make sure it's *really* okay." Sara leaned forward and reached out to him, taking his hand across the table.

"Is it okay with you?" he asked.

"It is." She nodded. "I've seen her in action, in the costume and everything. It's like she's always been Black Canary. Not that anyone can replace Laurel."

They both went silent for a moment, lost in their own memories of Laurel. One as a sister, the other as a daughter, both of a strong, complicated woman they missed terribly.

"I saw her," Sara said.

Quentin frowned deeply and shifted in his seat. "You mean, you saw her in the past, with that Legends thing you're doing now?"

Sara shook her head. "No, not quite. It's—it's hard to explain. There was an alternate timeline made by the Spear of Destiny and—"

"Wait," Quentin interrupted. "You saw an *alternate* version of Laurel?"

"It was Laurel," Sara's voice was firm. "She, well, she came to me. I don't know everything, but I think she's fine with Dinah taking her mantle."

A tear trickled from the corner of Quentin's eye.

"It's okay, Dad. That's what I'm saying, it's okay."

He wiped his cheek. "It's not. I mean it is, with what you said, but—"

"But what?"

"There's another Laurel."

"What?"

"We've got another Laurel running around here."

Sara didn't know what to think. "Explain."

"I don't know how, some Earth-2 thing or something. I just know your sister is here, but it isn't her."

"Where is she? Should we go see her? I know it's not her, but—"

"She's evil, honey. This new Laurel is bad."

"Laurel has an evil twin from an alternate world?"

"I guess so. A doppelganger, or whatever you call it."

Sara sat there for a long moment.

"I've thought a lot about it," Quentin said. "You remember, your sister had her demons. Hell, I think both of you girls got that from me, things you have to fight."

"Dad—"

"Let me finish," he said. "I don't know what this other Laurel went through before coming here, but it put her on the bad side. I don't know if she can be brought back. She's not our Laurel."

"Maybe, maybe she could be redeemed." Sara thought about her own past, the things she had done, things she couldn't be proud of, things that she should be ashamed of. "People can change. We know they can."

Quentin didn't say anything. He took a sip of his coffee, making a face.

"What?" she asked. "Tell me what you're not telling me."

"You know that thing on that island?"

"The thing that has all of you shaken, even now?"

"Yeah." He rubbed his hand over his head, as if he were stalling. "She was there, this other Laurel."

Sara just waited, letting her father come to whatever he was trying to tell her.

"I shot her." Quentin looked up, not crying but with wet eyes. "She was going to kill Dinah and, even though I knew it wasn't my baby girl, it was still my baby girl and I shot her like an animal." Tears streamed freely.

"Dad, it's okay. You had to do what you did."

"You don't understand."

"I know, but it's okay."

"It's not." His voice was empty, as hollow as his heart. "I left her there and then the island exploded, it just exploded into a fiery deathtrap." He put his face in his hands and she could barely hear the last words he said.

"I left my baby girl there to burn to ashes."

7

William sat on the couch, two action figures in his lap. He clutched a tablet in his hands, thumbs moving as he played a video game, the sound on mute.

Oliver watched his son just sit. William hadn't moved in more than an hour, just stared at the television. All attempts to talk were met with sullen stares or grunts for answers. Part of him wanted to grab the tablet and turn it off, to *make* William talk to him, to confront the problem head on.

But he knew that was just his trigger response to almost any situation. His default setting was confrontation, and had been for years. First as an angry young man, then stranded on Lian Yu, and finally solidifying once he returned home and donned the mantle of the Green Arrow. He solved problems head on, charging in, using his own power and strength to overcome whatever stood between him and his goal.

Every tool he had to solve problems was the absolute

worst way to solve the problem of a traumatized son he barely knew.

Part of him was also happy that William seemed to find even a passing peace by watching whatever he was watching.

He wanted to talk to his son, but couldn't, so he watched him from across the room.

William flinched when the doorbell rang.

"I've got it, son," he said, keeping his voice as gentle as he could while moving to the door. He opened it, and smiled. Standing there was a dark-haired woman with large, kind eyes.

"Hello, Oliver," she said.

"Hello, Raisa," he said. "I am *so* glad you could come."

"You called, and I could not say no."

He stepped back to usher her inside. "Welcome to my home." She entered, looking around at the fully furnished apartment.

"When are you going to decorate?"

Oliver glanced around, unsure of what she meant.

"It is lovely, Oliver," she said. "But this is all someone else. You should add your own personality to it, make it feel more like home."

Her words startled him, cutting to the center of something he had already been feeling. The apartment wasn't truly his, and now he realized it wasn't truly William's either.

"I will do that very thing… tomorrow," he promised.

"Good boy," she said, moving toward the couch. "And who is this handsome young man?"

Oliver waited for William to introduce himself, but instead his son just stared at the television. Finally Oliver spoke up.

"This is my son, William. William, this is Raisa."

William said nothing, and simply turned ever so slightly away, his eyes still on the screen.

"I'm sorry," Oliver said, "he—"

Raisa cut him off with a quick hand motion, moving until she was in front of William. She sat on the coffee table in front of him and just stayed still for a moment, waiting for some signal only she would be able to interpret.

William ignored her.

Oliver wanted to step in, to say something, to break the silence in the room, but instead he stood and watched. He'd done enough hunting to recognize it as such, even if the prey at stake was the attention of a young boy, instead of food for survival.

He didn't see what William did, and he knew that William may have done nothing, but Raisa reached out, her hand moving very slowly between them, until she touched the tablet. Leaving her fingers on the edge of it for a long moment she waited. After a full minute passed, she carefully lifted the tablet and put it beside her.

William didn't move, but he also didn't object.

"Do you know how long I have known your father, William?" Raisa asked.

The boy said nothing, but his head moved a scant inch.

"I have known your father since he was in short pants, much younger than you are now." She put her hand on the couch between them, the edge of it barely touching his leg. "Do you know how old your father is now?"

William shook his head, not even enough to make his hair move, but it was just enough.

"He's old!" she cried. "Ancient, as old as dirt." Her laugh sang across the apartment.

William's lips twitched, just barely, at the corners.

"So, you know I have been here a *very* long time, even though this is the first time we are meeting, and I will be here for a long time from now."

The words came, just barely loud enough to hear.

"How long?"

"As long as you need me."

William's head bobbed in a tiny nod.

"Now, I think you need me to make dinner," Raisa said.

"Do I get to pick?" The question was a little louder this time.

"You can pick from two choices, but you have to come to the kitchen with me to do that." She stood. "Okay?"

William used his legs to pull himself forward to stand from the couch.

"Let's go then, young William." She turned and moved toward the kitchen, with William following. After a few steps she stopped. "Your father has to go to dinner with friends, William. Tell him goodbye, and we will consider dessert of some kind."

William turned around and looked up at Oliver.

"Goodbye, Oliver."

Oliver knelt beside him. "Goodbye, William, I'll see you in the morning."

"Okay."

"I—I love you, son."

William nodded solemnly. "I know," he said, turning back to Raisa and the kitchen.

Oliver stood and mouthed *thank you* to Raisa. Then he left with the first glimmer of hope for his son he'd had in a long time.

Felicity pushed past a group of fresh-out-of-high-schoolers and stepped into the middle of Big Belly Burger's lobby. She looked around until she saw Diggle waving at her. Moving quickly, she arrived at the table for four. Diggle pulled a chair out for her and she sat across from Lyla.

"Oliver is running a few minutes behind," she announced once Diggle settled in next to his wife.

"Of course he is," Diggle said with a smile on his face.

"I think the only thing Oliver is ever on time for involves a hood and arrows." Lyla's smile matched Diggle's.

"No comment," Felicity said, "but I concede your point. Not this time, though. He's still having issues with William."

Diggle and Lyla shared a knowing look.

Felicity didn't say anything. She knew her friends meant nothing by it, but the smug exclusion really chafed at her. She didn't spend a lot of time thinking about kids—well, lately she had, not kids in general though, but one kid in particular. She'd thought long and hard about William, not just worried over him because he was Oliver's son, but considering what William might mean to whatever she and Oliver had.

Felicity already felt bad about her feelings, no matter which way they fell at any given moment. Thinking about William didn't help.

The waitress appeared with a tray of cups and began setting them on the table.

"We ordered a round of orange sodas," Lyla said by way of explanation. Felicity picked hers up and took a sip, the carbonation making her nose tickle.

"I love orange soda."

"Did someone say 'orange soda'?"

Felicity turned to find Oliver pulling his chair out and sitting down. She leaned close to him and said, "How did things go?"

"It went well, very well. Raisa will be as good for William as she was for me." He looked over at Diggle and Lyla, "Sorry I'm late."

They both waved away his concern.

"Have we ordered?" he asked.

"No," Lyla said, waving over the waitress. "But we can now."

The woman appeared, and it only took a moment for everyone to order their regular favorites. The waitress left and they were back to being by themselves in the busy restaurant.

They laughed around the table, enjoying each other's company. The same as the other patrons of Big Belly Burger were doing that very evening around them. No, they weren't accountants, or software analysts, or welders, or retail clerks. They were two vigilantes, a chaotic good hacker, and the head of a secret government agency that dealt with meta-human crime and terrorism. Yet their easy laughter was the same as the people around them.

It felt… right.

And then the conversation did what conversations inevitably do when adults spend time together. It turned to work.

"John tells me you have a copycat," Lyla said.

Oliver frowned.

"He's not happy about it," Felicity said.

"I can see that." Lyla laughed. "You should never play high stakes poker, Oliver."

Diggle put his arm around his wife. "Didn't Dinah talk to the vic?"

Oliver nodded.

"What did she say?"

"Apparently the copycat is looking to do something with the drug trade in the city," Oliver said.

"Taking it over?" Diggle asked.

"She doesn't think so. She thinks he's targeting the upper-level distributors. I trust her judgment, but…" Oliver let the sentence trail off.

"She definitely has the experience to know," Felicity said. "That's why you sent her in."

"True." Oliver shifted in his seat. "She said he attacked this Mr. Chavis to get information."

"Did he get any?" Diggle asked.

"He gave up someone named Manny Cross." Felicity and Lyla shifted in their seats. Oliver looked from one to the other. "You know that name?" he asked both.

"It's come up when I was researching the influx of drugs in Star City," Felicity said.

"Manny Cross has been on A.R.G.U.S.'s radar for a hot minute," Lyla added. "We don't have cause to take action, but it's only a matter of time." She looked sideways at Felicity. "I'm surprised you don't know more about him."

Felicity began tearing at her napkin, looking down as she did.

"Why would you think that?"

"I just assumed you read our files."

"Um…" Felicity's cheeks grew warm. "I try not to hack our allies' systems."

"That's very… polite of you."

"I said *try*," she said. "Remember that, if your cyber-security guys do a deep check on your systems."

Lyla smiled. "Well, if you find anything too easy to

get past, let me know so I can send a message to IT."

"What did Dinah recommend we do about the copycat?" Diggle asked.

"Nothing," Oliver said. "She thinks like you."

Lyla looked over at her husband. "How do *you* think the copycat should be handled?"

"I think he should be left to do his work," Diggle said. "Maybe even brought in to work with the team."

Felicity turned to Oliver. "You don't think that's a good idea?" She shook her head. "Wait, of course you don't think that's a good idea."

"Wouldn't a new vigilante just help the cause?" Lyla asked. "If he's skilled and needs discipline, perhaps A.R.G.U.S. should scoop him up. I can always use an effective agent, and you know he *will* be disciplined."

"I don't think that's a good idea," Oliver said.

Diggle leaned toward his wife, but spoke loud enough for everyone at the table to hear.

"Oliver is mad that someone's biting his style."

"No," Felicity responded, and she shook her head again. "He's bothered by the fact that he inspired someone else to go all *Dirty Harry*."

"*Death Wish* is a more apt analogy," Oliver said.

"Is that the one with the guy in the hat?"

Oliver smiled. "That's *Billy Jack*."

"Then the one with the ponytail?"

"No."

"It doesn't matter," Felicity said. "You get my point."

"What I don't understand," Lyla said, "is why being

an inspiration would bother you. You did it for the team you have now. You've done it in the past. This just seems like another in a long line."

Oliver leaned forward. "Something about this one just seems almost… sinister. I don't know why, but I don't think this guy is on the same side of the law as us."

"He was pretty brutal in dealing with the victim," Diggle said, reaching for his drink. His hand shook, splashing orange soda up onto the back of it and over to the table. He set the cup down quickly.

"Are you okay?" Felicity asked.

"It's just caffeine," he said, moving his hand off the table to his lap. "I had an extra-large Flash with double-speed force shots at Jitters."

Oliver was about to question his friend when Lyla's phone began to vibrate. Within seconds, all their phones began sounding alarms.

Felicity was the first one to say it.

"I guess we should get this food to go."

8

"What the hell is this?"

Faust turned to the black man standing at stage left. Two of his new mercenaries—El Tigre and a younger merc built like a quarterback on a semi-pro team— had him and his band held at gunpoint alongside the speaker tower.

"This," Faust said as he sauntered over, extending his hand out to the area in front of the stage, "is a hostage situation." More of the mercenaries were herding the audience into the center of the open soccer field by pointing their rifles and yelling orders.

"Man, this is supposed to be a blues festival! You can't come up in here with all this and make this a hostage thing." The man shook his fist in Faust's direction. He had a scar that ran from just below his left eye, curled under his cheekbone, and ended on his chin.

"Why goodness, I like your gumption!" Faust cried. "What *is* your name?"

"My name?" the man cried. "That's my name, fool!" He shoved his finger up toward the banner hanging from the top of the stage.

STAR CITY BLUES FESTIVAL
Featuring Papa Legbone!

"You're Papa Legbone?" Faust cried, clapping his hands in front of his face. "I'm your biggest fan!"

Papa Legbone stepped back, frowning in confusion. "You are?"

Faust's face went flat and expressionless. "No," he said. "Never heard of you."

Papa Legbone's face darkened, making the scar appear to glow. He shook his fist toward Faust. "You... why I oughta take my fake leg and shove it—"

"Now, now." Faust shook his finger at the tall blues singer. "Let's keep it family friendly."

"Please, fool," Papa Legbone dug at the waist of his pants, "I ain't been 'family friendly' since the summer of sixty-nine." He pulled a heavy, snub-nosed revolver from under his shirt. Its chrome barrel and cylinder gleamed under the stage lights.

Before he could pull the trigger, El Tigre stepped up and smashed the butt of his rifle across the musician's forehead. The gun tumbled to the stage, rolling end over end three times before landing against a coil of electric cables. Papa Legbone dropped as if his feet had been yanked out from under him, slamming face-first to the stage.

The other band members crowded back, pressing against the speaker stack, just wanting to be as far from the violence as possible. Most of them turned their backs on the fallen blues singer, frozen by their fear, consumed with their helplessness, shamed by his "don't-care-if-I-live-or-die" bravery.

Faust squatted in front of the fallen blues legend. Papa Legbone looked up at him from the stage, blood coating the side of his face where his eyebrow split open.

"I hope you don't have anymore guns on you, old dog," Faust said.

"If I do, you'll be the first to know." Papa Legbone didn't reach up to wipe his face, just let the blood run like a red badge of courage.

Faust sighed. "Well, I guess I wouldn't expect anything else from a man with a scar like that." His hand disappeared into his jacket pocket and came back out with a thin disc. He held it in front of the musician. It wasn't much larger than a coaster and only an inch thick. Its plastic surface was a uniform blue that shone as if it had been oiled. In the center of one side was a black triangle the size of a thumbprint.

"This," Faust said, "is a miniature version of the devices my men are planting all around this stadium. If I press this—" His finger pushed the black triangle, and as he lifted it the triangle began to glow. "—then it is armed."

Papa Legbone pushed himself up and spat out a

bit of blood that had seeped into his mouth. "Why should I care about that little old firecracker?"

"This 'little old firecracker,' as you put it, is powerful enough to blow a hole through three inches of steel."

"Maybe I should put that where I was going to put my wooden leg then." Papa Legbone's voice was strong, but a small tremor ran underneath it.

Faust stood, signaling El Tigre to pick the old bluesman up. The merc did it, lifting him to his feet as if he were made of paper, instead of flesh and bone. Faust leaned in.

"I think strapping it to you in center stage, and letting this audience see it turn you into half the man you are now, should keep them as docile as Hindu cows." Faust motioned for Papa Legbone to be dragged to the center of the stage, ending the gesture with a flourish of the hand holding the bomb.

An emerald arrow plucked it from his grasp.

It moved faster than he could see, let alone react, catching the device and pinning it to the stage where he had intended to place the blues legend. Faust jerked his head around, bewildered. A roar came from the field in front of the stage as the captured audience began to break ranks and run. It took a second to realize that his mercenaries were dropping.

"No, no, no," he babbled, "not yet, I don't want to see the inferno just yet!"

The Green Arrow dropped to the stage, swinging from the light rig above, and landed in front of Faust.

He rose like an avenging angel in emerald, staring down with eyes that were filled with anger.

Dinah pivoted on her left foot and kicked out with her right. The heel of her combat boot snagged her adversary's shirt, pulling it to the left and knocking him down. She used the momentum to twist into a downward punch that landed hard across the bridge of his nose. The collapsed steel baton in her hand loaded the punch with more weight and reinforced her fist. The skin between his eyes split, blood splashing hot over her knuckles.

The merc dropped to his hands and knees, head down, blood dripping on the fake grass of the soccer field. She lashed out with her foot one more time, caught him in the temple, and knocked him flat unconscious. She pivoted back up, fists at the ready, looking for her next opponent.

"Hit these guys hard." Felicity's voice came through the comms. "A.R.G.U.S. is so sweetly batting cleanup, so they'll gather any bad guys you put down. They'll also handle the civilian evacuation. All Team Arrow has to do is fight the forces of evil."

Felicity paused then added, "Wow, that was melodramatic. Accurate, but way over the top. Sorry guys."

The mercenaries were scrambling under Team Arrow's assault, unable to form up in groups of more than two or three before being taken down. Once that was done, A.R.G.U.S. agents swept in behind the heroes and put the mercs in cuffs. They had also cleared the exits and were guiding the civilians out. She didn't know how Oliver had managed the backup, but she was grateful for it.

Wild Dog rode the mercenary to the ground, feeling the solid thud of impact through his shins. The gun for hire exhaled sharply, all the air driven from his lungs by the sudden weight. Even through his mask it was foul enough to make Rene gag.

"You need some freshmaker," he said. "Try some of this." He grabbed the merc's Taser and shoved it up against his throat, depressing the button. The mercenary began to jitter underneath him as 50,000 volts of electricity lit up his nervous system. Wild Dog pulled it away and the man stayed locked, immobilized in the position of the last jerk and twist.

"Damn, stun gun don't play." Wild Dog looked at the Taser and nodded his head. "I might need to get me one of these."

Mister Terrific landed flat on the ground next to him, the result of being punched by a mercenary twice his size. He twisted, slipping the next punch. Wild Dog leaned over, stuck the Taser against the guy's side and depressed the trigger.

The mercenary twisted, bowing back until his head almost reached his boots.

"Thanks, man." Mister Terrific sat up, pushing off the immobilized opponent.

"Don't mention it, Hoss." Wild Dog stood, offering a hand to his fellow vigilante. "Now you owe me."

Mister Terrific let himself be pulled to his feet. He shoulder checked Wild Dog, knocking him to the left as his hands went under his jacket. They came out in an arc and at the end of it, his fingers opened, flinging out both his T-Spheres. They kicked on the moment they left his hand and flew, straight and true, into a mercenary with his rifle aimed at Wild Dog's back. The two spheres hit like mini-rockets, both crackling as their own Taser capability engaged.

First his rifle fell to the ground, then the assailant did the same.

Mister Terrific smiled widely. "Now we're even."

Wild Dog shook his head. "Shut up."

"This ends now!"

Green Arrow lashed out with a hard kick to Faust's stomach, which sent the psychotic bomb maker tumbling across the stage. The archer glanced over his shoulder. The rest of Team Arrow were on the field and engaging the mercenaries there.

Movement caught his eye. He spun, pulling flechettes from the back of his glove, flinging the tiny blades in one smooth motion. *Zip zip zip*, they hit a mercenary who had aimed his rifle at the back of Green Arrow's head. The steel projectiles stuck in a line across his chest. He fell and rolled off the edge of the stage.

Green Arrow had just a second to raise his bow to block a short, massively built mercenary from hitting him across the face with a rifle. The blow vibrated through the bow and down into his arms, making his teeth hurt. The hulking assailant swung the rifle around, aiming the barrel to shoot him in the stomach. He dove to the left in a roll as bullets chewed the space where he had just been standing.

He lashed out with his bow, hitting the man in the knee. The mercenary skipped to the side, but did not go down. It was like hitting a boxing bag. He didn't seem to feel pain.

Pushing off, Green Arrow used his momentum to hook a powerful blow to the man's temple. The mercenary staggered back, and shook his head. Green Arrow chopped down with his bow, knocking the rifle from the man's hands.

His attacker's fingers closed on his arm, squeezing tight like the jaws of a pit bull. The mercenary growled through blunt, square teeth and yanked him to the left. Green Arrow stumbled forward, unable to resist the pull. While he was off balance the man drove a big, meaty fist into his kidneys, punching with all his considerable weight and leverage behind it.

Nauseating pain sank deep inside him, all the way into his core. Then a second blow struck him in the middle of the back, robbing him of the ability to breathe.

He dropped to the stage floor, the world going black at the corners of his eyes. Splinters from bullet holes dug into his cheek. From behind him he heard the merc growl.

"Time to earn your stripes, son."

Something inside him, his sixth sense for violence earned from years of living it and giving it himself, called out for him to push, to roll, to just get out of the way. It took all he had to move away before the knife sliced the space where he had been. He pushed hard, working through the pain that filled his torso, scrambling to his feet. His brain started separating the pain, parceling it off to the corners so he could function.

His foe had a knife as long as his forearm, and a wolfish grin on his face.

"Time to dance for El Tigre, little man."

Reaching over his shoulder, Green Arrow pulled two arrows from his quiver. Gripping them low, he held the scalpel-sharp broad heads out in his hands, the carbon-fiber shafts braced down his forearms.

El Tigre nodded then rushed in, moving far faster than a man his size should be able to go. He was like a great white shark, all power and fury. Green Arrow jabbed the broad heads forward. The attacker knocked them aside with an almost casual swing of his muscular arm while his blade drove up, seeking the soft space in his target's side, between hip and rib.

Green Arrow barely had enough time to shove his arm down between them. He used the bandoleer of flechettes strapped to the back of his hand as a shield to keep from being sliced open like a fleshy envelope. El Tigre's knife cut the leather holding the tiny blades and they tumbled out onto the stage in a clatter.

Grabbing another arrow, the archer swung up. The broad head in his hand sank deep into El Tigre's tricep, cutting muscle like a razor through paper until it struck bone. This time the mercenary howled with pain, jerking away. The blades of the broad head curved back on themselves, making pronged points that hung in the fiber of the muscle they pierced. They stuck fast and El Tigre's flailing yanked the arrow from Green Arrow's hand.

El Tigre lashed out with the handle of his knife, striking Green Arrow in the forehead. White light exploded across the back of his eyes and he went down, unable to see.

Get up, get up, get up! his brain screamed at him. *If you stay in this spot you're dead!*

Before he could move, however, El Tigre struck, driving his blade straight into Green Arrow's chest. The reinforced layers of his costume stopped the knife from penetrating, but couldn't dissipate all the force of the strike, compressed to such a small point. It felt as if he had been stabbed deep between his ribs. The pain shot all the way through to his spine, unspooling all the mental discipline that had been keeping it at bay.

El Tigre grabbed the strap of his quiver and lifted him off the ground. The mercenary put his face close to Green

Arrow's. It was twisted in a mixture of pain and fury.

"I'm going to cut your throat," he growled.

Green Arrow flailed weakly at El Tigre's arm, but it did no good. He could only watch as the man moved the knife to slash his throat. As he watched death come for him, he had just one thought.

William.

And then there was a *BOOM*.

Spartan threw a hard punch, catching the mercenary in the mouth. The blow landed with a satisfying crunch.

He'd added some equipment to his outfit—sap gloves on his hands, the weight of them adding power to his punches, high-impact plastic elbow pads, and steel-toed boots. His smartgun hung on his hip in its holster. He didn't trust his hands to grip it, though—they were much better as fists.

The mercenary dropped to the field and Spartan stepped over him, wading into another group. Throwing fists and swinging elbows, he reveled in the feel of his body doing what he had trained it to do.

He dropped one with a back-fist to the temple, another with a knife hand straight to the throat, and the third with a hard-torqued uppercut punch to the stomach. The mercenary doubled over, retching from the blow. Spartan drew his lead-covered fist far back over his head and drove it down onto the back of the mercenary's skull, putting him down for the count.

Deep in the muscle, his forearm throbbed.

He shook it off.

Another mercenary who didn't care about the innocent bystanders or his fellow brothers-in-arms fired a burst of bullets his way. High on adrenaline, Spartan dove toward him instead of away from the bullets, rolling under the gunfire and coming up slamming into the trigger-happy assailant. His shoulder drove deep into the man's torso, lifting his feet off the ground. Spartan carried him a few steps before slamming him into the ground. His hand grabbed the man's rifle barrel, shoving it up into the air while he thrust an elbow down in the man's face.

It took three blows before the man lay still.

Spartan pushed himself up, looking for the next merc he would take down. His arm was on fire where muscle met bone, but it was ice cold and tingling in his fingertips. Nevertheless, he could still make a fist.

White Canary flipped over the pile of mercenaries she had laid low, using her bō staff like a vaulting pole. Her foot lashed out on her way down, smacking the rifle from an enemy's hands. It slung around his body on the strap attached to it. He fumbled to catch it, trying to get a hold so he could use it to shoot her.

She landed lightly in front of him and smiled.

"You should just put your hands up in the air and surrender."

He looked up at her, eyes wide, but his hands didn't stop fumbling for his gun.

She shook her head. "Two hits."

"What?" he said, his hands finally on the grips, pulling the gun into position as his finger sought the trigger.

The end of the bõ staff whipped up with the velocity of a sledgehammer, clipping the merc on the chin. He went up on his tiptoes, standing on them for a long second before his body realized it had been knocked unconscious. He folded in on himself like a popped balloon.

"I hit you. You hit the ground."

El Tigre's eyes were wide open as he slowly spun on his heel and tumbled off the edge of the stage.

Green Arrow looked up to find Papa Legbone holding the snub-nosed revolver.

"I told that fool he'd be the first to know," Papa Legbone said.

As he climbed to his feet, Green Arrow's chest hurt in a way that told him his sternum was bruised badly. He pulled himself tall and took a deep breath, regaining control of his body, once again pushing the pain aside until later.

"Where did Faust go?" he asked the bluesman.

"That crazy guy? He limped off that-a-way." Papa Legbone pointed to the rear of the stage.

Green Arrow stepped close. "Thank you. It's an

honor to meet you. I'm a big fan."

Papa Legbone blinked at him. "You okay to go after him?" he asked. "I've taken some beatings before, son, and believe me, you took a beating there."

"I'll be fine." He reached out and took the revolver from the bluesman's hands. "Don't shoot anyone else."

He turned and took off after Faust.

Papa Legbone watched him go.

"Damn."

"Is that all the bad guys?" Mister Terrific asked. "Because if so, go Team Arrow."

"Don't be smug," White Canary said, with a smirk on her face. "It doesn't look good on you."

All of Team Arrow had gathered by the stage to touch base. Wild Dog looked out at the field, watching A.R.G.U.S. agents lead away the last of the mercenaries.

"I like this backup thing," he said. "Maybe they can bat cleanup for us all the time."

"*Not likely*," Felicity's voice said in their ears. "*But we may be able to call them anytime there's a hostage situation, or a demolitions expert gone bad.*"

"So are we all done?" White Canary asked.

Diggle shook his hand out, grimacing. "We are," he said. "Thank you for the help."

Dinah studied him with her head cocked to the side. "You okay there?" she asked.

"Yeah," Diggle said, thinking, *I wish she'd stop asking.*

He pulled the sap glove off his trembling hand and shoved it into his jacket pocket, leaving the trembling hand inside, out of sight. "One of those guys nailed me in the funny bone with the butt of his rifle. It'll go away soon." He looked around. "Where is Green Arrow?"

Felicity's voice came on. "*His GPS tracker puts him in the corridors of the stadium behind the stage.*"

"What's he doing?" Wild Dog started to ask.

"*He's not answering his comms,*" Felicity interrupted. "*But he's moving fast.*"

From somewhere deep behind the stage a low rumble rolled out.

His boots pounded down the formed concrete corridor that led into the stadium's lobby. He rounded a corner at full speed, his body pumping his bloodstream full of endorphins, making his pain dull to nothing as long as he kept moving.

Tomorrow, if he survived, it would be a different story.

Some motion or blur of color caught in his peripheral vision and he leaped behind an abandoned concession stand. An explosion sucked the air from where he had been, slamming into the stand and making it shudder and slide across the floor, dragging him with it. A rack of candy in colorful wrappers spilled down from the counter, peppering him.

He stuck his head out and saw Faust clambering

down the stopped escalator, headed somewhere below. He guessed it would be the parking garage.

He probably has a getaway vehicle.

If Faust got into a car, it was over until the next time he struck.

Not on my watch, he thought, jumping to his feet and running after the explosives expert. Faust turned down a hallway, and Green Arrow followed, picking up speed in the determination to catch him. He nearly lost his footing, sliding to a stop, because Faust stood facing him, hands in the air.

The archer had an arrow notched and pointed at Faust before he fully stopped.

"Get on the ground!" he yelled. "Now!"

"While I appreciate what your sharp sticks can accomplish," Faust said, "I do believe I will listen to the man with the gun."

Green Arrow pivoted, bow still at full draw. A man in a mask and a dark green hoodie, and with a big pistol, stepped out from the shadows.

The copycat.

"Are you with him?" Green Arrow growled.

"Why would I be with him?" The copycat's voice was amplified and distorted, unrecognizable. "I'm here to stop him. I'm on your side."

"I've seen your way of doing things. My side doesn't kill."

"Well, maybe that's your side's problem," the copycat said. "Too many criminals doing too many

dirty deeds, and not enough permanent solutions."
He raised his gun, leveling it at Faust's head. The
psychotic bomb maker flinched, but kept his hands up.

"You are *not* killing this man."

"You've gone sally on this city, Green Arrow. All
weak sister about crime."

"Drop the gun!"

"No."

The word was said simply, spoken plainly by the
copycat—no inflection, no lilt, no rising syllable, just a
plain statement.

And a tightening trigger finger.

The Emerald Archer let his arrow fly.

The copycat jerked to the left, swinging his gun up.
The barrel of the pistol struck the shaft mid-flight with
a chime of metal on metal. The arrow kicked away and
flew, wobbling, off into space.

Before Green Arrow could follow up the copycat
fired three rounds at him. He dropped low and they
missed, spiking through the air where he had been.

Behind the copycat he saw Faust, grinning ear to ear,
pull something from inside his jacket. The demolitions
expert pushed a button and tossed an object between
the two vigilantes.

"Look out!" Green Arrow cried, then the world
became white light, white heat, and a concussive force
that knocked him off his feet.

* * *

They walked through the cloud of dust on high alert, not sure what they would find. Spartan and Wild Dog moved with the cribbed, fluid steps of military training. Black Canary stepped cautiously but quickly, always finding solid footing. White Canary strode forward, her casual demeanor belying her readiness and awareness of her surroundings. Mister Terrific simply walked, looking at the destruction around them.

Felicity's voice came over the comms. *"Tell me something as soon as you can, guys."*

"Will do," Spartan responded.

Half the fluorescent lights above were dark or flickering, taken out in the blast. This left the hallway filled with shadows and pools of solid darkness everywhere. The further in they moved, the more debris there was. A toppled concession stand spilled its contents across the floor, a spray of hot dogs and Polish sausages and weirdly meat-scented water. A few feet further, hats and T-shirts smoldered in piles along the floor. A scorched light fixture hung by wires off the wall, spitting bright sparks of electricity into the air around it. Wood and brick debris lay underfoot, waiting to turn an ankle.

None of them spoke, forming a V pattern with Spartan in the lead, taking point. He was the first to spot the Green Arrow. The archer lay on the floor, face down and covered in dirt-colored dust. He sprawled, arms and legs at odd angles, his upper body curled in on itself.

Moving quickly, Diggle knelt beside him. The carbon-fiber quiver on his back looked as if it had been chewed on by a pack of rabid wolves, the top edge of it rent in a big tear, the rest of it gouged and pitted where it had taken the brunt of the explosion. He reached down and put his fingers to his friend's throat, pressing alongside his trachea, feeling for a pulse.

"Is he..." Sara asked.

He found a pulse, a steady one.

Before Diggle could answer Oliver groaned, and moved.

"Easy, Hoss, easy," Rene said, lifting his hockey mask off his face.

Dinah spoke into the comms. "Overwatch, we have Green Arrow. He's alive."

Felicity's voice was tight with apprehension, *"What is his status?"*

Diggle leaned in. "You okay, brother?"

Oliver took his help sitting up. "Do you have Faust?"

Dinah spoke to the comms again. "He seems fine. Banged up but okay."

Even though she whispered, all of them could still hear Felicity say, *"Oh dear God, thank you."*

"Looks like Faust got away," Rene said.

The Emerald Archer cursed under his breath. "Help me up," he said.

Diggle stood and helped him to his feet, grimacing as he did.

Curtis wore a puzzled look on his face as he stepped close and squatted down.

"Um, hey, G.A." He looked up with a quizzical expression. "Can I call you G.A.? I like the sound of it."

"I just got done being blown up. What do you think?"

"Oh, I totally understand, got it. Felt too casual when I said it, anyhow. I'll stick with Green Arrow. Much more professional, especially since we're the only ones who can ever hear our comms."

"What were you going to say?" Oliver's voice was harsh. The pain was returning in solid waves throughout his body.

"Oh, um yeah, did he shoot at you?" Curtis lifted up a single spent shell casing. "'Cause he always seemed like a bombs-only kind of guy."

Oliver stared at the empty shell casing.

"No, *he* didn't."

9

"What *was* that?" Tall Man slammed his hand on the steel table. The sound of it reverberated through the small room.

His voice dripped from his mouth like acid as he loomed over Faust, who slouched in a tatty office chair.

"What was that?" Faust studied his fingernails, instead of the angry man in front of him. "That was overexuberance, and hubris on my part. It's something I have always been prone to. Ma Faust used to try to beat it out of me, but she never succeeded."

"That stunt at the soccer field cost me forty men," Tall Man snarled.

"That little stunt of mine cost me a million dollars."

"I don't give a damn about your money."

"Oh, really?" Faust raised an eyebrow. "Then perhaps I should stop paying you."

Tall Man frowned, a deep crease between his bladed eyebrows. "If you stop paying my men I will kill you."

Faust smiled widely, exposing nearly all the teeth in his head. He spun in his chair, and put both feet on the floor, then leaned toward the tall man.

"Do you know the mistake of all great leaders throughout time?" he asked. "Their most common failure is that, eventually, no matter how powerful they are, they forget that they have men of power underneath them. Men of authority, enforcing their rule of law. They become secure in their power, viewing the men who help them hold it as mere extensions of themselves, instead of men with ambitions and desires of their very own. Most empires fall from within. Most kings topple at their right hand. No matter how many great men come before them, they fail to see the pattern."

Faust stood. "Now, do you think someone as meticulous as I am, with all of the dangerous things in my toy box, would be so foolish as to not learn that lesson?"

"That sounds an awful lot like a threat."

"Oh no, no, no, no, not a threat. Instead think of it as an illustration, an illumination, without which there is no way for us to continue this association of ours. I would never threaten you." Faust held his slender hands out, palms up. "Understand first, I'm not some fool. I recognize that, to your military mind, I look as solid as ice cream in the summer heat. However, the process to my chaos simply isn't your process.

"For one thing," he continued, "you suffer under

the illusion that I do not have all of my bases covered. I mean, I wouldn't at any point—" Faust opened his jacket and Tall Man tensed. "—be caught unprepared for any and all circumstances."

Then Tall Man gaped.

Under Faust's jacket was a canvas vest. Long, thin rectangles of plastic explosive circled his torso in three rows. Fine, multi-colored wires looped from rectangle to rectangle. Wire leaders ran from the vest ending in flat white electrodes that stuck to Faust's collar, ran down under his shirt, and trailed up, over, and into his sleeve. Tall Man recognized it from his time in the sandbox.

It was a suicide vest with a dead man's switch.

"I'm taking a cue from the man who put me in motion," Faust said. "If I go, this is enough of my homebrew to make sure even the best sniper would go too." He dropped his jacket lapel, letting it close over the suicide vest. "So would anyone unlucky enough to be caught nearby."

Tall Man felt hot and cold at the same time, sweating underneath his clothes, freezing along the tops of his bones. *This man is insane*, he thought, *but I have taken his money. What have I done?*

He was a mercenary—had been one since leaving the military. He worked with mercenaries, guided them. They were his men. Mercenaries were in the business of making money, and he wasn't always particular about how he did it. He had done—and had led his men to do—criminal acts. He preferred working with criminals because their money was far better than contract work. Bank heists, security for transports of all manner of illegal merchandise, from drugs to weapons, even providing armed support for human traffickers. All doing bad things for bad men for money.

Faust was in an entirely different league.

Faust was a terrorist without an ideology.

It was one thing to walk beside the abyss, it was another thing to try to cross it. He felt as if he were falling.

Faust walked around the table.

"My dear friend and employee," he said, "no need to worry so much. I learned my lesson from the last outing. No more exposing ourselves again that way. This game should be played from a distance. I apologize that I got ahead of myself."

Tall Man tried to regain control. "No more reckless actions."

Faust held his hand up in the Scout's Honor position. "As an apology, I extend a bonus to the family of any man that we lost." He studied Tall Man's face. "I see you doubting, my friend. I promise you that I have a plan, and next time you and your men simply have to provide security for me. They won't be involved in any conflict.

"Trust me," Faust added. "It's all about the long play now."

AUGUST 2017

1

Oliver stepped out of the bathroom, wearing only pajama pants, drying his hair with a towel. The shower had felt good, the hot water easing away some of the ache he still had from the incident at the Blues Festival. Between the fight with the big mercenary and the explosion that allowed Faust and the copycat to get away, he still had bruises.

He looked at them in the mirror. They were fading, but still stood out, sickly greens and yellows with pockets of fading purple as his body broke down and absorbed the contusions. Wiping the last of the water away, he continued toward the dining room.

He found William sitting at the table.

His son was also in his pajamas, hair tousled from being in bed. It stuck up as if placed that way on purpose. Oliver read it as a sign that William had been sweating, and sleeping badly again. That would be why he was awake at this late hour.

William glanced up as Oliver came in, then went back to eating cereal from a bowl and flipping the pages of a comic book on the table. Oliver spread the towel over his shoulders and chest, trying to hide the worst of the marks, and walked over to see what his son was reading.

A comic-book version of his friend Barry, the Flash, zipped through square panels, punching bad guys in colorful costumes.

He searched for something to say and came up with, "What're you reading, William?"

"*Showcase Comics*," William said, taking another spoonful of cereal.

"Wait," Oliver said. "Are you eating Chocolaty Poofs?"

William nodded.

"I used to *love* Chocolaty Poofs. Do we have any more?"

William pointed to the kitchen.

Oliver went to the pantry. There on the first shelf was an opened box of cereal. He poured some into a bowl, filled it with milk, and went to the table, sitting across from his son. His first bite of Chocolaty Poofs flooded his brain with memories and his mouth with sugary goodness.

"Where did we get these?" Oliver asked.

"Raisa brought them."

"Of course she did. Do you like them?"

"They're pretty good."

Three simple words made Oliver's heart lift. It was progress.

"Oliver?"

"Yes, William."

"What's it like shooting an arrow?"

Seven simple words made Oliver's heart skip a beat.

He should have seen it coming, some form of this question. William had seen him in costume on Lian Yu. He knew, but through the rescue and all of the aftermath they hadn't spoken about it. He thought for a long time that the trauma of Lian Yu—of being kidnapped, seeing his captor kill himself, discovering his mother had died—might have caused William to forget that his father, the man he barely knew, was a costumed vigilante.

Was the Green Arrow.

Did William want to talk about that?

He decided to answer the question as it were.

"It's—" He stopped, searching for the words. "It's a moment where you feel everything inside you is in perfect order."

William stared at him closely. "Do you enjoy it?"

"Enjoy isn't the right word."

"What is then?"

"It's satisfying." That seemed appropriate. "Knowing I can make a shot, even a difficult one or one under... pressure," Oliver faltered at his own words. He hadn't been able to save William's mother. "In that way, it makes me feel good."

"Do you get scared?"

"Sometimes."

"Do you get hurt?"

Oliver took the towel from around his neck, revealing his scars and the ugly, still-fading bruises. William's eyes went a little wider.

"Yes," he said.

William studied his father's torso, not blinking as he read the map of scar tissue that documented all the injuries Oliver had suffered over the last several years. After a moment he slid off his chair. He closed his comic book, put it under his arm, and picked up his bowl of cereal, nearly empty. He carried it over to the sink, then turned and walked down the hallway.

Oliver heard the click when he shut his bedroom door.

"This guy doesn't exist. He's like the Invisible Man."

Felicity turned to Curtis, who hunched over a keyboard on the other end of the computer console. He sipped a fruit drink in a silver pouch made for kids. His hands clicked the keys on the keyboard as he stared at the computer screen.

"Okay, first of all," she said, "we don't have an Invisible Man."

"We don't?"

"Nope. A Nuclear Man, yes, and Barry and Cisco have an invisible woman. Doctor Light."

"Seriously?" Curtis asked.

Felicity nodded.

"I'd kill to be able to be invisible," he continued. "That would be hella cool."

"Not as cool as flying."

"True." They'd had the super-powers discussion many times. "Our guy here can't fly, but he might as well not exist."

"He has to exist—we have his fingerprints. And Curtis, seriously, move back away from the computer. You're going to get cathode ray burn on your eyeballs."

Curtis sat up. "First of all, I've run that print through the NCIC database, the SCBI database, Interpol, and Run DMC, and found nothing."

"Run DMC is a hip hop group, not a database."

"Hip hop legend," Curtis corrected. "Just making sure you were paying attention." He picked up his juice pouch and took another sip. "Secondly though, this is an LCD screen, it doesn't emit cathode rays. That's a CRT monitor, which has never been seen in a state-of-the-art secret base like the Arrowcave—"

"Oliver hates when we call it that."

"And yet we continue to do so," he said. "But LCD screens only put out low-level EMF fields which are, mostly, harmless."

"Nerd," Felicity said.

"Geek."

"Easy with the insults there, people." The voice came from behind them. "I'm going to think you two can't work together." Dinah climbed the stairs that led up to the dais, toweling off from the workout she'd just completed in the Bunker's gym.

"Oh, we were just blowing off steam," Curtis said. "We get along fine, it's just how we…"

"Blow off steam?" Dinah smiled. "Take it easy. I was just yanking your chain, Curtis."

"Oh, okay." He laughed.

"Any luck tracking down our copycat?"

Felicity shook her head. "He doesn't come up in any criminal database at all."

"You've tried them all?"

"All one hundred and forty-three of them."

"There are that many?" Dinah leaned against the rail.

"If you include international."

"Which you did?"

Curtis nodded. "Even the Markovian crime database."

"Well, there may be your problem."

Curtis frowned. "The problem might be that he isn't a Markovian criminal?"

"Ah!" Felicity shot up in her chair. "Ah! What an idiot I am." She spun and began typing. "Our problem is that he might not be a criminal at all."

"Wow," Curtis said. "That makes so much sense."

"Dinah, you're a genius," Felicity said over her shoulder.

Dinah waved away the praise. "Not a genius, just a really good detective."

"Got him!" Felicity cried.

"Is he Markovian?" Curtis asked.

Felicity shot him a look and began reading. "Arthur Hallsey, father of two, lives in—lives in a nice suburban neighborhood. Owns a car and a boat, not too extended on his credit cards, bit of money in the bank. IT technician, which explains how he knows where the action is." She looked up. "This guy is so straight-laced he doesn't even have a parking citation."

"Maybe the system mismatched his fingerprints," Dinah said.

Felicity and Curtis laughed in unison.

"Okay, maybe this guy had the gun, and it was stolen and used by someone else."

Curtis fanned his fingers quickly over the keyboard. "Nope. There'd be a police report, if that were the case. Guy like that would report it."

"If he isn't a gun nut, then he might not even know it's gone," Dinah offered. "Lot of people have a gun for protection, and just put it in the closet or between the mattresses and forget about it. If it were stolen, they wouldn't know until it popped for being used in a crime."

"Maybe," Felicity said, turning in her chair, "but Arthur Hallsey did order a paintball mask, several green hoodies, and—the nail in a rather circumstantial coffin, I will admit—a bulletproof vest."

Dinah pushed off the rail. "Good enough for me. Text me his address, and I'll pick him up for questioning."

"What's your probable cause?" Curtis asked.

"Probably 'cause I want to," she said with a smile.

Agony seared in a thin line along the bottom edge of his pectoral muscle, causing it to spasm. The convulsive movement seemed to make the needles sink deeper.

"I know it hurts, Mr. Diggle," Dr. Schwartz said, her eyes covered with dark goggles, "but I need you to remain as still as possible."

He gritted his teeth and tried to relax as Dr. Schwartz lowered the apparatus, moving toward the elbow. The needle it held slid into the thin skin as if it were made of air. He felt every millimeter of surgical stainless steel that pierced him, fully aware as it punctured through skin, muscle, and tendon. He didn't feel the shaky scrape of it hitting the bone.

New pain pulsed into his elbow, and immediately he felt it begin to swell even as the machine pulled back, leaving the needle embedded in his arm.

Another needle cycled into the now empty slot.

"It's okay, Mr. Diggle—we're over halfway done."

Diggle turned his head and glanced across his body. A line of needles stuck out of his dark skin, shining in the harsh beam of the exam light. They looked like miniature fence posts all in a row from his sternum, across his chest, and down to the elbow. Thin tubes connected to the top of each needle, gathering in a bundle and running up to a dispenser unit. Under each of them, down deep where the tips were embedded in his flesh, were tiny pools of hot, liquid pain as they slowly released whatever medicinal concoction was being injected into him.

"It's okay, Doc." His voice sounded almost guttural as he forced his words through clenched teeth. "It's worth it if it works."

"Remember our odds," Dr. Schwartz said. "This gives us only a seventeen percent chance of improvement." She lowered the device again.

He turned his head away as another needle pierced his flesh.

2

He was a normal-looking man.

Mid– to late forties, in decent shape by all appearances with a straight spine and wide shoulders. Dark brown hair over dark brown eyes in a fine but forgettable face. He was every man, someone who could blend into a crowd without leaving a ripple.

Arthur Hallsey sat in a metal chair at the metal table in the small interrogation room. He did not look scared or anxious. He didn't even appear to be annoyed. He simply sat, lightly tapping his fingers along the sides of a half-full paper cup of cold coffee from the vending machine down the hall. Tapping to some tune only he could hear.

Oliver thought about that coffee as he watched Hallsey through the one-way glass. He had drunk that coffee before. It was garbage. The vending machine was a relic of late eighties coin-operated machinery and had been in place probably before he had even been born. The coffee it put out certainly tasted as if the machine had not been cleaned since then.

He made a mental note to have it replaced.

The door to the room opened and Hallsey stopped tapping. Dinah walked in. She wore a dark pantsuit, her lieutenant badge swinging from a thin ball-bead chain around her neck. Her hair was tightly tied in a ponytail that gave her a very intimidating look. She sat in the chair across from Hallsey and leaned back, just watching him without saying anything.

Oliver waited, watching. Whenever they did speak, he would hear it all through the intercom on the wall to the left of the window.

Hallsey resumed tapping on his cup. After a few minutes he picked it up, shook it slightly, and tossed back what was left. He grimaced as he put the empty cup on the table.

"Your coffee is terrible," he said.

"That's how you want to start?" she asked.

Hallsey shrugged. "You could tell me why I'm here."

"You *know* why you're here."

"I was working on my screenplay when you showed up at my house, put me into a car, and brought me here."

"What's your screenplay about?"

"About two acts long at this point. I was starting the third when you arrived." Hallsey smiled at his tiny joke.

Dinah didn't.

"Is your screenplay about a man who dresses in a costume and goes out trying to find crime to stop?"

"No," he said. "I think that story's been done."

"How do you feel about it?"

"The idea that it's been done before? Doesn't bother me in the slightest. All ideas have been done before."

"How do you feel about vigilantes?"

"We have a lot of them here in Star City."

"Do they help stop crime, or do they just get in the way?"

"Well, officer, I think you could answer that better than me." He leaned forward. "But it does seem like no matter what they do, crime keeps rising."

"So you think they get in the way?"

He considered it. "Not so much 'get in the way' as more 'don't go far enough.'" He frowned slightly at the thought.

"So, you think normal people should put on costumes and try to fight crime?"

"I'm saying it's not the worst idea."

"Are you a vigilante, Mr. Hallsey?"

"That seems pretty silly," he responded. "What do you think? Don't I look like a normal citizen with a normal family and a normal life?"

"That is not a denial."

"It's not a confession, either."

"Do you hate criminals?"

"Doesn't everyone?"

"Other criminals don't."

Hallsey chuckled. "Oh, I bet they do. The only reason you police get any crime solved is that they hate each other and turn on each other like rats. They do your job for you."

Dinah raised an eyebrow. "You don't like police?"

"Police are fine. Mostly good people."

"Fine?"

"Someone has to clean up after a vigilante stops a criminal."

Even though her face and body language did nothing to give it away, Oliver could feel Dinah's frustration through the glass. He understood her predicament. There was nothing with which she could charge Hallsey, so she couldn't use her normal interrogation tactics. She was handcuffed by circumstance because she was a police officer.

Good thing I'm not, he thought. *I'm just the mayor.*

He turned toward the door.

Oliver knocked and stepped inside the interrogation room.

"Lieutenant Drake, could I speak with Mr. Hallsey, please?"

Dinah stood without answering and walked out through the door, shutting it behind her and leaving the two men alone. Oliver knew she would go to the observation room, primarily to keep anyone else from listening in.

Oliver crossed the room, his hand extended. "Hello Mr. Hallsey, I'm—"

"I voted for you."

Oliver stopped short, then moved to the chair Dinah had just vacated and sat down. The metal legs scraped on the concrete floor.

"Thank you for that."

Hallsey waved it away. With a twinge of resentment, Oliver noticed that he didn't seem to suffer any physical discomfort, even after the explosion.

"The reason you're here today is that the police think you are dressing up and going out at night to be a vigilante."

"You say that as if you're very sure of it."

"Mr. Hallsey…" Oliver leaned forward. "I'm not a police officer. I cannot arrest you. But I am in touch with the Green Arrow, and so I know a thing or two about vigilantes."

"If you're so close to him, you should ask him why he went soft on crime."

"Soft? The Green Arrow and his team have helped the police put an end to several major crime organizations."

Hallsey shrugged. "That was last year. This year he seems to be letting criminals get away with a lot more. Even murder."

"I assure you, he's fighting as hard as he can."

"Criminals go to jail and come back out doing even more. They need to be stopped—permanently."

"The Arrow is trying very hard to not kill anyone," Oliver said, doing his best to keep his face calm and his voice even. "He works in extreme situations, but he and I agree that killing isn't the solution."

"Some people need to be killed."

Oliver leaned forward. "Yes, sometimes they do. And sometimes it's the vigilante who loses their life. Laurel Lance, for example. People still honor her death as Black Canary."

"So criminals are dangerous? Hmmm... I never thought of them that way." Hallsey rubbed his chin as if contemplating, "Sounds as if Green Arrow needs to be more... *thorough*. You know, get them off the streets for good."

"You think he should kill these people."

"Mayor Queen, I think the most important thing is for my daughters to grow up in a safe time, a safe place. If some of the bad guys need to go down to make that happen, well then, so be it. I'd applaud anyone who makes that happen."

"You should think about your daughters," Oliver said, "and your wife. They need you to go home to them."

"I didn't say I was a vigilante."

"No, Mr. Hallsey, but you didn't deny it."

"Look, Mayor Queen." Hallsey shifted in his seat. "Your friend the Green Arrow is a good guy. I've felt inspired by him for a long time. But you should tell him I was more inspired when he used to give the bad guys the justice they deserved."

"Justice is more than killing."

"If there is harm, then you shall pay life for life, eye

for eye, tooth for tooth, hand for hand, foot for foot," Hallsey said flatly. "Burn for burn, wound for wound, stripe for stripe."

"Did you just quote the Bible to me?" Oliver asked.

"It's the truth," Hallsey said. "You can nail that to the cross."

"I can't charge him with anything."

They watched Hallsey through the one-way glass. The man had turned his empty cup upside down and was tapping on it like a miniature drum.

"I can't even hold him much longer," Dinah said.

Oliver took a deep breath, held it, and then let it slide out through his nostrils.

"Cut him loose," he said.

"He's the one."

"I know." Oliver didn't turn. "He couldn't resist at the end there, dropping Cross's name. He's the copycat."

"What are we going to do about that?"

"First thing is to take Cross off his list."

3

"Hello, ladies and gentlemen, welcome to your main event! It's Shock-and-Awe Night in Star City! Bad guys beware, drug dealers be scared. You can hide but you'd better not run, because—" Felicity rolled up the volume on the comms link, leaning into the microphone she had chosen over her normal ear bud unit. Her voice deepened in her closest impersonation of a movie trailer announcer.

"—We. Are. Bringing. The. Justice."

The push of a button caused the sound effect of a bomb dropping to roll out over the comms. As it faded, Wild Dog's voice replaced it.

"You are having way too much fun with this."

"Hush," White Canary's voice said. *"She's adorable when she's cute."*

In the Bunker, Felicity ignored them both as she started a playlist and cracked her knuckles. Frantic drumming under sleazy guitar chords came over the cave's speakers where *she* could hear it, but it wouldn't go over the comms to distract the teams as they worked.

As a bonus, it would help her ignore the danger they might face.

She brought up the appropriate screens and leaned into the microphone.

"First up, Team Wild Terrific is a go for launch."

"Don't call us that," Wild Dog growled over the comms.

"I don't mind it," Mister Terrific said.

"You wouldn't."

They crouched beside a runny dumpster, the entire thing glistening black in the harsh sodium lights of the alley behind Wo Fat's Chicken And Waffles. The stench was stifling, a combination of stale fat, old meat, and rotting vegetables. In the late summer heat, there was a shimmer in the air around it. And flies. Hundreds of flies.

"*Okay,*" Felicity's voice said in their ears. "*Fire alarm is disabled. Whenever you're ready.*"

"We're going now." Wild Dog stepped out. "This dumpster is killing me."

"That's excessive hyperbole," Curtis said.

"Hyperbole my ass, you try having that smell trapped under your mask."

They moved to the door at the back of the restaurant.

"I used to come here with Paul," Mister Terrific said. "This should take us to the kitchen, then it's straight through to the dining area. It's a simple layout."

"I can't believe you used to take your boyfriend to a drug distribution front."

"It's not like they advertise it on the menu."

"Still—" Wild Dog shook his head. "—seems like something a crime fighter should've picked up on."

"Their 'Barbecue and Belgian Combo' is delicious."

"What?"

"Barbecue chicken with Belgian waffles and a spicy mustard maple syrup."

"No wonder that dumpster smells so bad." Wild Dog put his hand on the doorknob. "Ready?"

Mister Terrific nodded.

Before either of them could move, the door swung wide, making both crime fighters jump back. Wild Dog had his gun out before the steel door crashed into the brick wall beside it.

In the doorway, partially silhouetted by the light from within, stood a tall, raw-boned, ropey man in a very expensive suit. An unlit cigarette dangled from his mouth, hung there on his bottom lip. He held a lighter, the flame flickering between his cupped palms.

The cigarette fell from his mouth, tumbled down his chest, and dropped to the ground.

"Who the hell are you guys?" he said.

"Team SBC, you're up," Felicity said in their ears. *"We're going dark side of the moon in five, four, three—"*

Spartan looked over at Black Canary. She nodded

her readiness. They stood in a dark storage room that smelled of cleaning supplies and the distinctive shiny-rubber odor of sporting equipment.

They'd entered Lifters Gym together, using the fake identities of Mr. and Miss Conroy, longtime members of the Blüdhaven location, but new to Star City.

"Yes, we just moved for her new job at Palmertech, isn't that great. We love the city so far, much better than the crime-ridden war zone Blüdhaven is turning into."

None of the staff looked twice at the large duffel bags they carried, even though they arrived in workout gear. After a few minutes doing a circuit around to familiarize themselves with the layout of the gym, they both agreed that their target was the third-floor locker room. A crudely written sign hung on the door.

CLOSED FOR REMODELING

Despite that, there seemed to be a steady stream of bodybuilders going in and out. So they located the nearest storage room and suited up in less than five minutes. Both wore night-vision goggles.

"—two, one." The lights in the gym went out, throwing the whole place into darkness. Felicity was thorough, so not even the emergency lights came on. They were

out the door and moving as the first panicky screams began to roll through the building.

Moving as a unit they closed on the locker room and stepped inside. The air was thick, indicating that the air conditioning was off along with the lights. The noise was loud and chaotic—too many voices to identify, most of them panicked, talking over one another and echoing off the tile and metal.

Flashes appeared as the people inside began lighting up their phones and using them as flashlights. Four bodybuilders stood around a counter laden with boxes of white pill bottles and crates with small glass vials next to stacks of plastic-wrapped syringes.

Black Canary pulled the collapsed steel baton from its clip on her belt, extending it with a snap of her wrist.

"Left," she said, peeling off. Spartan went right and they moved in on the four men. She closed the distance quickly, shaking the baton to loosen up her arm. The desire to unleash her canary cry was heavy on her, but in the enclosed space and with the amplification of the tile, she wouldn't have the focus she would need. The echoes would make her scream ineffective as a precision weapon.

So she was ready to get her hands dirty.

Dinah kept the baton back and low, difficult to see and poised for use. The man in front of her was swollen, skin thin from steroid infusions. His arms boasted a map of veins, and he held his phone in one hand, the light on it shaking wildly as he came at her.

One quick swing of the baton and the phone went sailing. It crashed into the row of metal lockers to the left. The light went out as the device shattered. The bodybuilder's scream of rage echoed around her as he swung at her head. As muscular as he was, he was clumsy. She ducked, stepping nimbly to the side and sliding under his arm.

Lashing up with the baton, she cracked him along the inside of the elbow. The impact made the steel baton sing a bit, the sign of a good solid blow, and he howled. She stepped up on the low wooden bench in front of the lockers, using it to lift her above the muscle-bound brute, then spun, whipping her foot around in a kick with all of her body weight behind it. It connected with his jaw, snapping his head to the side.

The howling stopped.

He crumpled to the ground in a mound of moaning beefcake.

Black Canary quickly scanned the room. Spartan was holding his own against two more bruisers.

Where's the other one? she thought. Then she spotted him ducking around a corner, headed deeper into the locker room. She jumped down and sprinted after him.

"Team—"

"We are *not* Team White Arrow, or Team Green Canary." The archer cut her off. He shifted his position in the rafters of the warehouse.

"God, please not Green Canary," Sara groaned. "We have enough canaries out and about tonight."

"*Fine, fine,*" Felicity said. "*Team Sourpuss, it's all you now.*"

White Canary smiled. "She got you."

Green Arrow said nothing.

"*The doors are electronic,*" Felicity said. "*When I shut them you have to work fast, because those fumes will build up in less than four minutes.*" The air already had the stringent, eye-glistening sting of chemical fumes, smelling like battery acid and candy.

"We'll be done before then."

"I'm going to move into position." White Canary didn't wait for a response before dropping down onto a rack of pallets. Green Arrow watched her until she disappeared, then turned his attention to the scene below.

In the center of the warehouse was a large-scale drug lab in full production. Three men in dirty yellow coveralls moved around large flat pots filled with steaming chemicals. Propane tanks hooked to the burners underneath provided fuel that kept the pots bubbling. At the end were rows and rows of trays holding large crystallized chunks. To the left sat a group of fifty-gallon drums of different colors.

Red for flammable.

Blue for toxins.

Yellow for oxidizers.

White for corrosives.

The whole enchilada of bad news. Chemicals that

should never be stored in the same facility, much less next to one another. He had found that people cooking up drugs usually weren't concerned about safety infractions, though.

Two guards with shotguns leaned on the colorful barrels, surrounded by empty cans of energy drinks. Both were smoking from a shared vape, sending out large white clouds with each hit. They were cut from street-thug stock. Big by genetics and diet, but not exercise or training. The use of the shotguns indicated they probably weren't marksmen, either.

It didn't make them not dangerous.

Another one sat in a chair by the loading dock. He leaned back, either napping or blessed-out on the product being manufactured here. He wasn't going to be a concern.

The other men's coveralls protected them head to toe from the hazardous chemicals they mixed. No weapons showed and if they wore them under their overalls then they wouldn't be able to reach them in time anyway.

They'd assumed this lab was safe from trouble because it was on the far edge of Star City, on the fringe where city began to disintegrate into country, and coverage by law enforcement began to thin dramatically. The warehouse was an old tire factory that had closed its doors almost a decade ago, when the business secured a large account overseas and moved closer to the docks. Along the walls and all around the building outside were stacks of tires of various sizes. Some had toppled, spilling out onto the open floor, and a few had rolled clear.

The electric hum of the door motors made a tiny vibration in the rafters.

It was time to go to work.

4

The raw-boned man crashed into a stainless-steel prep table, knocking aside piles of vegetables and rocking it up onto two legs before he tumbled off the other side. He pulled himself up, using the table for support. Mister Terrific shoved it.

The table screeched across the tile floor of the kitchen, slamming into the man, pinning him against the wall. He flailed out, trying to get ahold of the vigilante. Instead Mister Terrific pulled out his T-Spheres and let them fly. They zipped up, and then down, lining up next to the trapped criminal's neck. They arced out a big *zap* of electricity, tasing the raw-boned man into a loose-limbed pile of humanity slumped over the table.

The spheres flew back around, circling Mister Terrific as he stepped back and looked about. Wild Dog was pushing through the swinging door that led into the dining area, gun held out in front of him. Suddenly he dove back into the kitchen as a spray of bullets punched through the thin metal door. Scrambling on the tile, he put his back to the wall.

Mister Terrific crouched and moved over beside him.

"I think they know we're here."

"Yeah, Hoss, I'd say so," Wild Dog muttered. Into the comms he said, "Hey, Overwatch, think we could get some kind of distraction here, so we can get through this doorway?"

"*Let me see—*" Felicity said. "*Ah-ha! One distraction coming up. Sorry guys.*"

"Sorry?" Mister Terrific said.

A loud rattle sounded overhead, the noise of pipes rumbling against each other. Wild Dog groaned behind his mask.

"Oh, no."

The sprinklers burst forth with a shower of water and foam.

On the other side of the door, men started yelling.

"You wanted a distraction," Mister Terrific said.

"Shut up."

Wild Dog rolled and crashed through the door, gun out. In the center of the dining area stood three men around a group of square tables they had pushed together. One man stood sputtering, wiping water and foam off his face, his submachine gun hanging loosely from the strap on his shoulder. Noticing their arrival, he jerked his head up and scrambled for his weapon.

Wild Dog dropped him with a double-tap.

The other two men didn't look up as the two

costumed vigilantes came through the door. They were too busy trying to keep the open buckets of illegal pills from being ruined in the falling deluge of water and fire retardant foam.

"Hands up!" Wild Dog moved closer to them.

They jerked to a stop and both raised their hands, straightening and looking wet and miserable.

"Okay, we're in, you can knock it off with the distraction," Wild Dog growled over the comms. Immediately the sprinklers shut off with another rattle-pipe gurgle.

Mister Terrific moved around the two men. He zip tied the first one's hands behind his back and pushed him to the floor. The man went down without a struggle, sitting on the floor with his head down.

He stepped to the second man and grabbed his wrist to pull it down. Before he could, the man whirled around, flicking his hand out. A knife with a six-inch blade dropped down his sleeve and into his hand. He jabbed upward, trying to hook his captor under the ribs.

Mister Terrific twisted away, the blade just skimming the front of his body. Using the wrist he still held for leverage, he drove his other hand into the man's shoulder and rolled forward. The shift of his weight on the man's back drove his assailant to the ground face-first.

There was a wet celery sound of the criminal's shoulder separating followed by a loose animal noise of pain.

Mister Terrific put the zip ties on him, and stood.

Wild Dog nodded. "That was quick, man. I didn't even have time to do anything."

Mister Terrific's chest swelled with pride at the acknowledgment. "He should've just let me cuff him."

Wild Dog spoke into the comms. "All wrapped up."

"*Good job, Team Wild Terrific,*" Felicity said in their ears. "*SCPD is on its way, three minutes out. Now find me something to connect Cross to this, and hit the bricks.*"

"On it."

"We are not Team Wild Terrific," Wild Dog said.

"You know you like it."

"No."

"Not even a little?"

"No."

Mister Terrific began looking for evidence, smiling to himself.

"Team Wild Terrific for the win."

Each punch sent a shock of pain that ran through the muscles of his forearm, liquid fire coursing from wrist to elbow.

He had dropped one of the bodybuilders, slamming the guy's face into the sink so hard that the basin came loose from the wall and hung to one side. Water leaked slowly onto the floor in a widening puddle, coming from pipes pulled loose but not completely separated. The puddle tinged pink around the bodybuilder lying under it, bleeding from the nose and mouth.

The other guy was a problem.

He was taller and thicker than Spartan, probably had forty pounds of extra muscle, and was younger by at least a decade. Worse, he wasn't just a massive pile of muscles—he knew how to fight. Spartan traded blows with him for what felt like an hour. He got some hits in, but so did the thug. If it hadn't been for his helmet and the reinforced uniform he wore, Spartan would have already been beaten down.

The thug stood in a classic boxer's stance, fists raised and elbows in. He was breathing hard, but to keep oxygenated, not sucking air because he was struggling. Spartan was going to have to get ruthless.

With dead fingers he clawed his gun out of its holster. His arm felt like wood with hot embers lodged deep in the muscle. When he closed his fingers around the grip it caused the hand to begin trembling. He held the gun to his side to steady it.

The bodybuilder's mouth dropped open.

"You're gonna shoot me now, freak?"

"Yeah," Spartan said. "You're too big a target to miss." He raised the gun and pulled the trigger twice. Two darts took the bodybuilder in the stomach, knocking him down to land on his backside. He shook his head slowly as the tranquilizers began coursing through his system.

"I thog we wuz fightttiin…" The words slurred out of his mouth as he slumped over, unconscious from the double dose of tranquilizer.

Spartan had only meant to pull the trigger once.

The second time had been a spasm.

He almost lost his grip on the pistol as he put it back in the holster.

It's worse, he thought.

The sound of a metallic clatter came around the corner from the back of the locker room. He began moving toward it.

The first one to notice the lowering steel doors was the guard sitting in the chair, outside on the dock. Even oiled they made a low drumming sound like an old-time thunder maker, the thinner-gauge sheet steel flexing as it vibrated on the way down. Jumping up, he craned his neck, foggily trying to locate the source.

He didn't see White Canary until she was on him. She swept low, her outstretched leg taking him at the knees. He dropped forward and she rose, her knee coming up as she did, catching him just under the chin and snapping his head back.

Spinning, she saw that the door was about waist high. She dropped, tucked, and rolled under it.

Green Arrow shot down on a grapple line, crashing into one of the two guards standing at the barrels of chemicals. He hit boots-first in the man's chest, driving him back over the fifty-gallon drum. The henchman's body acted as a cushion that prevented the archer from slamming into the hard steel of the barrel.

Coming to his feet he kicked out, sending the man's rifle spinning off across the warehouse floor in a clattering bounce of metal on concrete. Its user was already unconscious. An instant later he heard the distinctive *clack-CLACK* of a shotgun being racked. That sent him into a rolling dive behind a stack of tires, just ahead of the echoing *boom*.

Pressed against the tires, he felt them rock as the blast struck the spot where he had been only a moment before. The top tire of the stack slid off, falling and hitting his shoulder in a *thud* of hurt before bouncing away. He shook his hand, trying to work out the pain so he could draw an arrow.

The shotgun racked once more, and the henchman fired. The stack rocked again. One of the pellets made it through a gap in the tires, sending a line of sharp pain lancing through the bicep of his good arm. Blood welled and ran freely down his limb like a tiny river.

The shotgun racked a third time.

Green Arrow dove, rolling out and away from the tires. He grabbed an arrow from the quiver, pulled, and fired. The arrow sailed past, narrowly missing the man with the shotgun, but it made him spin to avoid it, jerking the gun upward.

The archer pushed off, closing the distance in an instant. Using his carbon-fiber bow like a club, he knocked the shotgun from the henchman's hands. It dropped straight to the ground underfoot. The henchman reached for it, but Green Arrow took him off his feet with a vicious uppercut that put him down for the count.

Kicking the shotgun clear, he turned to find that White Canary had already zip tied the three drug cooks, their hands behind their backs. He walked over, blood still dripping from his arm.

"They didn't put up a fight?" he asked.

"They were too busy watching you take out the shotgun brothers. I just walked up and they went docile as little lambs." She glanced down at his wound. "Serious?"

He shook his head. "I'll go bind this." He gestured toward his unconscious opponents. "Zip up those two over there while I do."

"I'll handle it."

Green Arrow nodded, moving toward the door.

"Open us back up," he said into the comms.

The bodybuilder she had chased caught her coming around the corner of the shower. He had pulled down one of the shower curtains and used it like a net, tangling her in it.

Before she could fight her way free he slung her around, lifting her off her feet, and threw her into the tile in a hard, bruising bounce and skitter. She rolled to a stop, the air knocked out of her and her head ringing. Something tangled in her hair and pain fired across her scalp as she was dragged up from the floor and lifted.

The blinding curtain fell away and she found herself in the grip of the man she'd been chasing.

"Say, aren't you a pretty little thing?" His voice echoed off the tile in the shower room. She threw her elbow up, aiming for his face, but her actions were slowed by the lack of oxygen in her lungs. He moved quickly for someone so muscle-bound, and a hand the size of a chuck roast caught her elbow, blocking her strike.

That same hand lashed out, slapping her across the face. It was like being hit with a two-by-four.

"Put her down!"

She blinked through the stunning pain and saw Spartan at the shower entrance. Relief rushed through her. Diggle would put this guy down with a single shot.

"Not a chance." The bodybuilder shook her. "I think she's the reason you'll let me go."

"You're not getting away," Spartan said.

Pull your gun, she screamed in her head, pushing the thought at her teammate. *Shoot him!*

The bodybuilder shrugged, his free hand moving up. "Then I should just snap her neck so I don't have to worry about her anymore."

"Don't do that!" Spartan bellowed the words. They, too, echoed around the shower room. Black Canary grabbed the rising arm, pushing down to keep it off her throat.

Shoot him shoot him shoot him, her brain screamed.

The bodybuilder smiled. "You aren't strong enough to fight me off." He jerked his arm free and shoved it toward her throat.

She sucked in a gulp of air.

And screamed.

The cry ripped out of her, blasting him across the face. He snapped back, dropping her. She let loose, and her canary cry hit the tile in the room, echoing, doubling back on itself, and building. The sound waves crashing through the air lifted her hair like a wind. Blood shot from the bodybuilder's ears, spilling onto his shoulders, staining the straps of his tank top.

Then she dropped to her knees, out of oxygen, the dark room lit in her eyes with white sparks. She pitched forward, falling toward unconsciousness. Arms grabbed her, keeping her from striking the cold tile. Just before she slipped into the oncoming dark she heard him speak.

"I'm sorry. I'm so sorry."

The night breeze was cool on his skin, but it made the blood on his arm dry until it felt like sticky dust. The binding had stopped the bleeding right away. Now his arm throbbed, each pulse pushing just a few red drops from each of the two small holes. *Through and through.* Always the best kind of wound. He'd have Felicity wash it and pack it with antibiotics, and he'd be fine.

White Canary walked through the one open door. The rest were still shuttered.

"Bad guys all strung together a safe distance away, with a pile of evidence in their pockets. SCPD should find them without a problem."

He nodded and pulled a red arrow from his quiver. Laying it across the bow he aimed at the open door of the drug lab, and let fly.

The arrow arced across the lot. Midway to its destination it sparked and a long thin flame curled out from the broad head, swirling in the air stream, wrapping the shaft of the projectile.

It disappeared through the open door.

Only a few seconds passed before the first barrel of chemicals exploded.

In less than a minute the entire drug lab had become a chemical-fire inferno.

5

"Hey."

Felicity started, jumping in her chair at the voice from behind her. She turned to find Oliver on the platform. Reaching over, she turned down the volume of the music she had blaring from the Bunker's speakers.

"I didn't know you were behind me," she said. "Why didn't I know you were behind me? You should have tripped the sensors I installed to let me know when someone's coming."

"I didn't mean to startle you." His mouth quirked up even as he said it.

"That's just not true," she said.

"No, it's not, but only to test our system. That's why I avoided your sensors. You should upgrade, because if I can get past them then someone else can, too."

Felicity shook her head, making her ponytail bounce. "There aren't that many people we know of who could get past those sensors. Not everyone has

League of Assassin training like you do."

"I do." A voice came from across the room. Felicity turned to find Sara Lance standing there, grinning at her.

"Did you two plan this?"

"No, but it's a good illustration."

"Okay," she said. "Is anyone else coming?"

"Diggle said he was stopping by," Oliver said. "But before we drop the issue at hand…" He raised his finger, beginning to count off. "Malcolm, Nyssa, a whole league left behind who could want revenge, actually, a lot of people we know have League of Assassin training, or the equivalent."

"Plus," Diggle said, entering the room, "there are always new people popping up who could. Chase did."

Felicity looked from one person to the next. "Did I hit 'send' to the wrong people? I only meant to message Oliver."

"You sent a message?" Oliver asked.

"Yeah, I just texted it. I thought that's why you were here. Not to scare me straight, or force me to buy an upgraded security system."

Oliver pulled his phone out, and peered at the screen.

Found Cross

He slipped it back into his pocket.

"Got it."

"So I see," she replied. "He's on his yacht."

"I would have thought that after we shut down so much of his operation, he would have fled the country," Diggle said.

"He has too much business to go too far." Felicity shook her head. "But he should have. Curtis found connections that tie him to the drug business in Star City, enough to put him away for decades. Once we deliver him and the evidence we have, no more problem."

"Where is his yacht?" Oliver asked.

"It's out in the water—no, *duh*—not far off shore. I have the specs pulled up." She slid over. Oliver stood behind her shoulder looking down at the computer monitor. Both of them kept their eyes forward. Nevertheless, it was obvious how distracting the nearness was for the two of them.

Sara and Diggle shared a smirk.

"Comparatively, it's a fairly small yacht."

"Why, Mr. Cross, your yacht is practically tiny," Felicity mocked.

Oliver straightened. "I don't think this needs the full team. No need to call in everyone. Better to do this with two or three operatives." He looked pointedly at Diggle and Sara.

Sara immediately stepped forward. "Count me in."

Diggle looked down and shook his head. "Lyla needs me to take care of John tonight. I have to pass."

Oliver moved over and put his hand on Diggle's shoulder. "I understand. Go, take care of your family."

"I'm sorry."

"John, *brother*," Oliver's voice became stern, "family is the most important thing in this world. Go."

"Thanks," Diggle said. "I appreciate it." He turned and walked away without looking back. In a moment he was gone.

"Dinah has SCPD duty tonight. Do we know if Rene is available?" Felicity asked. "Do you want me to call him? Or Curtis?"

Oliver looked down at the yacht schematics on the screen, then up at Sara. She gave him a cocksure grin. He thought back to the Skulls on the car carrier, and taking down Cross's drug lab.

"Sara and I can handle it," he said. "No need to call anyone else in. We'll go tonight."

Dark water lapped the sides of the yacht as it rocked slightly up and down. Green Arrow pulled himself up and over the railing, landing lightly on the open foredeck. He crouched in the shadow of the lifeboat that dangled where he'd chosen to climb up, knowing it would provide some cover. From there he scanned the area around him. A small pool and hot tub sat in the middle of the deck, surrounded by deck chairs that were bolted in place. The deck was clear of people.

He turned, reaching down. White Canary grabbed his wrist and he pulled her up beside him.

"What's the plan?" she asked.

"You circle the main deck, head to the bridge, and

put down anyone you find along the way. I'm going below decks to find Cross."

She shook her head. "That's a dumb plan."

"What would you suggest?"

"We stay together, clear the upper decks, incapacitate the ship, then together we go after Cross. You *know* he'll have some kind of security, and the two of us would do better than the one of you."

He considered her plan. It was indeed the better way. He let the logic of it sit with him and cool his desire to take down Cross as soon as possible.

Before he could tell her so, something caught his eye out on the water. Pulling a small telescope from his belt, he raised it to his eye, and cursed under his breath at what he saw.

It was a military-grade rubber boat, far out on the water but headed toward the yacht, piloted by a man in a hood.

"What is it?" White Canary asked.

He handed over the telescope.

She looked out for a moment then turned and said, "I'll give your copycat this, he's got good info, and big balls."

"The last thing we need is him interfering."

"What are you going to do about it? He's coming this way."

Green Arrow watched the boat on the water, tracking it. It was far out, barely close enough to see with the naked eye. He stepped back and drew an arrow from his quiver. Laying it across the bow he took a deep breath, inhaling the salty air. His mind slipped sideways, unlocking itself and disengaging with the higher functions that ruled it. He dropped into the Zen of being an archer. Feeling a light breeze on his face, coming from the right. Tasting the concentration of salt on it and considering how that would affect the density of the air itself.

He became one with the rocking of the boat on which he stood, one with the water underneath it, his bodily rhythms syncing until he breathed in unison with the motion, and his heart beat in time to it. He drew the bow, feeling even the moisture that micro-beaded along his bowstring. His brain worked, synapses firing, calculating without math, the addition and subtraction of instinct, the physics of spirit.

All in an instant.

He tilted, aiming the arrow at the moon.

His eyelids parted, focusing on the oncoming boat.

Oliver's body moved, ever so slightly, adjusting the most minute of angles and lines.

The boat lifted, then dropped.

He let the arrow fly.

It arced high, cutting through the salt air. It reached its apex and tilted, angling down, accelerating until it was more than just an arrow, more than just a projectile, it was a streak of his will. It hit the raft like lightning, cutting through the rubber as if it didn't exist, passing through to the water and disappearing into the depths.

White Canary watched through the telescope, suppressing a chuckle as Hallsey scrambled in his rapidly deflating raft, cutting his small engine as the rubber folded on itself. He ungracefully tumbled over the side, into the water.

"Hell of a shot." She handed the telescope back to him.

They crouched outside the ship's bridge. Inside were two men enjoying their conversation. They laughed loudly enough to be heard even through the closed steel and glass door. Green Arrow put his hand on the handle, waiting for the laughter to reach a crescendo before pulling the door open and stepping aside so White Canary could move past him.

The two men jumped up, laughter ending in one quick moment as if it had been cut off with a knife. White Canary crossed the room, pivoted and spun into a high sweeping kick that took one man down to the floor. She immediately lashed out again, hitting the other man in the face, flipping him back over the chair he had sat in.

Green Arrow stepped into the room.

Sara blew a lock of hair out of her face and grinned over her shoulder. "Don't worry," she said, holding up a pair of zip ties. "I got this."

The two men didn't get up.

Green Arrow nodded and touched his comms link.

"Overwatch, we're on the bridge. How do I disable the ship?"

"You should be looking at a wide bank of instruments, the gaugey kind, not musical," Felicity responded.

He didn't smile at her humor but he felt it in the corners of his mouth.

"I am."

"Okay, to your left you should see a silver key below a T handle."

A large ring of keys lay on the console, one of them inserted in an ignition.

"Got it," he said.

"That's it. Without that key the ship is going nowhere."

As White Canary stood, he pulled the key, taking the entire bunch. He nodded and they went back out the door. On the way down the steel staircase he tossed the ring of keys over the rail and into the water. It hit the surface with a faint wet *plop*.

They moved to the door that led below decks. Light spilled from beneath it. Green Arrow slung his bow over his shoulder. Down there it would be tight spaces, small confines. No room for archery. This would be close-quarters combat, fists and feet, knees and elbows. He was glad he'd chosen White Canary for backup.

Quietly throwing the door open, he stepped in.

He was on a short, narrow stairwell that split left and right at its end. Music and laughter came from below. Moving silently, he stepped down, Sara right behind him.

At the bottom the noise came from the passageway to the left. Contrary to what they had joked, it was a roomy hall, the yacht built for luxury, not compactness. Here in the living quarters everything was carpet and polished wood accents. At the end of the passage there was a wooden door.

Through it they heard the music and a high, giggly laugh.

Green Arrow leaned back and took down the door with one solid kick that splintered the jamb. The door crashed open and he was inside the room.

To the right were a low couch and table. The couch contained Cross, wearing only a pair of slacks, his chest bare, and two young girls wearing less. The table contained a string of multicolored pills and a pile of white powder cut into long lines.

To the left of the room, sitting at the small bar, were two sides of beef acting as bodyguards. The farthest one jumped off the stool, reaching to his waist for the small snub-nosed pistol tucked there. Green Arrow closed the distance in four steps, knocking the pistol out of the man's hand with a sharp back-fist. The weapon flew to the rear of the bar, smashing bottles of expensive whiskey that lined the wall. The archer gave two hard strikes to the bodyguard's throat, feeling the pop of the man's trachea under his hand. The man's face went purple and he lurched forward. Green Arrow sidestepped as the bodyguard fell to the carpet and vomited the contents of his stomach.

Arrow turned to find White Canary flipping the other bodyguard in a brutal hip toss that slammed him to the carpet. She had it covered.

He looked for Cross.

The man was gone.

Only the two girls remained, clutching each other with looks of terror on their faces. One of them, a redhead, was crying, her face a wad of tears and fear.

"Where is he?" He loomed over them, knowing he was frightening them even more, but needing the information as quickly as possible before Cross escaped.

In the back of his mind, he remembered Hallsey.

The one with the short brunette bob pointed across the room. He looked and saw, beside the flat-screen television, a crack in the wall, a hidden sliding hatch. In his haste to escape, Cross hadn't pulled it completely closed.

Reaching the far side of the room, he jerked open the hatch and was gone in an instant.

White Canary looked down at the weeping girls. Her heart hurt, just a touch, as little as she could allow. She had been one of these girls, once, wild for her own reasons, in situations that started fun and wrong and even illicit, but went horribly upside down without any warning.

"How old are you two?" She shook her head. "Never mind, I don't want to know. Get dressed and get out. Wait on the deck up top and go with the police when they arrive."

The brunette nodded vigorously.

White Canary moved to follow Green Arrow. At the passage she stopped, turned, and spoke.

"Say no to drugs from now on."

She grimaced as soon as she said it, then kept going.

The passage cut through the hull of the ship. He could hear the water against the sides, mere inches away. The stairs went up, and then down, twisting as they did. Cross was close enough he could hear him, but far enough that he never got a clear shot.

The footsteps ahead went silent.

Two turns later he ran out onto the rear deck. His target was a short distance ahead. He drew an arrow across his bow and yelled, "Hands up!"

Cross stopped running and raised his hands. Slowly he turned, shuffling bare feet on the wooden deck.

"Ah, the vigilante. I assume you're the one who's been causing me all the trouble recently." Adopting an air of calm, Cross put his hands behind his head and lowered himself to his knees. Green Arrow relaxed his draw.

"It's over, Cross. You're done in Star City."

"I don't suppose there's a chance of coming to some financial agreement over this?"

"You can't buy your way free of this."

Cross laughed. "From the first time I went to jail to the last time I went, I've bought my way free. I don't see how this will be any different."

Green Arrow said nothing.

Cross sighed. "Let's get this part over with, so I can have my lawyers working on getting me cleared of this. I can't imagine it will be too difficult. Since you were the one who caught me I doubt you have any evidence."

A shot split the night and Cross's chest folded in on itself.

Damn!

Blood and gore gushed from his back as if someone had tossed a bucket of chum across the deck boards behind him. The open water drank in the sound of the gunshot, leaving a hollow of silence that contained only the dull melon *thunk* of Cross's head hitting the deck as his corpse slumped forward.

From the shadows stepped a dripping wet Hallsey, holding a chrome revolver.

"What did you do?" Green Arrow bellowed, whipping his bow up to aim at the newcomer.

"I keep telling people," Hallsey said, his voice muffled slightly by the mask he wore, "I'm doing what you *should* be doing. Stopping crime."

"You *committed* a crime—you killed him."

"That's shortsighted. I prefer to look at it as you should. He killed himself when he chose a life that could only end by violence. I am merely the instrument of Judgment."

"You don't have the right."

"I have the *obligation*," Hallsey snarled.

Green Arrow stepped forward. "Drop your weapon or I will shoot you."

"We've already established that you won't kill me." Hallsey slipped the revolver into a holster on his hip. "But thank you, I did learn something the last time we got together." Hallsey extended his hand, opening his fingers. A metal cylinder rolled from his palm, striking the deck between them and bouncing once. On impact it began rapidly spewing thick yellow smoke.

White Canary stepped out in time to see the smoke clear, torn apart by the night breeze off the water. She took in the drug kingpin, dead from a bullet hole, and her fellow costumed crime fighter shaking in rage and staring at the otherwise empty deck.

SEPTEMBER 2017

1

"How much longer is this going to take?"

Miranda gripped the steering wheel and pulled herself forward. It really hurt her back driving in stop-and-go city traffic, but her son's school wasn't free. The man behind her could pay for it. He could pay for a month's tuition with just the price of the new smart phone he furiously tapped with his thumbs.

She extended her hand out toward her dirty windshield, indicating the line of traffic in front of them.

"Gonna take as long as it takes," she said.

"I have a meeting to make, a flight to catch and, basically, a million things to do that are *not* sitting in this traffic." He said it without taking his eyes off the screen.

"I understand."

"No doubt you also understand that the longer we sit on this bridge, the more money I owe you," he commented.

You're the one who called a cab, she thought—but she

said, "No one works for free."

He looked up from his phone, catching her eyes in the rear view mirror. "Honey, I bill at three hundred and forty-nine dollars per hour. I know all about not working for free." His eyes dropped back down, dismissing her.

You just can't get that one more dollar out of them, canya son? Miranda thought. The little bit of meanness made her feel better. Her fingers touched the knob on the radio, seeking something new to distract her. Looking down, she didn't see the explosion that rocked the bridge underneath her taxi.

Miranda looked up in time to see the fireball that engulfed the cars in front of her. It rolled over her hood, blistering the paint as it did, turning her windshield into a blackened, bubbled mess.

The door to his office opened sharply, and Quentin Lance walked in. Oliver looked up, taking in his deputy mayor's face, creased with anxiety.

"What's wrong?" he asked.

"We have a situation," Lance said. "Somebody just blew up part of the Star City Bridge."

Faust, Oliver thought.

"Give me the details," he said.

"First responders on scene, and more on the way. As far as we can tell, the bridge is still structurally sound, and not in danger of collapsing. Every indication so far is that it was all smoke and flame. Early reports have injuries—mostly from the panic of drivers hitting other cars—but no deaths."

"So this is a way of getting our attention."

Lance nodded grimly. "If I were a betting man, and I *am* a betting man, I'd put money on it."

"Is there anything I can do to help?"

"As mayor? Yes. As the other guy? No, not yet." Lance leaned forward. "The city needs a voice of comfort, and a show of leadership."

Oliver nodded. He often thought of being the Green Arrow as doing night work. Yes, they could—and did—operate during the day, but this would be too exposed. It wasn't like the attack on Dearden Tower, where they needed to pitch in with search-and-rescue. Here the sight of costumes would just be a distraction. If the bridge was sound, he would leave the police and others to do their jobs.

Standing, he squared his shoulders and buttoned his suit jacket.

"Let's go to work," he said.

Outside his office stood a short, dark man holding a wide white envelope. One word was written on it, in thick green sharpie.

Queen

Oliver and Lance stopped short.

"Can I help you?" Lance asked.

"Are you Mayor Queen?" the man asked.

"Yeah, this isn't a good time, pal." Quentin moved to put the man aside. "We're a little busy."

"I stay here until I give this to the mayor."

Oliver stepped forward. "I'm Mayor Queen."

The man looked at Oliver, nodded, and held out the package.

"Who is it from?" Lance asked.

The man shook his head. "No idea. It was prepaid over the internet, then delivered to us with proof of payment. I was told to deliver it here, precisely at this time." He raised his hands. "That's all I know."

"Thank you for the information." Oliver tilted his head toward Lance. "We'll have our team look into it."

"Don't bother." The man raised his hands. "I don't have anything to hide, but I don't want anyone looking into me."

"Not your choice, pal." Lance put his hand on the man's shoulder.

Without waiting, Oliver tore open the envelope and looked inside. There he found a flash drive, with the crude symbol for fire imprinted on the side.

2

Oliver, Lance, and Dinah stood around Oliver's desk, watching the video on the computer monitor. The film was clear.

"Hello, Star City!" Faust grinned at the camera. "It's your favorite mother's son, and I have to tell you it's a real blast being here." He bowed his head, holding his hands up. "Sorry, terrible joke, just awful."

He adjusted his face, adopting a deadpan expression.

"This is serious business, and as such I won't waste any of your time, Mayor Queen. You know I blew up the Star City Bridge—well, not exactly blew it *up*, more set it on *fire*. Now, you know I'm both able and willing to blow things up if I don't get what I want."

Oliver watched the bomb maker. The man never sat still, always moving in some small manner—a twitching finger, a tic under his left eye, always some part of him in motion, even when he wasn't dancing around like a fool. It was a mystery how this frenetic, *spastic* individual could be steady enough to ever wire a bomb.

But they knew firsthand that he could, and once more Oliver was stunned at the depths of Adrian Chase's hatred for him. It ran so deep that he'd set this maniac loose on Star City, just for revenge.

"Simply wire twenty-three hundred bitcoins to this account."

A number flashed across the screen.

"Or I will use *this* to blow up a significant landmark in Star City."

The camera pulled back to reveal a ballistic missile. It hung in the air behind its maker, a stubby-looking thing despite its size and sharply pointed nose cone. It looked like a brutal piece of equipment, and had just one purpose.

Destruction. On a large scale.

Faust jumped in front of the camera, filling the screen with his face.

"You have two weeks," he said. "The deadline— and I mean *dead*—is midnight, October twelfth." The screen went blank.

"That guy is crazy," Lance said.

Dinah's eyebrows creased. "He is," she agreed, "but what do you mean?"

"Well, I don't know how much a tactical missile goes for these days, but they don't come cheap. Like *millions* not cheap. This clown is going to use one, just for twenty-three hundred dollars? It makes no sense."

"Bitcoins," Dinah corrected.

"Bit what?"

"Bitcoins. It's a cryptocurrency."

Lance looked at her, his question plain in his eyes.

"It's digital money," she offered.

"Okay, it's internet dollars. How much is the exchange on these bitquarters?"

Oliver spoke for the first time. "Roughly ten million dollars."

"You just knew that?" Lance asked.

"The Russian crime bosses love bitcoins."

Lance nodded. "Ten million isn't that much, not for a city budget."

"That's the point," Oliver said. "A good extortionist never asks for more than their mark can afford to pay."

"The Russians again?"

Oliver nodded.

"Damn those commies," Lance said.

Oliver pulled the flash drive from the computer. "Quentin, hold things together here," he said. "Not a word about this to anyone—not yet."

"You're taking it to the brainy part of the team?"

Oliver nodded.

Lance turned toward the door. "Tell Miss Smoak I said hello," he said, and he turned. "Dinah, it was good to see you." They said their goodbyes and Lance shut the door behind him.

"Can I talk to you?" Dinah asked.

"Yes, of course."

Suddenly, she didn't know how to say what she wanted to say. The words sat in her throat, behind her teeth.

"Is everything okay, Dinah?"

"You should talk to John."

"Does this have anything to do with how little he's been involved with the team recently?"

"I don't know, maybe, probably—but you should check in on him. I think the stuff on the island might still be bothering him."

"Is there something I should know?"

"John's your friend, just talk to him."

Oliver frowned.

"Hello, Mother."

Felicity held the door open as Donna Smoak stepped inside her apartment. They embraced, hugging tightly. Donna jerked back, loosening her grip.

"Oh dear," she said. "I didn't mean to squeeze so tight."

Felicity frowned. "Why—oh, don't worry about my back. You won't hurt me."

Donna shook her head, amazed at the weird science that gave her daughter back the ability to walk. Not understanding it, but grateful for it. She stepped inside, and Felicity closed the door behind them.

"I can't believe it's been so long," Felicity said.

"I can't believe I'm back in Star City."

"You're always welcome here."

The area around Donna's eyes grew tight. "You can't say that for everyone."

"I can say it for *me*."

"Does Quentin—?"

Felicity reached out, placing a hand on her mother's arm. "You know that's not his way." She said it as gently as she could. Donna waved her hands, shaking off the sadness that threatened to well up inside her.

"What is going on in your love life?" she asked. "Are you seeing someone special, or have you and Oliver stopped being dumb?"

"Getting right to it—well, okay," Felicity replied, grimacing and smiling at the same time. "No, no one special. Things with me and Oliver are… complicated."

"They always have been. You need to—"

"His son lives with him," Felicity blurted out.

"Son?"

Felicity nodded. "William."

"Oh."

"He's twelve."

"Oh."

"His mother was killed in an explosion. A car accident, her car exploded."

Donna stood there for what seemed like entirely too long, her mouth open but no sound coming out. She closed it and gave a sharp little shake of her head, trying to organize everything her daughter had just said. Gathering her wits, she finally found her voice.

"Felicity, dear, are you okay?"

"I worry about Oliver and William, and sometimes I can't sleep very well, but otherwise I'm fine, just fine."

Donna stared at her daughter. "Sounds like you're not really very fine at all."

Felicity just shrugged.

"That's a lot to deal with."

Felicity shrugged again.

Donna's eyes narrowed. "Felicity Megan Smoak."

"I hate it when you use my full name."

"And I hate it when you aren't being honest with me," Donna countered. "What is on your mind?"

"Well, my severance pay from Palmertech is almost over."

Donna stared at her daughter, who just looked at the wall.

"What are you going to do?" she asked.

Felicity shrugged.

Diggle answered his door, and found Oliver standing there.

"I didn't expect a visit from you."

"I need to talk to you, John."

"Come on in." He stepped aside, allowing Oliver to enter. "Would you like a drink?"

Oliver shook his head.

"What's on your mind?"

Oliver looked at him for a long moment. Diggle knew that look. He was trying to figure out just how blunt he could be. As much as he loved Oliver for all his faults and strengths, sometimes the man was lousy with his interpersonal skills.

"Are you quitting the team?" Oliver said.

Fairly blunt, he thought. "Why would you think that?"

"You've missed the last few missions, to be with your family."

"It's just the stuff from Chase, it's bothering me more than I thought it would, but family is the most important thing..." Diggle bit back the *brother*, not wanting to throw Oliver's words back in his face.

"It is. I understand that even more now that William is with me. So, I understand if John Junior has made you begin to rethink the life we've chosen."

"But you're here to talk me out of quitting?"

"No." Oliver shook his head. "I would support that decision. Completely."

"What's the 'but'? I know there's one coming."

"Faust is still out there, waiting to create a crisis, and the copycat is still on the loose. Plus, you know this city—every day, every week could bring a new threat."

"I know all of this."

"So, my point is," Oliver said, "I will support you quitting, but if you aren't quitting, then I need you. I can't keep this city safe on my own. *You* taught me that. And the team functions better with you as a part of it."

Diggle felt Oliver's words like punches. He also felt the burn, deep in the nerve clusters of his arm, a constant low throb of pain that the medicine hadn't been able to touch. Earlier that night he'd dropped a glass, his hand unable to maintain a grip.

He looked down at Oliver.

"I'm not quitting. You can count on me."

3

"You wanted to see me, Hoss?"

"Come in, have a seat," Oliver said. "I wanted to talk to you for just a moment."

Rene walked in and stood beside the chair across from Oliver's desk. He didn't sit down. "Is everything okay?"

"Yes, I just wanted to see how you were doing with your new position. I know Thea left a lot behind, and now that several weeks have passed it will be hard to catch up." He waved his hand, walking back what he just said. "Not that I doubt your abilities at all."

"It's been a lot of work getting things organized." Rene took the chair now. "I think I've got a handle on it, though."

"You know, Quentin's very proud of the way you're handling all of this."

"Really?" Rene shot him a side-eye.

Oliver nodded. "He won't say anything, at least not to you. Trust me, I spent many, many years trying to win that man's approval. I know what it looks like."

The words made Rene sit a tiny bit straighter, and look directly at the man behind the desk.

"However," Oliver said, "it seems as if there's a bit of a struggle where your daughter is concerned."

Rene looked off to the side. "Zoe is fine."

"I want you to know that I understand," Oliver said, standing and moving around the desk. "Believe me, things aren't easy at home with William."

Rene looked up at him.

"I don't know what to say, what to tell him, and what not to tell him," Oliver continued. "I don't know how to speak to my own son. And I don't know whether I can keep him safe. I think I can, but is that my own arrogance? I don't know." Oliver shook his head at his own words. "My being the Green Arrow puts him in danger, and yet it gives me the ability to protect him. We truly help this city, and I don't think that I can give that up."

"I understand that," Rene said.

"I just want you to know that you're not alone, even though it may feel as if you are sometimes."

"I know I have the team."

"No, Rene, not just the team." Oliver propped himself on the edge of his desk. "I know I can be a bit… distant, sometimes."

Rene nodded.

"And I know that most of that is me trying to be a leader, whereas I'd rather do things on my own. If

I'm by myself, there's no one to blame if I get hurt, or make a mistake. I won't have to feel guilty over it, because whatever I've done, it was my choice. My life. My fault." He shook his head. "With the rest of you, it becomes so much more complicated."

Rene leaned forward. "I think that's the most open you've ever been, the entire time that I've known you."

"Well," Oliver said, "I've been trying to work on things. Learning *why* I do things instead of simply doing them. I think it's realizing I can lose people—people who are close to me—that makes me act the way I do."

Rene knew how much strength it took to disclose such hard, heavy feelings, and he was touched. It was hard for him to talk about his own emotions, to share how he felt about things that truly mattered. He couldn't imagine how much harder it had to be for Oliver, after all that he'd been through.

That touched him. He had no concept of how to respond to that level of honesty, especially between two people who put up walls, just to hold the world at bay.

So he went to the joke.

"Damn, cut it out, Hoss," he said. "I'm getting misty."

Oliver chuckled, releasing the tension between them. Rene leaned back in the chair, and relaxed some. The moment had passed, but not without leaving a mark.

The door to the office opened and a plain, dark-haired man leaned in.

"Sorry to interrupt, but do you remember me?"

Suddenly Oliver's voice was hollow.

"What can I do for you, Mr. Hallsey?"

"I'd much rather speak with you alone." Hallsey's eyes slid to the left, indicating Rene.

Tension vibrated off Rene's shoulders, and his teeth clenched.

"I can stay."

"It's okay," Oliver said. "I've got this, Mr. Ramirez. If you will leave us to it, I'm sure Mr. Hallsey will only take a moment of my time."

Rene walked toward the door, passing close to the newcomer. When they were side by side he spoke, his voice low.

"I'll be right outside." With that he stepped out and shut the door.

"He's an aggressive one, isn't he?" Hallsey asked.

Oliver moved around the desk, closing the distance between him and his visitor, gaining ground, establishing a position of authority in his own office. Hallsey moved forward and dropped himself into the chair Rene had vacated.

"Mr. Hallsey," Oliver said, "what can I do for you?"

"My... work brought me close to here today, and it seemed like the perfect opportunity to continue our conversation, from when I was in lockup," Hallsey explained. "There were things you said, and didn't say. You kind of stepped around… certain topics. Well, I'm not one to beat around the bush, Mr. Mayor. I will tell you the truth—confirm that I have been taking an active part in cleaning up the streets of Star City."

Oliver listened to what Hallsey said, thinking about it for a long moment.

"Why would you do that?"

"Which part? Clean up the streets, or tell you that your suspicions are true?"

"Let's start with the first part."

"I'm just doing what needs to be done." Oliver waited for him to elaborate, but the man remained silent.

"I'm not sure that we have a shortage of vigilantes in this town," Oliver said, filling the silence. "We have more than Blüdhaven and Central City combined."

"I understand that, Mr. Mayor." Hallsey leaned forward. "We also seem to have more criminals." His voice took on the fervor of a preacher. "Every day there are people suffering from the lawlessness that goes on in this city. Crime isn't being stopped, it's only being deterred, and often not even that. The police are a joke—the ones who aren't corrupt are ineffective because they rely too much on vigilantes to do their job and keep people safe. They've gone soft."

"Mr. Hallsey, I'm not sure if I understand," Oliver said, keeping his voice even. "You just told me that you are a vigilante, and implied that you feel the ones I'm familiar with—the Green Arrow and others—aren't going far enough in stopping the criminals."

"Not going far enough by far," Hallsey said, and he smirked at his own play on words.

"Are you confessing to me that you've been killing people?"

"That would be a ridiculous thing to do, even though you're not the police."

"That is, however, what it sounds like."

"For the record, Mr. Mayor, I'm not saying that I'm guilty of anything."

"You're not denying it, either."

Hallsey shrugged.

"Then what did you come here for?" Oliver asked. "To unburden your soul, or recite scripture like last time?"

Hallsey put his elbows on his knees, leaning forward. "It has been long established that you allow vigilantes to operate in Star City. In fact, you actually endorse them, as you did with the memorial to Laurel Lance. I stood in front of that statue, Mayor Queen, inspired by the speech that you gave that day."

"Are you blaming my speech for your actions?"

"You inspired me, but I am my own man," Hallsey said, "with my own motivations for what I do."

"Again, what do you want?"

"I seek your endorsement."

"No." There was heat in Oliver's voice.

"You misunderstand—not with the city," Hallsey said. "I prefer to operate in the shadows, like all the other crimefighters you know. Speak to the Green Arrow, tell him I'm going to continue to operate in the city. I'm going to stop criminals from hurting innocent people. This is my city, and nothing is going to stop me."

His phone buzzed and he glanced at it, then stood, looking at Oliver.

"I'd like to stop having to look over my shoulder all the time, just because my fellow vigilantes think I'm not good enough at my job. I don't care about their opinions, not really. They're not effective enough at what they do, either. But I cannot abide their interference."

"Why would Green Arrow listen?" Oliver asked. "If he's decided to stop you, he will. There's no doubt of that."

"Call it a hunch," Hallsey replied. "Just let the Green Arrow know to stay out of my way, or suffer the consequences. Now if you'll excuse me, I have an appointment to keep." With that he turned on his heels and walked out of the office.

The mercenary in the town car lowered the camera. He began pushing buttons on the back.

"What are you doing?" his partner asked from behind the wheel.

"Uploading the pictures to the remote server."

"Why?"

"I think we got enough shots of the building."

"Better be sure, 'cause that Faust guy is a weird one." The driver shivered. "You saw what he did to Rickson."

"Rickson was an idiot."

"He was a good soldier."

"Like the two things are mutually exclusive?"

The wheel man looked over. "You're a soldier, too."

"But I ain't an idiot—and we got enough pictures of City Hall. Let's roll."

The wheel man dropped the car into gear and pulled forward, easing onto the road. Glancing in the mirror, he saw a high-performance sports bike pull out at the same time. When it peeled off in another direction, though, he put it out of his mind.

Oliver moved quickly down the hall.

Rene rounded the corner.

"Which way did he go?" Oliver didn't break stride.

"Toward the main entrance."

"Hold the fort here. I'm going after him."

"Let me suit up."

"I've got it." Oliver broke away, entering the stairwell that provided access to the basement, digging his phone out of his pocket.

"It's an MGM dash one forty ATAC dash MS."

Curtis nodded. "Run the specs."

Felicity went through the details, her voice almost staccato. "Surface to surface guided missile—it's one of ours, range of one hundred-plus miles, and can be fired from a bunch of different kinds of launchers."

"Fuel?"

"Solid propellant."

Curtis nodded.

"Payload is a unitary blast fragmentation warhead."

"Those damn unitarians," he said. "Guidance system?"

"GPS and inertial navigational system."

"Interesting."

"Is it?"

"We know he's close." Curtis nodded, fingers steepled in thought. "Short range on that thing."

"Hundred-mile radius really narrows it down." Sarcasm hung heavy in Felicity's voice. "We're just *seconds* away from catching him."

"A journey of a thousand miles begins with a single step."

"Lao Tzu? Really?"

Curtis looked sheepish. "I was doing some reading on ancient Chinese philosophers. He's no Gongsun Long or Wang Bi, but it's hard to avoid him."

Felicity gave him a look.

"It's been a good distraction since Paul left."

Felicity felt a pang of terrible guilt at having inadvertently reminded her friend that his husband had left him. She tried to keep that feeling off her face, and was pretty sure she'd failed.

"It's okay," Curtis said. "No problem at all. Just me and philosophy from Chinese monks who have been dead for thousands of years." Suddenly the comms buzzed, jolting both of them to attention. It was the signal for an incoming emergency call.

Felicity hit the button. "Overwatch here, go."

Oliver's voice came over the speakers.

"Hallsey is here at City Hall, leaving by the main entrance. Track him and tell me where he's going."

The bike under him roared as he whipped it out of the parking garage. The wind whipped over his battle suit, snagging in the scoop of his hood, snapping the edges of it.

"Where am I going?" he growled over the comms.

"We picked him up outside. He's on a bike and heading north on the main drag."

He twisted the throttle and cut left, separating from the pack of traffic and heading in the direction he'd been given.

"Did that car make the same three turns our guy made?" Curtis pointed at the monitor.

"It did." Felicity leaned forward, clicking her mouse to grab a screen shot from a surveillance camera and move it to its own screen.

"Before our guy made them?"

Felicity nodded, squinting at the fuzzy picture she'd grabbed, enhancing it. There were people who claimed it couldn't be done—that it was just a trick made up for television. If only they knew. She read off the license plate under her breath, fingers moving over keys to type it in.

"What do you have?"

Felicity read the information on the car, clicking on hyperlinks to learn more. She clicked on the comms.

"Um, we have a problem," she announced.

He jerked left, shoving the bike into a cut-through alley by throwing his body weight to one side. His front tire scrubbed the brick wall, but it stayed intact, so he dropped it and kept moving.

Emerging from the alley, he cut right again.

"Talk to me, Overwatch."

"He's chasing a car," Felicity said. "The tag is a dead end, probably a cutter."

"Cutter?" Curtis asked.

"Chop shop trick," she explained. "Take two license plates, cut them both in half with a torch, then weld two unmatched halves together and you have an untraceable plate for your car."

"That really works?"

Felicity nodded.

"How did you know that?"

"I don't just know how to hack computers."

Oliver's voice came through the comms. *"Who is he after?"*

"One moment."

Both she and Curtis began running through the traffic cam footage of the car Hallsey was tailing, scrolling quickly on their monitors.

Curtis jumped. "Got it." He typed quickly, fingers moving like lightning over the keys as he cut the frame of footage he'd found and performed a zoom and scrub on the face of the man in the passenger seat of the car. He assigned the nodal points to the photo and zipped it through the facial recognition software. In a moment it spit back a list of organizations and names.

"He's part of a group of paramilitary mercenaries," Curtis said, "selling their services to the highest bidder."

"Why would Hallsey be tracking them, if he's so on fire to snag drug dealers?"

Curtis pointed at the screen. He'd found another picture of the man in the car. This time he was wearing a dark blue uniform, with other members of his crew.

"These are the guys who were with Faust at the Blues Festival."

Felicity relayed the news.

Oliver rolled his bike around the corner and into the junkyard. Towers of twisted metal that once were cars and appliances loomed over him, making solid walls thirty feet high along the twisting dirt driveway. Some of them leaned crazily, hanging out overhead, cutting jagged, geometric abstracts from the sky.

He hoped they were welded together.

Noise filled the air, machinery working all throughout the property. Over the wall of scrap he could see a magnetic crane swinging overhead. A low, grinding *thrum* filled the air, and he could feel it on his skin. Shrill screams of metal on metal split the fog of noise in sharp jags.

Feeling like he'd been wrapped in a cocoon of junkyard, he breathed in the heady mix of fuel and exhaust and rubber and metal baking in the sun. It enveloped him, choking his senses. Even his sight was curtailed by the bends of the dirt road hemmed in with mountains of junked vehicles.

He rolled forward at a slow pace, sticking to the left curve. Hallsey and Faust's men were here, nearby, he felt it. Not logic, but intuition shaped by years working against criminals. This place was full of cover and off the law enforcement radar, out in the open but twisty enough to let them feel safe. There were a dozen ways to slip free if things went south, but only a few people would know them.

A perfect place for a meet.

Is he chasing them, or working with them?

A wall of stacked shipping containers crossed the path he was on. He went right, riding along their length. At the end of the row the road turned back on itself. He followed the switchback and found himself in a large opening, boxed in on three sides with more stacked shipping containers. He kept his bike idling and found a niche from which he could observe, unnoticed.

In the center stood Hallsey, gun drawn and pointed at two men who knelt beside a town car with its doors flung open. The copycat's sport bike jutted, crumpled into the wheel well on the front passenger side of the car.

The sounds of the junkyard were louder here. Hallsey yelled something at the men, but he couldn't make it out—from where he stood, still unnoticed, it was just noise. One of the men yelled something back.

A large SUV rolled up the road across the opening. It stopped at the edge of the clearing. He was too far away to see inside the tinted glass, but the sight of it made his stomach clench with dread.

Hallsey began swinging his gun back and forth between the men on the ground to whoever was inside the SUV. The passenger-side window rolled down and a slender arm slid out. Its owner held something in his hand.

He could see a red button.

He hit the throttle.

Hallsey fired a shot at the SUV.

The town car exploded in a ball of flame and screaming metal shrapnel. A wave of heat and concussion knocked Oliver off the bike, lifting him completely from the seat and tossing him to skid in the dirt. He rolled to a stop, and sharp pain radiated from his shin. Some small piece of metal had cut through his boot and lodged itself in the muscle there.

Everything was a blur of light and shadows, and

the sounds of the junkyard had been replaced by a roaring in his ears that slowly diminished. As his vision began to return, shapes slowly resolved and became recognizable. He pushed himself up and began moving. The wound forced him to limp.

The town car was a hunk of twisted burning slag, just the steel ribs of it showing through the flames and black smoke it spewed into the air. The two mercenaries had been torn apart by the blast. Pieces of them scattered in a half circle in the dirt. For the most part the containers stood intact, though several had holes in them, and here and there a few seemed to teeter precariously.

The SUV was gone.

Hallsey lay in a heap, thrown a dozen feet from where he had been standing.

Oliver limped across, dropping beside him, rolling him over.

The man's face was a wreck of torn and shredded flesh. Scorched bone showed along his temple and cheek where the skin had just been scrubbed away. His right eye was gone. The fabric of his mask had melted, fusing with the skin along his scalp.

Just below his collarbone jutted a thin, spiraled piece of shrapnel. It sank deep, embedding itself in his body cavity. The edges of it were serrated and fluted—they would have destroyed anything they cut through. The ugly wound pumped dark blood from along its edges.

Green Arrow was holding a dying man.

Hallsey's eye rolled wildly as he gasped, trying to breathe around the metal that was killing him.

"I—I—should…"

"Don't talk," he said. "It will be over soon."

Hallsey gripped the strap of his quiver.

"Shld've listnd to—Mayor… Queen."

Oliver didn't say anything. Hallsey had brought this on himself, but he should have stopped him, should have saved him… Green Arrow shuttered the conflicting thoughts away at the back of his mind. They would do no good for anyone.

So Green Arrow did the only thing that was left to do. He bore witness to the death of a man. Hallsey spoke, his voice too low and garbled to understand. Oliver leaned down, putting his ear close.

"I—I think Faust—is water…"

Hallsey's last breath chased his final word away.

4

He sat in a low spot on the couch. It was a nice couch, leather rich and brown, well stuffed, only slightly worn even though it was of a style that had been popular nearly two decades past. The place he sat dipped just slightly, the springs precompressed, the stuffing of the cushion slightly displaced, the wood frame gently curved.

It was someone's favorite place to sit. *Their* spot.

Across from him was a flat-screen television surrounded by framed photos. A family doing family things.

He heard a noise from the kitchen around the corner, followed by soft footsteps. The woman who came into the room held a cup and wore a cheerful, bright yellow sweater. It contrasted harshly with her sad brown eyes.

"Here you go, Mr. Queen." She handed him a steaming cup of coffee. It had a picture of a squished-faced dog and the words PUG MUG on the side of it.

"Should I call you Mayor Queen?"

"Oliver is fine, ma'am." He sipped the coffee. It was bitter in his mouth.

"Yes, of course." She didn't offer a first name for him to use.

"I wanted to stop in and offer my condolences on the passing of your husband."

"That's very kind of you."

"I also wanted to offer to your daughters the Queen Foundation scholarship, to help with their school. It won't cover everything, but it will pay for their tuition."

"That's very generous." Mrs. Hallsey smoothed her hands over the arms of the chair she sat in.

"It's the least I could do."

"Why do it at all?"

"Excuse me?" He leaned back, surprised at the venom in her voice.

"Do you feel guilty over Arthur's death?"

He thought for a moment how to answer. "I do."

She nodded. "You should."

He sat, holding his pug mug of coffee, unsure of what to say.

"If you hadn't encouraged these masked vigilantes, this, this, Green Arrow, to take the law into their own hands then my husband would still be here," she continued.

"The vigilantes had been in this town long before I became mayor."

She refused to look at him.

"Mrs. Hallsey..." He shifted forward, moving toward her slightly. "I don't want to be insensitive, but Green Arrow didn't kill Arthur."

"I know that."

"People like him, they do things to keep this city safe—things that our regular police can't do." He tried to keep his voice soft, trying to comfort even as he defended. She took a deep breath, held it, and let it out slowly.

"Mr. Queen... Oliver... I know. I know." Another breath, then another. He recognized what she was doing, centering herself. Her voice was even when she spoke again.

"Our daughter Demetria was saved by Green Arrow. He was just called the Arrow then. Some soldier men had attacked the city and she got caught up in it."

Oliver nodded. He remembered, not the daughter, but the attack. Slade Wilson's men under the direction of Sebastian Blood.

Mrs. Hallsey kept talking. "We were so happy to have our girl returned to us. That was when Arthur began obsessing over the vigilantes. He scoured the news and the internet for information about them. He started the neighborhood watch in honor of them, started monitoring the police communications, learning ways to dig up information even they couldn't find. As for the vigilantes, he was their biggest supporter, and their biggest fan—especially the Green Arrow."

Oliver swallowed. Her words didn't make him feel proud. Instead they piled more guilt on him, and it sat heavily in his mind.

"Is that why he chose to become one of them?"

"No, just the opposite. After a time he became concerned that his heroes, the people he had given so much of his love to, had betrayed their mission. He got so angry that they had changed their tactics."

"Changed their tactics?"

"That's what he called it," she continued. "He said the Green Arrow had gone soft, and was letting criminals return to do more harm." She shook her head. "I don't know what exactly he meant, what happened that made him change his mind. I loved him but I didn't join him in his obsession. I mean, superheroes and supervillains are just part of the scenery here in Star City, a fact of life. I don't like it, but we were both from here, grew up together. This was our home, in our city." A tear trickled down her cheek. "I wish we'd have sold this damned house."

"I am truly sorry," he said.

"Don't be." She waved away his sympathy. "It's not your fault."

But it is *my fault*, he thought. *In ways I can never tell you, I am the reason your husband is dead and your daughter is fatherless.*

Mrs. Hallsey stood. Her hand slipped into the pocket of her sweater and came out holding a flat external hard drive.

"I didn't know what Arthur was doing. I knew he was doing something, but he said it was just work for the neighborhood watch so I thought nothing of it. After he…" She paused, swallowing hard to keep from sobbing. It took a moment to gain her composure. "After he died and all of it came out, I found this in the place where he kept the things a man doesn't want his wife and daughters to find."

She held it out to him.

"What is it?" he asked, taking it from her.

"A lot of things, files and notes and even a short journal of what he had been doing. For *months*. He had been doing this for almost a year." She looked down at him. "He mentions you in there, and that's why I'm giving it to you. Take it out of here—I never want to read that again. That was not my husband. My husband made me hand-stitched chapbooks of terrible love poems and made blueberry smiley faces in my daughters' pancakes on Sundays."

Oliver stood. "Mrs. Hallsey—"

She pointed at the door. "Go, Mr. Queen. Thank you for the scholarship, but just go."

Oliver left.

"Wow."

"Wow, what?" Rene said, climbing up the platform steps. He was in costume, his Wild Dog jersey tattered and torn. Sweat covered his brow.

Felicity turned in her chair. "Sorry, didn't mean to say that out loud." She scrunched her brow. "Why are you in your hero gear?"

"Working out. I prefer to do it in uniform, so I'm comfortable when it's time to rock 'n' roll."

"He wanted a lesson in stick fighting before I took off back to the Legends," Sara said, following him up the steps.

Rene turned to her. "That seems like a pretty sweet gig."

"You looking for a new team?" Oliver entered, climbing the stairs. "We'd hate to give you up."

Rene shook his head. "You can't get rid of me that easy."

Oliver smiled then looked down at Felicity. "What are we wowing?"

"I'm just going through Hallsey's files. The man was able to obtain an impressive amount of intel. He'd been gathering it for a long time, and he kept meticulous records. He didn't know where Faust has the missile, but he was on the scent for it. I think with this, we'll find him soon."

"You can get a lot of information if you're a computer geek," Rene said. "Or if you're willing to beat your informant to death."

"That's not how we operate," Oliver said.

"I was just saying it's effective, not advocating that we do it."

"Advocating?"

Rene nodded. "I got this new job so I gotta speak eloquently."

"You know what's not eloquent?" Felicity asked. "That jersey. It has seen better days."

"Smells great, too." Sara laughed. "Like burnt sweat socks."

"I know, I know." Rene raised his hands. "These are expensive, but I'll replace it soon."

"Actually," Oliver said, "I've got a lot of new equipment coming from Lodai. There might be a jersey in it."

"Man, I hope you didn't mess up my style."

Oliver's voice turned solemn. "I'd never do that."

Sara sat on her bike.

"Thank you for your help with all of this," Oliver said. "You're welcome on Team Arrow anytime."

She grinned at him. "I appreciate that. You never know when I might want to pop in, kick some normal bad-guy ass, and then ride off into the sunset."

"Tell Ray and the others I said hello."

"I will." She reached up and drew him into a hug. They embraced, feeling the closeness only they could feel—former lovers, fellow warriors, and closest friends. They shared the same losses and triumphs, and it bonded the two of them as family. As they pulled apart, she grabbed his head and put her mouth by his ear.

"Don't wait with Felicity," she whispered.

Before he could say anything she fired up the bike and rode away.

There wasn't a sunset.

Epilogue

October 2017
Star City

"Do you think the Mayor will pony up?"

The mercenary asking the question did so over cupped hands. He blew on them again to warm them. The night breeze was cool coming over the water, especially high up on the deck of the freighter. He didn't like heights or open water, but he could handle it. He *did* like the money he made. Better pay, less danger, and he got to stay stateside for the most part.

The man to whom he spoke just shrugged, adjusting the machine gun on its strap over his shoulder.

"Seems like he would have already."

"Those electronic payments go in seconds," the first man offered, "so they *could* wait 'til the last minute."

"Don't worry about it," a third man said as he approached. He wore a matching uniform and carried a matching weapon.

"I didn't know you could hear me."

The third man stopped next to them. "Sound carries further, out on the water."

"The salt air?" the second man asked.

"Hell if I know," the third man said. "The important part is to know it happens, not the why."

The other two nodded at his wisdom. The newcomer looked out over the water. In the distance the lights of Star City glimmered like jewels displayed on black velvet. "It's kind of pretty."

"Star City is hell," the first man said. "I got popped three times by those masks."

The third man swept his hand out. "Look at the way it shines under the moonlight."

The first man spit on the deck. "Don't start waxing poetical or anything, I can't handle it."

"Art thou attempting to offend me?" The third man's tone took on mock outrage.

"Take your offended self back on patrol. Team one or three come around and find us chit-chatting we'll get reprimanded," the second man said.

The first man spoke up again. "I wonder if the masks will make a move tonight."

"If they do, we have the guns and the open water." He swung his hand out to indicate the dark water that surrounded the freighter. "We'll see them coming a mile away. Now back on task."

They all went back to their patrolling, parting ways to cover their quadrants of the deck. The first man adjusted his machine gun, and looked out over the water.

I see a mask coming, I'll plant a bullet in them.

Something punched him in the shoulder, making him stumble and fall to the deck. He looked down and over.

There was an arrow sticking out of him.

It didn't hurt, wasn't bleeding, it just stuck out of him like some kind of special effect.

The arrow was green.

Then he was hot. Not just 'not cold' anymore, but burning up, and his legs felt funny.

What?

That was all he had time to think before the pain burst over him like a jackhammer, and his mind gave out. He didn't have time to make a sound. He was already unconscious.

Machine-gun fire ripped the night air around him as the mercenaries on the ship began firing into the water. More arrows sliced the air, taking each of them down in rapid succession.

A grapple arrow appeared from below, arcing up over them to lodge in the upper deck. The cable trailing behind it was taut and a second later it dragged up something from below the ship.

The Emerald Archer dripping with water and vengeance.

The new bow swept out from his hand in an elegant curve, the lines of it almost artistic, blending ancient engineering that archers had used for centuries with modern tech improvements. It was sleek and powerful and already felt like an extension of himself. He angled his body as the deck loomed larger and larger with every passing second. His boots struck it hard, the shock of landing rushing through his bones. He absorbed the forward momentum by running with it.

Moving quickly, he scanned the deck. A soldier rounded the corner ahead, raising his gun to cut him in half.

Thwick!

The arrow was in the soldier before he got his gun level.

The sound of boots on steel rolled over him. He whipped around to find two mercs pounding toward him.

Thwick!

The first arrow caught the merc who was in the lead, dropping him in a howl of pain and a clatter of gun on deck.

Thwick!

The second arrow cut through the space where the merc had been, punching into the soldier who had been following. It took him just as he tripped over his fallen colleague. He dogpiled on the other merc in a sprawl of limbs and guns and straps.

Green Arrow turned and kept moving.

More bootsteps came around the corner. He slid closer to the wall, but kept moving. At the corner he collided with the mercs. They jumped back, trying to get enough room to bring their guns to bear. He didn't retreat, shoving himself into the middle of them.

Thwick!

Thwick!

Thwick!

He fired quickly, and from point-blank range, dropping the one in front of him then twisting to shoot the one who stood beside him. For the third he arched backward and fired from instinct, working off where it *felt* like the merc would be.

His intuition proved true as the beefy man howled and fell to the deck, clutching the arrow that was protruding from his thigh.

In motion again, Green Arrow stepped over them and kept going. He nocked another arrow, sweeping it back and forth as he moved on high alert. Convinced the deck was clear, he tapped the comms.

"I'm on site. No sign of Faust."

Blood spattered his jacket as his elbow smashed into the merc's mouth.

He looked down at it and thought, *This jacket is new!*

His opponent snarled at him through a bloody mouth. Spartan leaned back and kicked him in the throat.

The merc fell in a heap.

Spartan shook out his hands, clenching and unclenching them, trying to ease the pain running from his triceps to the ends of his fingers. He looked around the dim, dingy warehouse office. It had seen better days, but here and there he found evidence of recent occupation. A candy wrapper, a water bottle, and a trashcan half full of takeout. Flies buzzed incessantly.

He spoke into the comms.

"Not at his last known, either."

Green Arrow stood in front of a large square container, mounted on a platform. It had several gaps that revealed its contents. He could see a pointed nose cone through one of the openings, poking out of a metal tube. There was a control console only a few feet away.

He spoke into the comms. "But his ordnance is."

"*If Faust has gone from bombs to missiles, makes you wonder what else he's changed up,*" Spartan replied.

"Exactly," Green Arrow said, "Stay sharp."

It was a small noise.

It might have been nothing, some slight shifting of a thing dislodged by the violence. Or it could have been the rustle of cloth on cloth...

Spartan turned toward the noise.

The merc had his rifle held at waist level, finger on the trigger, one twitch away from cutting him in half.

Spartan spun, dropping as he did, trying to get out of the line of fire. *Ba-boom* came the throaty, chugging sound of a shotgun spitting lead. Plaster shattered loudly, sending a rain of debris down on him. He couched, body tensed against the flesh-tearing onslaught of a bullet swarm, his mind on Lyla and John Junior.

Nothing.

No organ-ripping pain, no thudding stabs of white-hot agony.

He turned.

Wild Dog stood in the doorway, holding his gun. He still had the hockey mask, but his new tactical uniform was sleeker, more menacing, than his old jersey. He racked the slide.

"Boss said to stay sharp, Hoss."

He approached the launcher, examining its lines. It was a large, blunt thing, all utilitarian. He could appreciate its bleak economy. It was a thing designed for a singular purpose, and that appealed to a part of him.

Nevertheless, he wouldn't hesitate to destroy it to save his city.

Something kicked deep in his lizard brain, some movement on his periphery, some sound he didn't consciously register, some change in the barometric pressure of his personal circle.

He didn't think, just twisted sideways.

A long wicked blade cut the air he had just occupied, missing its target—his throat. The edge of the blade struck the side of the launcher in a screech of metal on metal and a shower of grinding sparks.

He rolled out of his twist and came up to find a mercenary holding a knife so large it was virtually a machete. The merc who held it was so large that the blade looked almost dainty in his hands.

Green Arrow lunged forward, throwing his fist into the merc's midsection. It was like punching a side of beef.

The merc lashed out with the knife. Green Arrow stepped in, using his shoulder to block the arm that swung the blade. He launched his own assault, aiming his blows for vital areas in the merc's torso. Punch to the left mid-quadrant of the abdominals, seeking to send a shock wave to the merc's spleen. Shuto strike up under the ribs of the right side to make the diaphragm spasm, robbing the merc of his ability to breathe. Phoenix Eye punch, up and twisting into the solar plexus.

The merc took a step back and shook his head. Then, too fast for a man his size, he grabbed Green Arrow by the shoulders and used his superior mass and muscle strength to move the archer as if he were a toy.

A forearm the thickness of a two-liter bottle wrapped around him, applying pressure to his throat in a crush choke. The vertebrae in his neck popped as the thickness of the arm lifted his chin and squeezed. It took only a second to go from a chiropractic maneuver to a homicidal one.

Green Arrow couldn't breathe.

He flailed, driving his fingers into pressure points on the man's arms, using his feet to kick. The merc held him tight, squeezing harder.

A voice came from behind them.

"Apologies. Won't be but a minute."

Faust.

The wiry maniac circled around them, moving to the launcher. He stood in front of the console and began pushing buttons and turning dials. The launcher groaned to a start and began pivoting slowly. Then it tilted.

Aiming.

Faust picked up a tablet and climbed down the ladder. He looked up at Green Arrow, and raised a finger. "If you have the opportunity, please advise the mayor the *next* time someone threatens to launch a ballistic missile at his city, he really should pay up." With that he jabbed down, hitting a button.

The launcher began to vibrate as the ballistic missile inside ignited. Slowly the nose cone slid forward, creeping just an inch.

Then another.

It paused there, smoke leaking out of the tube in which it nestled.

With a loud noise like rolling thunder and a plume of spent rocket fuel it lurched forward. Moments later it tore into the sky in a gently curving trajectory. Even through eyes going greasy from lack of oxygen, Oliver could see it right itself and begin flying toward Star City.

Breathing hard in his ear, the merc applied more pressure. Green Arrow clenched his body, using the power in his chest and shoulders to pull himself forward.

The merc held him tightly.

Snapping his body around, the archer flipped the

merc, slamming him to the deck. He felt the snap of his assailant's nasal bone. The impact vibrated all the way into the man's teeth as his skull smashed his nose nearly flat. The merc's arms came loose as he gave a choked, muffled howl.

Green Arrow slipped to the ground, pushed off, and flung his body around in an acrobatic spinning kick that snapped the man's head back. The mercenary's body followed in the next second.

Pulling air in, Green Arrow turned to face Faust.

The bomb maker pulled a face.

"Disappointing," he said.

Green Arrow swooped up his bow, drew and fired. Twin shafts struck Faust in the chest, driving him back, pinning him to the freighter wall.

Faust's voice was smug, nearly condescending. "That's an MGM-one-forty AT-ack-MS SSM. It's fire-and-forget. You can't stop it. You can't disarm it."

"No, but I've got a very smart friend who can."

Mister Terrific ran, legs churning, breathing deep in rhythm with each footfall. He ran like an Olympian. The tar of the rooftop was solid as concrete under his feet, hardened with the cooler weather. He slid to a stop at the edge, eyes out on the night sky.

There was the oncoming missile, a slowly growing bright spot in the dark, close enough now to see the shape of it. Reaching under his jacket he pulled out a

T-Sphere. Taking a deep, centering breath he hurled it into the air.

The T-Sphere arced up, looped, then flew straight at the missile.

The shiny metal sphere crossed the missile's path and arced hard to the left.

Then the T-Sphere was in front of the projectile, and the effect was immediate. The missile bobbled, then turned, curving back on its trajectory. It began chasing the sphere, identifying it now as the primary target.

Mister Terrific keyed up his comms.

"My T-Sphere's spoofed the missile's guidance system," he said, allowing a hint of triumph into his voice. "I'm drawing it back to the water."

The missile came into sight, following a target that was too small to see from so far away. He watched as the projectile curved and fell toward the water. It exploded in a shower of flaming fragments that were thrown into the water.

By the time it reached him, it was simply a mist.

Faust grinned at him. "You look troubled. As if detonations stir unpleasant memories."

Green Arrow let his words—and the memories they brought—slip over him. Lian Yu was the past. It was water. He was the rock. Turning on his heel, he left Faust to hang until the SCPD could arrive.

It was time to put everything right again.

ACKNOWLEDGMENTS

This book is written from the inspiration of so many people. I will miss someone and for that I am sorry, my aim is not perfect.

Firstly to Marc Guggenheim, you rocked out a story I could run with, thank you. To Steve Saffel for making all the gears mesh. You kick all the ass. To the Arrow team and all the folks who make so many awesome hours of entertainment with these characters, you have given so much. The writers, the actors, the production team, all of you, thank you for letting me play in your toy box.

Same to the Titan team, including Nick Landau, Vivian Cheung, Laura Price, Cat Camacho, Joanna Harwood, Natasha MacKenzie, Steve Gove, and all the rest. Y'all keep it all happening on the book end and it's appreciated so much.

Thank you Mort and George for the original character.

Thank you DC Comics and the CW.

Thank you to the Dr. No's Dinner Crew, y'all keep me in the comic book way.

Thank you to each and every person who loves this stuff as much as me. Fan boys and geek girls and all the ones who just love the capes or masks or powers or metas, you are all heroes.

James R. Tuck
Atlanta, Georgia
November 2017

There are many people to thank. The largest portion of my gratitude goes to James Tuck because without his efforts, this book would literally not exist.

Back when I was in college, I interned for Steve Saffel in Marvel Comics' promotions department. I learned much from him and am privileged to still be working with him—lo, these many years later—on this project.

My assistant, Liz Kim, *Arrow*'s Script Coordinator, Jeanne Wong, and *Arrow*'s Writers' PA, Becky Rosenberg provided mission critical reads of the manuscript, assuring fidelity to *Arrow*'s continuity. Carl Ogawa of Berlanti Productions was another key pair of eyes and clearly missed his calling as a book editor.

Speaking of Berlanti Productions, none of the CW superhero shows would be possible without Greg Berlanti.

I don't know why you'd read these acknowledgments first, but in the unlikely event that you are, skip this paragraph: This novel ends with a recapitulation of the opening of *Arrow*'s Sixth Season Premiere, which I co-wrote with my fellow showrunner and partner in crime, Wendy Mericle.

Finally, thanks to *Arrow*'s cast, crew, writers and

post-production team. Their tireless efforts are the reason there's an audience that makes a book like this a viable proposition.

Marc Guggenheim
Encino, California
November 2017

ABOUT THE AUTHORS

James R. Tuck lives and writes in Atlanta. He is the author of the Deacon Chalk: Occult Bounty Hunter series, and co-author of the Robin Hood: Demon's Bane trilogy (with Debbie Viguié). James is an accomplished tattoo artist, loves dark fantasy novels, Golden Age comics, and the blues, and used to throw people out of bars for money.

Marc Guggenheim is a recovering attorney who has written for television, film, animation, comics, motion comics, and videogames. He is currently writing *X-Men Gold* for Marvel Comics and executive producing *Arrow*, *DC's Legends of Tomorrow*, and *Trollhunters*. His first novel, *Overwatch*, was published in 2014 by Mulholland Books.

ALSO AVAILABLE FROM TITAN BOOKS

FLASH™
THE HAUNTING OF
BARRY ALLEN

by Clay and Susan Griffith

The prequel to
ARROW: A GENERATION
OF VIPERS

Following the supercharged, crime-fighting
superhero with the power to move at
superhuman speeds, this first Flash adventure
pits the Scarlet Speedster against the villains
who comprise his meta-human Rogues Gallery.
But when the Flash's own abilities begin to
fail him, he must seek help from his closest
ally—the Arrow.

ON SALE NOW!

TITANBOOKS.COM

ALSO AVAILABLE FROM TITAN BOOKS

ARROW™
VENGEANCE

by Oscar Balderrama and Lauren Certo

Slade Wilson. Sebastian Blood. Isabel Rochev. Their
actions will determine the path of a hero.

SECRET ORIGINS

Oliver Queen returns from the dead to create
his persona as the Arrow. Yet others work in the
shadows to fashion his downfall… and plot the
destruction of all he holds dear.

Also a survivor of Lian Yu, Slade Wilson's
ultimate goal is Oliver's doom, and he recruits
Isabel Rochev, whose hatred for the Queens
knows no bounds. Brother Blood, while
seeking to do what is right, also finds himself
inextricably tangled in Wilson's machinations.

This is the untold story behind the rise and fall
of the Arrow…

ON SALE NOW!

TITANBOOKS.COM

For more fantastic fiction, author events,
competitions, limited editions and more

VISIT OUR WEBSITE
titanbooks.com

LIKE US ON FACEBOOK
facebook.com/titanbooks

FOLLOW US ON TWITTER
@TitanBooks

EMAIL US
readerfeedback@titanemail.com